How to be a Millionaire
by Next Wednesday

How to be a Millionaire by Next Wednesday

a novel by

Alistair Paterson

DI

David Ling Publishing Limited
PO Box 34-601
Birkenhead, Auckland 10

Distributed in New Zealand by Lothian Books

The publisher gratefully acknowledges
the assistance of the Literature Programme
of the Queen Elizabeth II Arts Council
of New Zealand

How to be a Millionaire by Next Wednesday
First Edition

ISBN 0-908990-17-0

First published 1994

© Alistair Paterson 1994

Design by Biggles & Co.
The cover features a detail from *Racing Auckland
Harbour*, by Lily Lewis.
Author photo: Sally Griffin
Typeset by Hazard Publication Services
Printed in New Zealand

One

Of course, Harry hasn't always been as he is now. That's what he tells himself, and he sees somewhere inside his head that other — well, one of the other Harrys — perhaps the one who used to be slender to middling in build and height, upright with square shoulders, and attractive (as occasionally, former events and his imagination sometimes suggest) to the opposite sex. He stares through the window, and looks out and down towards the trees at the far side of the car park. They appear to be constantly in motion and peculiarly dismal — dark green and depressing in the light rain and the southerly wind which bend them as if to breaking point before they whip back and bend again.

Yes, he reassures himself, things haven't always been as bad as they are now. Sometimes — and perhaps not all that long ago — women have found him attractive. He recalls first noticing it when he was seventeen. He'd just had his hair trimmed and was coming out of the hairdresser's. The man who had cut his hair, had sprayed some kind of tacky stuff onto his head, combed what was left of his hair into place and handed him a mirror so he could inspect the finished work from the back as well as the front. His hair was pale and shone in the bright lights of the hairdresser's salon. It shone in a way he wasn't happy with because according to the traditional view and the magazines on the hairdresser's coffee table, if men were to be interesting to women, they had to be 'tall, dark and handsome' — two of which attributes didn't apply to him. The third he wasn't certain about.

When he was outside and beginning to make his way along the pavement, she had looked at him — looked with what had seemed a prolonged stare but which he now knows must have occupied no more than a mere fraction of time. She had stared at him and then eye contact was lost and she moved off — but not before looking back, quickly, intently and with an expression of surprise. At least — and sometimes he still thinks about it — it must have been surprise and it was probably their age difference that caused it. She'd been about thirty — well, perhaps a little older — and married. He assumed she was married: an attractive woman with alert green eyes — a woman surprised at herself for whatever it was she happened to be thinking, and at having looked in that particular way at someone as young as he was.

He's often wondered exactly what it was she might have been thinking, and although he's come to believe he knows what it was, this is only in a general sort of way and excludes the details — the exact images and thoughts that occur in another person's head and remain there beyond reach, beyond any certainty of knowledge or identification.

He stares blankly through his office window at the trees on the other side of the car park and thinks about being seventeen years old — about the infinite possibilities still ahead — all very different from the way things are now. And he thinks about the woman outside the hairdresser's and about other momentarily glimpsed and unknown women — some he might and perhaps should have done something about but didn't because there wasn't enough time or if he's truthful about it, because he isn't the kind of person who's able to follow up a momentary glance. And he wonders about other women as well — women who are too beautiful — women that only the wealthy, the gifted, confident men ever do anything about.

But now he brings himself back to the present and looks at the screen in front of him — at what he's writing. It's boring, boring, boring! *While the optimum size of the operation can't be readily defined,* he types into his word processor, *the third year's activities will require a minimum of sixty-five full-time student equivalents if a financially viable and effective organisation is to be established.*

He's rewriting it and despite his every effort, the pomposity of the document offends him. The Qualifications Authority (not 'Education Authority' — as they keep reminding him) — the Qualifications Authority returned the original a week ago with a beautifully printed covering letter and disfiguring marginalia designed to clarify 'minor points' but as far as he could see, intended merely to make things more difficult. Or maybe the Authority was trying to slow things down, keep its own workload within manageable proportions by making the people it dealt with work harder and longer at what it believed they ought to be doing.

The Qualifications Authority requires sponsors to guarantee sufficient funds for living expenses, he types slowly and awkwardly, never having reached more than a three-finger stage of proficiency. *This money may be kept in a local bank, provided the bank certifies it can be transferred when needed. A list of suitable banks is given below...*'

'Hey, what's all this?' Frank interrupts him.

'Registration,' he says. Frank is staring over his shoulder, examining what he's written. 'I told you — we had two years to get things into shape. Time's up at the end of the month. We've only got twelve days left. The Authority wants us to prove we're doing what we said we'd do, that everything's ship shape and working out according to plan.'

Frank stares more closely at the screen. 'I don't understand it,' he says. 'Why do we have to write such stuff?'

'It's the rules, the way we have to do things — the way we're supposed to appear as if we're doing them.' He types another sentence into the machine and follows it up with instructions to print. There's nothing more he needs to do until the copy comes off the printer and he's checked it for errors. He knows that in theory he ought to get everything right before he prints it out, but nothing's ever perfect and there are always a few mistakes that have to be picked up later.

'It has to be in the mail in time for Annette — she's asked us to send it to her — so Annette can check it out before she turns up for the inspection.' He pushes his chair back and swivels round towards his questioner. Frank is tall with an urbane, almost childish face which never shows anything he's thinking and allows him to ask questions without being offensive. Harry doesn't like to think that a man with that kind of face could be seriously cruel or vicious, yet increasingly he wonders about it, whether he might have misread Frank — might not have understood the things Frank wants, the goals he's set himself — the direction he's moving in. He knows from experience that not understanding things, that taking them at their face value can lead to disaster — and disaster isn't an outcome he wants either of them to be involved in.

'What about this other letter, the one you've got in the in-tray?' Frank picks up the envelope, looks at the address on the back and then opens it. 'The Munwha Corporation — have we heard of it — do we know anything about it?'

'They're agents in Korea,' Harry tells him, 'one of the agents we wrote to.' He takes the letter from Frank and reads it aloud to him.

Dear Mr Houghton, it says, *Thank you for your letter and the information you forwarded. I was impressed by the material you sent. The contract conditions are very reasonable and we basically agree with them. But I would like to tell you of our company's policy before signing…*

'My God! An answer! Somebody's sent us an answer!' Although Frank's expression hasn't changed, Harry can tell from his voice that he's excited, that he thinks the letter's something of a break-through — and considering the difficulties they've been having, it could be a break-through! Personally, he's cynical about it. Too many things go wrong and with the increasing speed and frequency of changes in Government policy, recent newspaper reports of insider trading and political scams, the bad press language schools have been getting, things are more ~~likely to go wrong than right~~.

He'd like to share Frank's enthusiasm but the tone of the letter tells him there are going to be 'ifs' and 'buts', and there usually are when you're dealing with people who have more power than you do. They don't do business unless there's money in it, and they don't make concessions. It's not what the letter says but the way the words are put together that matters most. He's sensitive to words and he reads too much — particularly when he's under stress and doesn't want to make decisions. What he's been reading recently is a case in point — it's rubbish, but he doesn't mind it being rubbish as long as it keeps his eyes moving across the page and his mind off everything else.

We conduct an on site visit to the organisations we intend to deal with. Frank reads out to him. *This way we become acquainted with the facilities, programmes and staff. We especially check whether the equipment, curricula and personnel are suitable for students from Korea.*

In Korea there are many agents, some of whom have a bad reputation. We do not want to send students to companies represented by such agents because it would lower our company's credit and damage our reputation. Accordingly, it would be helpful if you would send us a list of agents in Korea with who you are already dealing, for our reference.

Could you send us letters of recommendation for your organisation in Korean, from Koreans for whom you are presently supplying training courses or services — people who know your organisation well.

If the points outlined above are successfully dealt with, we would be very interested in conducting business with you and hopefully, arranging for students from Korea to participate in your programs.

'Great!' Frank tells him. 'They want to do business with us. We're going to make it — we're really going to make it.'

Harry closes the file he's working on, and opens a new one. 'Let's send him a fax,' he says. 'The sooner he gets a reply, the better.' He doesn't feel as well as he ought to. There's a queasiness in his stomach that bears no relationship to their business problems — to Frank, or to whether they can make a success of things or not.

He ought to be accustomed to it, should be able to keep it under control, but every now and again it pushes its way up into his mind forcing him to think about things he doesn't want to think about, to give them attention he doesn't want to give them. It's why he spends so much time in the office or reading things: newspapers, magazines, novels, literary articles — anything he can get his hands on, anything that will fill up the bits of his mind that aren't being used.

'How many agents have we written to?' Frank asks him. He looks as if he's considering things Harry might have missed, as if he has private and esoteric knowledge that will suddenly and unexpectedly clarify everything and make life easier for both of them. It's a characteristic Harry doesn't like. It makes him feel uneasy about himself, that he's not as efficient, not as intelligent as Frank.

'We wrote to twenty-five — the most likely of the companies listed by the Trade Development Board — and there's only been this one reply.'

'We haven't done very well?'

'No, but it's not through lack of trying,' which is true. They've done everything right in theory, they should have developed a thriving and successful business, they should be operating within ten percent of the predicted cash flow. But it hasn't happened and there's still no certainty that it will happen. Frank stands behind him, silent, motionless, as if waiting for an explanation — an acknowledgement that their failure is the result of his having not done everything he should have done, or that he's made a mistake that's led to their present difficulties.

'No,' Harry says, 'we're not doing well, but we have this one favourable response — from the Munwha Corporation — it might make a difference. It's worth celebrating — and there hasn't been much to celebrate lately. A night on the town... how do you feel about it? What do you say to a night on the town?'

Frank smiles — it's something he doesn't do very often and has done increasingly rarely over the last few weeks. 'OK then, let's celebrate,' he says. 'Think positively and things get better — think negatively and everything falls apart.' He sounds as if he's giving a lecture — conducting a morale-building exercise. 'And it's Friday — maybe Bridget might like to come.' He turns towards the door. 'Don't worry about the fax. It can wait until later — until we've worked out the best possible reply.' He moves towards the door. Harry fights against the implied suggestion that he's there to receive Frank's instructions. He can see through the glass partition that Frank's telling Bridget the good news and hamming it up a little as well. He doesn't like that either — and he's not certain that occasionally he doesn't behave in the same way himself.

He watches what's going on in the next room, the enthusiasm Frank displays when he's talking to Bridget. And yet enthusiastic as he appears, there's a distance there, a formality between Frank and Bridget that indicates their separateness — clearly distinguishes employer from employee or in management terms, staff from line. It's something he's observed before and he's never liked very much. He remembers it was the same when he was in the Navy. No matter what the situation, people tended to keep a formal distance from each other. It varied, but it was always there and almost physically measurable — especially on social occasions and between the officers and everyone else. And the women — the women subscribed to the same invisible rule except that there was a sisterly cohesiveness between them. It was something he'd almost forgotten, that he'd stopped thinking about until a month ago, until the reunion.

'Harry!' they called to him when he walked into the mess — and there was a warmth in their voices he hadn't expected. 'It's good to see you, Harry!' Somebody placed a hand on his shoulder. It was an indecisive movement which started off as if it were going to be a friendly slap and then changed into something else, something more restrained. He hadn't been popular during his last year in the service — the pain of it was still with him — and he couldn't decide whether the restraint was due to the events of the past or the formality of the present. He persuaded himself it was the latter because there was no reason to believe the suspicions and animosities of the past still persisted. In any case — and it was something he kept telling himself throughout the evening — people tended to remember the good things rather than the bad, and ex-servicemen were no different from other people.

They bought him drinks, although in fairness to the others he should have been buying his own. But then he'd been senior to most of them, and hadn't visited a naval mess or been near an ex-serviceman (apart from Frank who had been Army — which wasn't the same thing and didn't really count); he hadn't been near any of them for more than seven years, and although he hoped they'd put it all behind them, a few of them still seemed subject to the formalities and obligations of their former ranks. It was understand-able — difficult not to revert to service habits in military surroundings — especially in a service mess most of them had belonged to at one time or another. It was the same room, the same bar, perhaps even the same furniture they'd used almost every day of the week. But while he recognised everything — the carpets, the plaques and pennants at the back of the bar — there was a foreignness about everything, the feeling of strangeness that came from seven years of absence and defamiliarisation.

The uniforms their hosts were wearing identified their service ranks and marked them out from the visitors who were dressed in civies and were therefore no longer distinguishable in terms of their former status. Doug, with his unusual height (unusual even in the Navy), looked no more than in his mid-forties, and still had the formal upright appearance and wide shoulders that had marked him out as a future brass hat almost as soon as he'd joined the service.

Harry and Doug were talking to each other when Harry noticed the women, two of them, in their blue uniforms — lieutenants, youngish, perhaps in their mid twenties. They had identical haircuts, wore identical smiles and might have been twin sisters except for their faces and the colour of their hair. They spoke softly, in tones which were impossible to catch unless they turned towards the person they were addressing. Service women had always been like that, he remembered, always with an air of formality about them as if they had entered into an unwritten agreement to efface their individual identities. The men could be like it too, but only when things went wrong — which was what happened during his last two years of service.

'There have been changes,' Doug was saying to him.

'Yes,' he said, not sure whether Doug was talking about the Navy or what everyone had been doing over the last seven years.

'No one guessed it,' Doug was saying to him, 'no one guessed what Mills was up to, and it would have been a court-martial if there hadn't been civil charges as an alternative.' It was a kind of explanation — almost an apology.

He wasn't listening closely. He was thinking of women — of the two women officers and how extraordinary it was that people appeared, disappeared and were replaced by other people who looked almost exactly the same as the ones who'd vanished. He wondered what had become of Anne Skiffington who'd come in as a women's divisional officer and to do secretarial work, Anne Skiffington who he'd persuaded to ask for a transfer to training staff. Over his dead body, Doug had said, training was men's work and women weren't suited to it. Well, she'd received her transfer — she'd become a trainer — and Doug was still alive, was standing in front of him and telling him about Mills.

'Forgery,' Doug insisted, 'it was forgery — his papers were forged, and that's what he was charged with — fraud and the presentation of forged documents for personal gain.'

Mills — John Stuart Mills had been the guy's name, and God, he'd never forget it! An absurd name and except for the extra letter on the end, identical to that of the nineteenth century philosopher who would almost certainly turn in his grave if he were aware of the similarity. Harry had asked Mills about it after he'd arrived at the naval base and discovered his father had been in the Army and worked his way through the ranks. Mills had been born in Hannover. His father had been stationed there for two years after the war. According to Stuart, John Patrick Mills had put some of his leisure time into Army Education and Welfare Service courses and had acquired an interest in philosophy. He'd become enthusiastic about the Greeks — particularly the early Greeks — and he'd developed an admiration for the nineteenth century philosopher he'd named his son after. Harry had thought Sparta and the Spartans might have been more appropriate considering Mills senior was an army man and — as far as he could tell — a disciplinarian, but then people in the services sometimes developed surprising and unexpected leisure interests: taking off in hot-air balloons, building model aeroplanes, breeding pedigree Irish terriers...

'He couldn't march,' Doug said, interrupting Harry's train of thought. 'Hopeless on the parade ground — so bad that the First Lieutenant and the Gunnery Officer used to quote odds on how long he'd last before he tripped over his sword.'

Harry laughed, not out of amusement, but from embarrassment because it had been he who'd had the problem of what to do about Mills and he hadn't found the situation either funny or amusing. And Stuart himself had had no sense of humour, had never laughed. It had been impossible to exchange casual gossip with him or get him to see the point of the most obvious of service jokes. It was a mystery how he'd got to be that way unless of course, he'd inherited the trait from his father. Harry had thought at the time that Mills senior must have run his household as if it were a platoon composed of military defaulters assigned to him for disciplinary purposes. Eighteen to twenty years of military discipline initiated at birth was all he could think of as an explanation for Stuart's deadly serious disposition.

As it was, he would have preferred never to have met Mills at all, and in view of such a meeting having occurred, never to have heard of him again. Before Stuart joined the service and had been appointed to his division, he'd always thought of himself as tough enough to handle anything that happened. Afterwards, he wasn't so sure.

T w o

Seated at a small table in the American Bar, Harry closes his ears to the voices around him and stares at the half empty glass in front of him. It's one of the recently redecorated bars which have suddenly lurched towards a younger, upmarket segment of the population — a segment which even after the stock market crash is still well provisioned with large incomes, larger mortgages and the hope of better things to come. Few of these people are as wealthy as they'd like to be, but they enjoy having money to spend and are easily enticed from their newly restored bungalows and villas that until recently crowded in on each other in disorder and decay near the inner margins of the city. Their owners like loud music, bright lights and the company of their peers — and are committed to the life-style magazines such as *Metro* and *More* have convinced them is exclusively theirs.

The floors of the houses they live in have been cleared of decayed carpet and long-dead linoleum, sanded back to the original wood, and polyurethaned. Scrim and water-stained wallpaper have been stripped from the walls and carted off with rusted roofing iron, rotting weather-board and broken glass to the council's nearest waste disposal facility. The rooms have been variously relined with Fijian kauri, Canadian cedar or gib board laid over fibreglass insulation and fireproof building paper.

A noisy and vociferous crowd is presently desporting itself in the American Bar. It fills up the tables, presses round the edges of the few square metres of dance floor and close to the stage from which a four piece band is hammering out music from the nineteen sixties — mainly Beatles' songs and occasionally something even earlier — rock and roll with a modest leavening of revivals from the fifties. Harry looks up from his glass and without noticing much of what's going on around him, thinks of the difficulties he and Frank are having, what happened while he was in the Navy and the lamentable state of his private life — each of which is sufficient to provide him with good enough reason to be disinterested in his surroundings.

He should, he tells himself and Frank has suggested it, be more positive but then, he and his partner view things differently and their personal situations are different. Frank, for example, is still married, still in a reasonably sound private financial situation. He'd survive financially if, or more accurately, when their business collapses — and ironically in view of their being there to celebrate, this is what's most likely to happen. It's depressing — too depressing to think about. He tries to distract himself, to imagine what Bridget and Frank might have talked about while they were driving into Newmarket. And why was it only Bridget Frank wanted to invite when it could have been any or all of the three other women their business employs?

He could have driven her himself but it seemed less selfish to let Frank do it. As his ex-wife used to tell him, he isn't interesting to women, and he knows from more recent experience he's not as interesting to them as Frank is; in any case because she works with him, failing to offer to drive her is more likely to be interpreted as a lack of interest than of confidence. Bridget is in her early twenties, and the kind of men who would impress her are either younger than he is or a great deal more confident.

'It's the Government,' Frank says, 'the Government and Tiananmen Square.' Frank's talking not only to Bridget but also to a second woman who's sitting next to her — someone Bridget seems to be acquainted with — who's turned up from nowhere and has miraculously in view of the number of people in the bar, found an unoccupied chair.

'Yes, Tiananmen Square,' Frank says repetitively, 'the Government and Tiananmen Square.'

'But you can't know for certain — you can't be sure it's the Government — that the Government's involved,' the woman next to Bridget tells him. 'There has to be factual evidence — some kind of proof.'

'It's the Government,' Frank repeats '— it has to be the Government.'

And that's not all it is, Harry thinks. He's put the morning paper, which he's brought with him and hasn't yet read, amongst the glasses on the table in front of him. He can see the headlines and a photograph of a former prime minister — overweight and with the little boy grin that not only won him political success at an absurdly early age but might also have contributed to his having an affair with his speech writer and leaving his wife. More than likely, it isn't only the smile that's led to the second event; there's the attraction power exerts over people. He thinks about it — about the advantages which seem always to accompany power and the exercise of power.

'That's why they made him prime minister,' he says, pointing at the photograph. 'It's because he's fat. People like men who are fat because they think they're unlikely to threaten anybody or do anything dangerous. And this one's solid — solid enough to suggest he's not only easy-going, but that he's trustworthy as well.'

'You read things,' the woman says, leaning in front of Bridget and looking at him. Her voice is flat and at the same time musical. She has bright red hair and her skin is so pale it seems almost white — as if she's purposely painted it that colour. Her eyes are green, ingenuous, and unreflective of any emotion he's familiar with. He doesn't like the clinical way in which she's looking at him and he doesn't know how to respond to her.

'Bridget,' she says as if she were a scientist offering an observation in the laboratory, or a school teacher talking to a colleague during a mid-morning break, 'Bridget — you never told me he could read.'

'The Government — it has to be the Government,' repeats Frank who's finished his beer and the whisky that preceded it, 'the Government ordered the Embassy in Beijing to stop issuing visas as soon as the tanks started moving into Tiananmen Square.' He gathers together the glasses, including Harry's which isn't yet empty, and turns towards the bar. 'That's what's ruining us,' he calls over his shoulder, 'the Government and the immigration service. They won't tell you anything — they don't want anyone to know what they're doing — and they've ordered the Embassy not to issue visas. It can't be anything else.'

'It's the newspapers,' Bridget breaks in, 'the newspapers sensationalising everything.' She pauses as if making sure she has their attention. 'The Sunday papers said — it was reported a few days ago that Harry seized his opportunity — went into the language business to get rich.'

'To make a million,' Frank suggests, 'to become a millionaire.'

From his seat near the window, Harry is able to look out and down onto the street below. The early evening traffic is a tangle of buses, cars, and trucks. The traffic lights at the intersection throw a red glow over the wet, velvet-black of the roadway. A light drizzle is falling — a drizzle that intensifies the encroaching darkness and adds an inexplicable melancholy to the scene. It reminds him of times when he's arrived in cities he's never been to before, where he's known no one. Almost always, it was raining — or at least drizzling — and in the same melancholy manner that depresses him so much he wants to stop the first woman who smiles at him and beg her to take him home.

He almost did once — ask someone to take him home. It was in a city as flat and monotonous as a pancake. He'd been booked into a dismally grubby hotel off the main street. It smelt of urine and damp and depressed him so much that he signed out after less than an hour, and left in search of something better. Crazy, of course — walking out instead of checking the AA ratings, and calling a taxi. And then, outside on the pavement there were only two directions to go: up the street to the left or down to the right. He remembers the absurdity of it — standing in the street wondering what the hell to do next.

He was still standing there looking at a shop window display when he saw her as an indistinct, smudgy figure moving in from the left: a collection of black dots on a yellow background. She was wearing some kind of short, yellowish fur jacket, high-heeled patent leather shoes, a white blouse, a pencil-thin skirt and a perfume he couldn't identify. He'd followed her half a block before she turned as if checking her watch and looked at him. He lost her outside a bus station. Maybe she took off, maybe he might have seemed threatening to her, but if she'd stopped and asked what the hell he thought he was doing or had come up to him with an inviting, 'Hello sailor,' he wouldn't have known what to say.

The woman with the red hair reaches across and gives him one of the glasses Frank has manoeuvred back to them through the crowd at the bar. Presumably Bridget has introduced her, but even if he might have heard her name, he's already forgotten it (he's not good with names) and now it's too late to ask.

'He doesn't say very much,' she says, turning to Bridget who's gone into her aloof blonde mode — the mode fair-haired, attractive women go into when they're being watched and admired.

'Of course it's the Government,' Frank says. 'They've sold Telecom and they're selling the railways so they can reduce public debt — balance the books.' He's bought another two drinks for himself — a whisky, which he swallows at once, and a beer he sips slowly with the pleasure of a connoisseur. 'And now they're looking for anything else they can get rid of — the power boards, the art galleries, the museums, the national archives — and the prisons for good measure.'

'We could sell the business and buy a prison,' Harry suggests. 'There'll always be gaols and imprisonment's become a growth industry.'

'He's an intellectual,' the red-headed woman tells Bridget, 'but he's not bright enough to have worked it out for himself — he must have read it somewhere.'

'No — no,' says Frank, 'you don't listen to what they say in Cabinet. The Minister of Justice has made it perfectly clear — and he's got the figures to prove it — it's not unemployment and poverty that create crime, it's the other way round: crime is the culprit. Get rid of crime, and there won't be any poverty or unemployment.'

'Harry never reads anything except newspapers!' Bridget says. 'Most of the time he sits round drinking coffee. The rest of the time he writes letters, works on files, calls the accountant, checks attendances, rounds up missing students, talks to Immigration... but he only does it when he's not drinking coffee or when he's bored.'

Harry pretends not to understand. Half of the American Bar is designed for drinking, the other half is given over to grey plastic tables on which are served steaks, quick fries and salads. This part of it is separated from the rest of the room by a glassed, shoulder-high partition. The half in which they're drinking is the one with the stage and the miniature dance floor. It's the noisiest half. On the stage the three-piece rock group is taking a break. Its leader, dressed in crumpled jeans and a denim jacket, adjusts the microphone and blows into it.

'An economist from America,' Bridget says, 'an economist from America thinks they've got it right — that they're on the right track.'

'Who says they've got it right?' Someone with a glass of beer in one hand and a briefcase in the other stands behind Bridget and stares down at her almost contemptuously. She stares back at him with what appears to Harry to be equal contempt. At least, to Harry it looks like contempt, but then it's something he's not always good at — making judgements about what's going on between people when they look at each other that way. The newcomer wears a business suit, could be a lawyer or an accountant but is more likely a minor public servant with a high opinion of himself. He takes a chair — perhaps only temporarily vacated — from a neighbouring table, slides it into place next to Bridget and waits for an answer.

'People from other countries,' Bridget tells him, 'see things differently — have a different point of view — just might be more objective than we are.'

Harry is surprised at her interest in politics — and her assertiveness. During the two years she's worked with him, Bridget has kept a politely formal distance between herself and her employers. Now he's seeing another side of her.

'He was talking on the radio this afternoon,' she says. Harry remembers Bridget has a Sony Walkman she listens to during lunch breaks or when she's working, if what she's doing is repetitive or boring.

'He's a retired Attorney General from the United States and he's... he's... a politician.' She emphasises 'politician' as if she considers it the major and the more important of the American's qualifications. 'He says the economic policies being developed here — the Government's economic policies — are necessary and irreversible. Protection can't meet the needs of consumers and doesn't produce enough overseas credit to pay for the things that need to be imported for industrial development — all that high tech stuff.'

'Card phones,' the red-headed woman interjects. 'Improved and better ways of making people pay more.'

Harry is surprised and he can see Frank is surprised as well. Neither of them has realised Bridget is interested in politics and even if she doesn't like the man she's talking to (and it appears she doesn't) he can't tell whether she approves or disapproves of the American's comments.

'Perhaps he's right,' says the man in the suit. 'State control's been around for so long now, nobody here knows how to deal with a free economy — how to compete in the real world, out there in the market place where everything's happening.'

'Yes,' Bridget comes back at him, 'controlled economies don't respond to market forces quickly enough. They don't allow for competition — for individual initiatives and external instability — changes in international trade and the world money market.' They stare at each other silently as if sizing each other up. Bridget suppresses a giggle and then suddenly she's laughing. The newcomer laughs with her.

Harry doesn't understand it — doesn't understand what's going on. He tends to disconnect himself from things, particularly if they bore him, and when this happens he doesn't really listen to what people are saying. A moment earlier he had the impression Bridget and the man in the suit were on the verge of quarrelling with each other and now unexpectedly, they're laughing. He doesn't understand it. Too often he listens to conversations without properly hearing them. It's not how he wants to be but how things are, and when it happens, his subconscious rushes off on its own, comes to some kind of an arrangement with itself to do exactly what it likes. The result is that the part of him that deals with everyday events loses contact with what's going on around him and he finishes up feeling stupid and afraid other people will notice his stupidity.

And his habit of not listening to people, of not paying attention to what's going on, is getting worse. It's been getting worse ever since his marriage broke up and started trying to work out why things went wrong. It means there could be a connection between the two — between what happened in his marriage and his absent-mindedness. Other people have problems, other people get into messes — all of them have things going on in their heads they'd rather forget about, and they have to make just as much of an effort as he does to listen to what's being said whether it's boring or not. But it's not only what goes on inside his head — not just trying to analyse the past — sometimes there are other things as well — things that don't make sense, that don't bear any relationship to ordinary, everyday events like... like strangers who stop you in the street and want to talk about nothing you know about, and there are problems with your car nobody at the garage can fix, letters that arrive from people you've never heard of... He's had letters like that. There was a letter only two or three weeks ago — from somebody he'd never heard of. Crazy! And it didn't make any sense. He can still remember it — at least he can remember the mess the guy made of the typing — and he still remembers the general tenor of the letter itself.

Dear Harry, the letter began, *You won't know who I am — nor does it matter — but I need to write to someone, and I found your name and address in the phone book.* He'd almost stopped reading at this point, but eventually, curiosity getting the better of him, he went on with it — kept going. *The day is washed out,* it continued, *grey is the colour of everything, including my thinking, so here I am writing from the kitchen — that is, from the kitchen table. There is little to choose from and nothing much to eat. I get by waiting for sleep to come, but sometimes it comes late and I spend the time thinking I don't have very much — nothing much at all.*

There is a compulsion which makes men want more than they have — the dominant drive in human society. Once a man is tolerably well fed, well housed, and clothed, the wings of acquisition begin to spread; I have none of these things, so my wings are clipped. Yesterday I attended 'A prayer for Israel' seminar because the advertisement said there would be a free supper afterwards and I particularly seek out such occasions. I heard many success stories concerning the benevolence of God, of prosperity in the blossoming land of Israel where anyone can tap this God on a private line, but somehow my friend (forgive my using the title but I'm writing to you, and for the time you're my friend), none of it seemed to match up with experience.

Sometimes I feel like the heroes of classical myth — always travelling between two opposing points, each equally deadly — the man-defeating rocks Jason had to pass, or Scylla and Charybdis past which Odysseus needed to go in order to find his way home. I remember these things which I once read, and think on them because it helps on days like these.

For the last few weeks, I've been walking into town every day and browsing for an hour or two in the local bookshop, but because I'm not well-dressed, have worn-out shoes and never buy anything, I've noticed many times and especially today, one of the shop assistants extract herself from the counter and move closer where she can busy herself watching me. It came to me sadly, to cease such entertainment as it seems she thinks that if I don't buy anything, I must be intending to steal something.

I have written the last paragraph in red (my typewriter ribbon possesses two colours), I've written it in red because that's how things appeared to me when I left the shop. I don't think I'm paranoiac — I've had experience of paranoia in times past and what I tell you is the direct truth from the inner man. These things happen because I have time on my hands — people take exception when they don't need to, can't cope with individuality — if you scratch your cock in the street, you're a potential flasher.

Following the long street home earlier, I thought, my God, can this be happening to me? You can see why people need things to keep them from getting lost — liquor, dope, that kind of thing. Perhaps I'm living beyond my capacity — too much hair, not properly shaven, lips slightly blue and never again to kiss a woman — carrying a sandwich in a plastic bag in my jacket pocket, a red apple, and a worn yellow notebook in which to scribble things that spook people.

I think I've lost touch with the walls in the place I'm supposed to be. On one of them — one of the walls — I have a picture of Lorca on his knees before the firing squad. Perhaps I should write poetry, produce a number of poems and ascribe the names of different authors to them. I could post them off and perhaps some of them might get published.

Looking at the picture of Lorca makes me think I'm losing whatever courage I might have, reminds me that I'm scared even of my own name. This afternoon I saw a guy selling coloured balloons. He was approached by two other guys in jeans. They started an argument about the price he was asking and then they beat the shit out of him and took off with the balloons. Another guy selling hot stuffed potatoes from a stall not far from the balloon seller, packed up his gear and quit. A woman went past trundling a trolley of canned goods. Just trying to be friendly, I said to her, 'We ain't got no money, honey but baby we got plenty of rain.' She pointed a finger at me and waved to the man looking after the car park. By tomorrow he will have told his customers to watch out for the man in the worn shoes, the torn jeans — the man with the red bandanna.

It's a week now since anything appeared in my mail box. Every now and again I wish I'd get a letter or a poem from somebody, even a circular from an insurance company — anything, just as long as it was personal. I think about music, money, cheese and macaroni. Soon I'll go to bed and watch the moon through the cracked window glass. Thank you for reading this far — it's good to be writing to somebody.

No date or address were given and the letter was unsigned. It worried him because there were things in the letter he didn't understand. He didn't for example, know for certain who Lorca was and although he'd heard of Scylla and Charybdis he wasn't sure what part of Greek mythology they belonged to. And it worried him because he didn't like to think of anyone being in the kind of situation the writer described — particularly when there was no way he could offer any assistance, nor even write back and say yes, he'd read what the guy had written, and thanks very much for sending it — and perhaps in another envelope, anonymously, send a few dollars to help him out.

'You've been taking a course in it,' the red-haired woman says. 'You've been reading that stuff the Chicago school puts out — market forces — the trickle down theory...' She seems to be party to whatever the joke is, to know what's going on between Bridget and the guy in the suit.

'No — no,' the man in the suit says, 'I'm really not into it. It's just stuff you can't miss, you pick up here, there and everywhere — the hard line stuff that didn't work during the industrial revolution, in the nineteenth century, and won't work now.'

Politics, eventually everything gets down to politics, Harry tells himself, and it makes no difference whether you're in the armed services or trying to get a business off the ground as he and Frank are doing. Everybody has bad times. He's had a bad time — Frank had a bad time in Vietnam. Of course, Frank shouldn't have had a bad time as the authorities who sent his unit there, did so unwillingly — not because they believed the war needed fighting, but because it seemed the best thing to do in view of what the Americans wanted and the Government's treaty with America.

'I forgot,' says Bridget, 'I forgot to introduce everybody. She waves towards the man in the suit. 'This is Richard. He's a politician — well, almost a politician. He's a member of the party and he's been nominated for selection — for selection as a candidate.'

The newcomer moves round the table and shakes hands with everyone, 'Richard,' he says, 'I'm Richard Vallant — like the Prince but spelt differently and not as famous. Well, not yet!' He laughs at the joke although none of them, not even Harry, sees the point of it. 'And I'm not really a politician — just running for selection, and then... maybe... well... who knows?' He sits down and smiling a little, looks around the table as if he expects formal acknowledgement of his political notability and future status as a parliamentarian.

'He's wrong,' says the woman with the red hair.

'He's not,' Bridget tells her. 'He's telling the truth — he always tells the truth. Richard really is running for selection and he could — he could become the candidate.'

'Not Richard — I'm not talking about Richard,' she smiles at Bridget.

'The economist — the American economist is wrong. Protected industries might not produce goods that can compete on the world market but they create jobs — and they do it here just like they do it in the United States. America isn't really a free market — it has import restrictions, it protects key industries...'

'I knew someone who stood for Parliament,' Frank says, 'but he didn't get in.'

'It's not easy to succeed in politics,' Harry offers, not because he wants to talk politics but because he feels an obligation to say something, anything at all. 'It's not easy to get started — you have to impress people — persuade them you're the best person for the job.'

'Yes,' Frank comes in again, obviously not wanting to be left out, but with no great enthusiasm for the direction the conversation's taken. 'You have to impress people who aren't up to it themselves but believe they're infinitely superior to whoever it is who's making the effort.'

'I read somewhere,' the red-headed woman says, 'that market theory isn't just theory — that it's not true that it hasn't been tested, hasn't had enough time to show an effect. This writer — she does something at the university — said we don't have to wait for an economic improvement because it's all been said and done before...'

It's Harry's turn to get the drinks. He checks out who's having what, and thinks he can remember everything including the export lager Prince Valiant's drinking. Before he's gone more than a few paces the band which has been taking a break, starts up again. A sudden clash of drums, guitar and saxophone throws the sound system out of kilter. The speakers emit a hideous shriek and drown out all conversation. By the time he's fought his way through the crowd round the bar he's forgotten the list he's been keeping in his head. 'Beer!' he calls out, dispensing with the niceties and catching what he thinks is a conspiratorial glance from one of the women serving behind the bar. 'Five beers!' It seems the simplest solution to his dilemma and likely to satisfy everyone.

While he waits for the drinks he tries to work out what he doesn't like about Richard. There has to be an explanation, something simple — perhaps from his childhood. Harry spends a lot of time thinking about his childhood even though it's something he prefers to forget. Small things bring it back to him: the smell of damp linoleum or decaying carpet (the predominant odours in his grandfather's house where he was brought up) — at other times it's the tone of a voice, the taste of food, the shape of a cloud, the colour of an apple. In the present case he thinks it's the voice. His distaste for the possessors of expensive, deep and meticulously cultivated voices causes him suddenly and irrationally to cancel the beer he's ordered for Richard and have it replaced by a sherry laced with raspberry — the sweetest cordial he can think of. It's a poor, spiteful action, but it puts him into a more comfortable frame of mind.

'It's the environment,' Bridget says while he's distributing the glasses and making sure the would-be politician receives his sherry, 'it's the environment we have to think about — not the economy.'

'No,' Frank tells the red-haired woman, 'it's the Government's fault — the Government's function is to find solutions. And it does, sometimes it does, but then it cancels everything out through its own stupidity — like not issuing visas when it's been encouraging people to sell education to students from overseas.'

'A market frenzy — like the feeding frenzies sharks get into,' says the red-headed woman. 'Freeing the market up the way they have brings out the worst in people — drives them crazy — convinces plumbers and school teachers that they're speculators and entrepreneurs when they'd be better off staying at home feeding the cat or digging the garden.'

'The Government didn't expect a student revolt in China, they didn't expect what happened in Beijing — in Tiananmen Square,' Richard tells them.

Harry remembers his recruiting trip to China, remembers walking across Tiananmen Square with his Chinese hosts after they'd shown him through the Forbidden City. He remembers the polite way in which the various architectural features and monuments of the revolution were pointed out to him — the oppressive heat and the brightness of the light, the almost pastel colours of the buildings — the way people went silently (almost stealthily) about their business as they walked across the enormous space and immense distances of the Square.

'The Chinese didn't expect it,' Harry says quietly. 'It wasn't supposed to happen.'

'Cherry Heering and a bloody great bucket of it! Generous!' the politician says. He sips appreciatively, waves to Harry and pushes his chair closer to Bridget's.

It wasn't just the size of everything — of the square itself, of the buildings, the monuments. It was the way the Chinese moved across the square — moved rapidly as if they had pressing business somewhere else and far off, somewhere far beyond the endless pavement they were traversing. There was the unnecessarily large number of policemen, all of them equipped with sidearms, who seemed to be moving in no particular direction at all. It was the police he didn't like, the police and their random, directionless movement — their extreme youth and the lethal power of the weapons they carried.

Thinking about it brings back the sense of unease, the heat and stickiness, the sweat and tension of the Square with its somnolent and unexpected trees — people everywhere — the sun moving overhead. His heart beats louder and faster, and he's standing in the almost unendurable heat of Beijing's mid-afternoon sun. There's a rush and clatter of feet, a burst of flame, shouting, the movement of personnel carriers, of armoured vehicles and tanks... a scatter of people... blood and broken bodies. He knows it's not possible for him to see exactly what happened or work out why it happened — but it's what he imagines might have happened, how he sees it...

'Wine — a carafe of house red,' says the Prince gathering up the empty glasses.

Harry's grandfather drank beer — and whisky when he could get it. He owned a garage, not much of a garage but it provided a living and allowed him to acquire a modest weather-board house and raise three children — two boys and a girl. The girl was Harry's mother, the two boys his uncles — not that he saw much of them. The garage itself was long gone by the time Harry was old enough to know it had ever existed. One of the sons worked as a hairdresser and seemed never to be able to present anything except the most dismal and lugubrious view of the world, the other was an eternal optimist and addicted to any form of sport that presented itself: rugby, cricket, hockey, basketball, bowls. The hairdresser occasionally attended to Harry's hair; the optimist sometimes visited Harry's grandfather, giving him an indirect acquaintance with the positive and nobler attributes conventional wisdom ascribes to physical activity and competitive human endeavour. Harry's mother and his father were usually absent — not that this worried him much or that he fully understood it... but combined with his other family relationships, it resulted in his seeing human circumstances and events — history itself — as varying combinations of chaos and confusion.

'History,' he says, when the various drinks he's consumed have had sufficient effect for it and a break in conversation gives him the opportunity, 'history's the cause of it all — not people — it's history that's the problem.'
'Susan St John says — she's a university lecturer —' the woman with the

red hair tells him, 'Susan St John says it's not history but the state, a question of what the state ought to be doing — how far it can go — whether it should be doing anything at all...' Harry thinks, although he can't be sure of it, he thinks he understands what she's saying and he likes it because... because it lends authority to what he's said... to what he's said already... about history. 'When people can't agree on what Governments are supposed to be doing, they — the Governments,' she hesitates, 'the Governments are supposed to...'

'More drinks —' says Bridget, 'the drinks are finished and we need to get more of them...' The red-headed woman and Bridget collect the glasses and weaving their way across the room, disappear into the crowd round the bar.

They are gone — they are gone a very long time — or so it seems to Harry. Frank and Richard buy the next two rounds. 'Vanished,' Frank tells them, when he comes back with the second round, 'vamoosed, disappeared...'

Frank and Richard make desultory conversation. Harry tries to join in but feels disappointed... guilty... as if he's personally responsible for some kind of a social gaffe — for the women leaving — and needs to offer an apology. 'You can't have much of night out —' he says, 'you can't have much of a night on the town...' But he doesn't finish, because Bridget and the red-haired woman unexpectedly reappear. They've not only bought everyone small and expensive bottles of imported beer — but they've brought Margueritas for themselves and a whisky each for the men.

'Ford... I think that's who it was... Ford said something about history...' Prince Valiant turns towards Bridget and stares into her eyes with such intensity that it appears he expects whatever it is he's going to say will change her life forever. 'Yes, Ford said something...' He pauses. 'But... but I can't remember what it was... well, not exactly...' Harry waits for him to tell Bridget what Ford said, but it seems that this is all he has to say.

'History is the highest... the highest... and most supreme form of human achievement,' the red-haired woman announces in an authoritative voice. Mysteriously, her chair has manoeuvred itself round from the other side of the table and she's sitting next to Harry waving her arms about. She's waving them so clumsily (it seems to him she's doing it clumsily), she's waving them so clumsily that they keep coming into contact with his shoulders and neck. He has no difficulty... no objection to her hand on his shoulder... no objection to what she's doing at all...

His problem is understanding... understanding what she means... history is the highest form of achievement... He can't remember having thought about it... well... he can't remember having thought about it deeply... but he recognises... it *sounds* as if it has the ring of truth about it. It probably makes as much sense as anything else anybody's ever said... perhaps it makes more sense... a lot more sense... And he's forgotten almost everything else — what everybody else has said — he's even forgotten what he's said himself... but then, he's never been a great conversationalist... which he puts down to his childhood... or maybe it was because he was in the Navy. People in the Navy don't talk very much — well not about anything that matters... People in the Navy have to be careful of what they say... because... because it can be taken up... it can be taken up and used... used in evidence... And it has to be written... it has to be written down first... has to be very formal...

Three

It is half past three in the morning. Harry knows it's morning because he's lying in bed in the dark — and through the darkness he can see the red glow of his digital clock which, unmistakeably, indicates that it's three thirty and in the morning rather than any other time of day. He's been dreaming about the Navy — about when he was in the Navy, and John Stuart Mills — but then he always dreams about the service when he's drunk too much or when it's been a bad week and he hasn't been able to get as much sleep as he ought to. This time it's alcohol — and he knows it's alcohol because his head aches and he has a bad taste in his mouth. The implications are clear and unequivocal: he's been mixing his drinks, and he's been drinking wine — and bad wine at that.

Drinking too much, going to bed too late are fine, he thinks, and even desirable activities for those who are too young to know any better. It's a different matter when you've lived long enough to have tried two — well, one and a half — professions and now seem to be failing at the third. He turns back the duvet — carefully, so that he doesn't have to experience the sudden glare of switching on the light, or go to the trouble of re-adjusting the bedding when he returns — stands up (unsteadily) and feels his way to the bathroom. It's through the bedroom door and immediately to the left — no distance at all, and really no further than an en suite would have been if he had one.

His head aches. Its dull throbbing is accompanied by a feeling of nausea and a slight ringing in his ears — what he deserves after staying up so late and drinking as much alcohol as it seems he has. Twenty years ago it wouldn't have been a problem. After four or five hours of sleep he'd have been up with the birds and looking forward to a second round of the same thing. Now is a different matter, now is now and he doesn't have the capacity for it. He gropes under the shaving mirror and finds the switch. Aspirin, a glass, and a little water from the tap are what he needs. He swirls the water round to encourage the tablet to dissolve. It takes longer than he thinks it should — but then, it always does.

The armed services — the Navy — why does he wake up sweating, why does he dream so often about the Navy? This time it was divisions, getting ready for divisions and wondering whether or not Mills would make such a fool of himself that he'd have to go to the trouble of speaking to him about it later. And then it had turned into a raw recruit's worst nightmare — not being able to find his full kit and wondering who the hell had taken part of it. And somewhere in the middle of the acute embarrassment of having to go on parade in his working rig instead of his number one uniform, he had woken up. Morning and a splitting headache — but at least it's Saturday and he doesn't have to rush off immediately — doesn't have to be anywhere at any specific time. He empties the glass, rinses it, puts it back on the shelf above the hand basin and switches off the light.

Back in the bedroom, he eases himself under the duvet and turns towards the windows. There's no light — no indication — not so much as a whisker of the eventual and unstoppable dawn. He closes his eyes and waits for the aspirin to begin its work, for the pain to leave his head and sleep to return. He has a few hours left before there's any need to get up and do anything — a few more hours of blissful, blank unconsciousness.

The bed creaks and unexpectedly, the duvet moves away, withdraws from him. He reaches out for it — to pull it back. 'Scuse me.' It's a voice he doesn't recognise — a woman's voice — the soft, sleepy, and slightly musical voice of a woman. 'Scuse me... could I... could I have a drink of water? With ice, please if... if there's any left.'

Harry props himself up on his elbow. His sleepiness has vanished and suddenly wide awake, he reaches for the light switch. 'Please,' says the voice, 'don't switch it on yet — I don't feel well, and... I would... I would so much like a glass of water.'

Harry gropes his way out to the kitchen. It's a mess. The bench is overflowing with empty glasses and used coffee cups, the sink is full of plates. They've not been washed but they've been stacked neatly, ready for washing. He can't remember stacking them nor anything much of what might have happened to get them into the state they're in now. The bar — yes — and going somewhere, drinking wine and eating afterwards — nothing special — but nevertheless, eating. He now sees that whatever it was he was drinking and wherever it was he was eating, some of these activities must have occurred in his own apartment — and judging from the quantity of used utensils, must have included all five of them — everyone who'd been at the American Bar earlier in the evening.

'Which of them is she?' he asks himself, knowing it has to be either Bridget or the red-haired woman, one or the other, and vaguely aware it's sometimes difficult to recognise voices when they're blurred by the stresses and strains imposed on them through their owners not getting enough sleep or subjecting themselves to the rigours of excessive drinking.

He switches off the light and goes back to the bedroom where he searches for his guest's right arm, locates it in the near dark and slides the glass of water into the hand attached to it. The hand is warm and soft and momentarily, its fingers have been in contact with his own.

When she's finished with the glass of water he's given her, she passes the glass back and he puts it on the table beside the bed. 'It's 'straordinary — it really is 'straordinary,' she tells him, 'how thirsty people get... when they stay up late... and drink too much. It's... it's — 'stra-ord-inary.' She has difficulty getting the words together — grave difficulty.

Keeping a safe distance from her, he retrieves enough of the duvet to cover himself and adjusts the top of it round his shoulders so that there'll be less likelihood of her pulling it off a second time. Somewhere far off in the darkness, a dog barks. The lonely sound is taken up by a second dog, and then repeated by a third animal at an even greater distance. Harry drifts back into sleep, hoping it's Bridget he's sharing his bed with but uncertain of it and willing (although he doesn't admire himself for it), willing to accept the red-haired woman if it turns out that it's she who happens to be his guest.

When he wakes the second time his headache's gone and there's a faint glow coming from the blinds which cover his bedroom windows — a warning of the dawn to come. He's uncomfortable and far from well. A hard, pointed object has forced itself up against ribs and is unpleasantly pushing into them. It isn't painful, but it's uncomfortable. He gropes around until he finds what it is — an elbow — a woman's elbow. Trying not to disturb its owner, he pushes the elbow gently — very gently aside. A movement of the mattress and a tug on the duvet tell him his visitor is also awake and that he's not been very successful.

'It's 'straordinarily difficult to sleep when there's someone else in the bed,' says the voice, 'especially when that someone isn't considerate — when he won't,' she pulls at the duvet, 'when he won't... keep... still.' Additional tugs on the duvet punctuate the last few words of what she's saying.

Harry is awake — wide awake. The coming dawn, the woman's voice, her tugging at the duvet, the movements of her body, the inhalation and exhalation of her breath, convince him he's awake and not going to return to that delicious oblivion from which her elbow has driven him.

'My God,' says Harry, 'you're the one who's keeping me awake — it's my bed, it's you who are tugging the bedding off me and it was your elbow grinding into my ribs — not the way it should be — the other way round!'

Another part of her body has found its way into contact with him. It's a hip, a bony but beautifully contoured hip that shouldn't properly be there and is therefore, in terms of his understanding of hospitality and good manners, none of his business — except that he's been pushed precariously close to the edge of the bed and there's nowhere else for him to retreat to.

'You're not very friendly, are you?' she says. 'Anybody would think we'd never seen each other before.' She wriggles into a more comfortable position — more comfortable for her, but balanced as he is on the edge of the bed, not so comfortable for Harry. 'It's 'straordinary — it's 'straordinary how inhospitable people can be...' He can see now the light's improving that she's not Bridget, but the woman with the long chin and the red hair. It's still too dark to see the colour of her hair, but he can tell from the way it spreads over the pillow and the shape of her face which of them she is, and therefore knows her hair has to be red.

'We don't know each other,' he tells her, 'we really don't know each other — at least, not well enough to be as friendly as that.' He pushes her away (gently), rediscovering in the process that neither of them is wearing anything — nothing at all — not even pyjamas. He's Harry Houghton, he reminds himself, he's Harry Houghton, formerly a naval officer — a *commissioned* naval officer — and therefore (although he's never thought much about it or felt any great certainty of it when he has thought of it), a gentleman — and more recently, a professional educationist and a... businessman... well, perhaps not much of a businessman. People like that aren't supposed to find themselves in bed with women they've scarcely met. It's possible — it's possible and it happens — but it's not supposed to, and in this case it's not women he's in bed with, but one woman... a particular women...

'The water,' she says, sitting up, 'could you pass me the glass — I don't think I drank it all.' He finds the glass and passes it to her. She drinks slowly but in short gulps until the glass is empty. He sees while she's doing it, while he's still up close to her and now the light's better, that her hair isn't simply red, but luxuriously, gloriously red and that her face is perhaps even more unusual than he thought it was — narrow, elegant, and nice — very nice indeed!

'I don't think we've been introduced,' he says, uncertain of what else to say. 'Harry Houghton,' he says in a formal tone and as if he's attending a diplomatic cocktail party, 'formerly of Her Majesty's service and currently of no particular status — military or otherwise.' He immediately regrets it — regrets it because his military status has no immediate bearing on anything and his naval career is over and done with anyway.

The light has increased enough for him to to see the shape and colour of the bedding and the furniture — the walls of the room. She's sitting with her back against the headboard and, presumably in order to combat the cold, with the duvet and the patchwork cover he bought in a moment of despair and at a price in excess of what he could afford, over her shoulders and clutched tightly round her neck. Fortunately it's an exceptionally large cover and there's more than enough of it to conceal the strategic parts of both their bodies — even if he's already observed enough of hers to have developed an appreciative interest in the bits of it he hasn't yet seen.

'The political situation,' she says, 'politically and economically it's not a good time for starting a business.' She's not looking at him, but is examining the room as if her mind isn't connected to what she's saying — as if she's familiarising herself with her surroundings and is almost as surprised at finding herself in bed with Harry as he's surprised at her being there. He surmises she has to talk about something, and is trying to pretend there's nothing unusual in the situation — but it's possible he's wrong. He's never been good at working out what women are thinking and why they behave the way they do.

'Politics — it's always politics,' he tells her because it seems to be what she wants to talk about and up to the point they've reached so far, it's the only subject they have in common. 'People always talk politics, but it wasn't long ago that they used to talk about other things: where they lived, what they did, the things they read, movies, theatre, the arts...'

It makes him nervous, being awake so early in the morning and lying in bed under his unnecessarily expensive duvet exchanging pleasantries not with his ex-wife or either of the two women who briefly followed her, but an almost complete stranger — a woman of completely unknown origin and interests.

'Yes,' she says, 'politics — politics are what goes on between people when nothing else is happening, like... now... like what's going on here in this room... between the two of us at the moment.' She turns towards him so that half of her face is in shadow and the other half is lit by light coming in through the venetian blinds and the curtains. It's still too early to see anything clearly, so he switches on the reading lamp. She stares at him, waiting for him to speak. Her eyes have changed colour slightly — are now somewhere between blue and green — and her face isn't quite as pale as it was before. If politics are what's happening between them, it's not the kind of politics he has any familiarity with.

'And business,' she says, 'business is the same kind of thing. It's what people do to earn a living — of course it is! Everyone has to earn a living. But it's more than that. It's what people do when there's nothing more interesting and there's no one particularly interesting to do it with.' She's wide awake, alert, and at this time of the morning, what she's saying is far too intelligent for him to deal with adequately.

'Coffee?' he asks her. 'Coffee and bread rolls?' He bought the rolls two days ago, on Thursday evening, he remembers, but hasn't eaten them because he's been running late, because Frank called on Thursday night and he'd had to go into the office early on Friday. They were still there, he'd noticed when he was in the kitchen. He could put them in the oven for a few minutes and then, well buttered, they'd seem as fresh as they'd have been if he'd rushed off to the corner dairy and bought them half an hour ago.

'Coffee,' she says and slides down into the full length of the bed, into precisely the position he himself would occupy if she were wherever it was she'd normally and — right now — ought to be.

In the kitchen in his red dressing gown with gold Chinese dragons on the back (the dressing gown he's purchased to provide for the kind of situation he's presently in, and which he never expected to arise) he turns on the oven, puts the rolls into it and makes coffee.

While he waits for the rolls to heat and the water to boil, he tries to work out what might have happened the night before. They — the five of them — must have come back to his flat instead of having something to eat at the American Bar. And they wouldn't have done that unless — unless the bar had become over-crowded and they'd been unable to get served in the restaurant. Alternatively, the restaurant might not have stayed open long enough for them to eat there. Either explanation would have been adequate although it didn't much matter which of them was correct. And then — then they'd have gone on drinking — which meant (and the empty wine bottles verified it) they'd drunk too much and the party must have gone on into the small hours. Frank would have gone home by himself, dropping Bridget off on the way, or Richard might have taken Bridget with him. He doesn't like it — he doesn't like the idea of Frank driving Bridget home, and he doesn't like thinking of Richard with her or anything that might have happened between them.

He puts the coffee and the cups onto a tray, takes the rolls out of the oven and while he's buttering them realises — realises Bridget would have known the woman with the red hair was being left in the apartment with him. And if Bridget had known it, then she either expected he'd take her home because she didn't have a car with her or... or expected her to do what she's done — stay the night. He finishes buttering the rolls and takes the tray into the bedroom. His guest puts aside the book she's found under the bedside lamp.

'Good,' she says, taking one of the cups and sipping from it appreciatively, 'you make good coffee.'

He passes her the rolls. 'Perhaps you'd like something more solid after you've finished the coffee — bacon and eggs — something like that.' She wipes butter from her chin. Her fingers are long, slender, and, in terms of Harry's opinion of how things ought to be, perfectly matched with the rest of her.

She laughs, emitting a slight, bubbly sound muted by the roll she's eating. 'After?' she says turning towards him and wiping more butter from her chin. 'Is there something else — are we having something else afterwards?'

'Yes,' he says, 'bacon and eggs — if you want them.'

'And after the bacon and eggs — what happens after that?' She's looking at him over the rim of her coffee cup. Her eyes are serious, unblinking — indecipherable.

'We shower and get dressed. You go home and I go into the office,' he tells her. He can't be sure that it's what he's expected to say, but it's all there is: he has to go into the office — she has to go home. He would rather she'd been Bridget and that there was more to it than coffee, rolls and possibly eggs and bacon — but there isn't and that's the end of it.

They sip coffee and nibble rolls. He can see by the quality of the light that it's going to be a beautiful day and he's pleased about it because he needs a few days of sun in order to dry up the soggy garden he seldom touches. He suspects the gum tree his neighbour is so proud of has pushed its roots into the drains and blocked them. Because the landlord's unlikely to do anything about it, sooner or later he's going to have to get out a spade and do something — dig up the drains, go next door and complain...

'You do a lot of reading,' she says, waving at the books on his bedside table and in the book case next to it. Again she looks at him longer that she ought to, but because her face is so thin and he hasn't known her for long, he's not able to decide what she's thinking — whether she's serious.

'I read a lot,' she tells him, 'but not what I want to — they're the things you read when you're a student — and they're boring.'

He finishes his coffee, rescues the tray from the foot of the bed, and takes her half-empty cup. 'Coffee's not very nice when it's cold,' he tells her, 'would you like some more.'

By the time Harry returns from the kitchen he's remembered her name and a few blurred flashes from the five hours he's been unable to account for — not enough to put everything together but sufficient for a reconstruction of some of the of events. He can remember that the party which began at the American Bar ended in his apartment somewhere in the early hours of the morning and that while Frank had departed alone, Bridget and Richard had called a taxi. Sometime after that, he'd given up and gone to bed. Angie had climbed in later, because she was tired, she told him, and because it wasn't necessary for anyone to go out of their way for her.

'Put them on the floor,' she says when the coffee's finished and he's begun to think about taking everything back to the kitchen. 'There's no need to do anything yet — it's Saturday.'

'I don't usually stay in bed very long — not even at the weekends,' he tells her, and he doesn't. He usually doesn't sleep long because there's always so much to do, because when he was in the service he had to be out and about almost as soon as he was awake, and the habit persists.

Colours, he remembers, morning colours or worse — going on watch when sensible people ashore were still asleep and likely to remain asleep for another six or seven hours. The middle watch, it was the middle watch he disliked most — crawling out at fifteen minutes before midnight and dressing in the dark in order not to damage his night vision. And on the way to the bridge, the duty watch sweeping up rubbish, scrubbing passageways — many of them seasick, and all wishing for another hour or two's kip — to get back to their bunks, to the warmth and snores, to the dubious comfort of their mess decks.

'Bridget's into politics,' she tells him, 'really into it. Did you know she stood for the local council? Yes, two years ago — she really did!'

'Bridget says if you don't like the Government, if you don't like the way the Government's looking after things you have an obligation to do something about it — to go out and do something yourself. She says old-style politics are dead. Tub-thumping, twenty years on the council and your name on a street sign type of politics, are dead. There have to be new ways of doing things, ways that begin at grass roots level and spread out from there — that include people who don't usually get a chance to do anything or influence anybody.'

'Last night,' he interrupts when the chance offers itself. 'I don't remember all of it.' He remembers waking up and finding himself warmer — almost uncomfortably warmer than usual — and he remembers getting a glass of water for her. And he knows that when he went to bed — he knows Angie joined him later. What he wants to find out... what he can't be sure of... is what happened after that... or whether anything happened at all.

'Politics,' says Angie, 'it's always politics — nobody thinks of anything except politics. People are always dashing off to meetings and conferences here, there and everywhere...'

'What happened,' he asks her, 'what happened last night after... after the others left?'

'Bridget says... she says the two major parties have a monopoly, a private arrangement... they don't talk about it... they have a private arrangement which allows them to squeeze other parties out and share politics and power between them — take turns at running the country. It's a private club. Bridget says that whatever safeguards there were before... before they created their monopoly... those safeguards have gone. Cabinet has control over everything that happens... inside and outside Parliament... and most of the things that happen anywhere else...'

He tries again, but Angie either doesn't want to or just isn't going to tell him what happened and because she's not going to tell him, and he suspects that if anything occurred he'd remember it, the safest thing to assume is that nothing happened — nothing at all.

'It's the New Right,' she says, 'it's subverted the democratic process...' He tries to listen but right now politics aren't what he wants to talk about.

'You're not political, are you?' she asks unexpectedly moving towards him and sliding a slim, cool arm across his chest. Her other arm goes behind his head and suddenly she's half leaning over him, her red hair drifting over his face, obscuring his vision.

'Excuse me... excuse me... I have to sit up... change my position.' He pushes her away — but gently in order not to cause her any hurt, not to offend her. 'Sometimes — sometimes staying in the same position gets to be uncomfortable. It's because — because my shoulder's... my shoulder's been smashed. It was smashed in the service and it's never come right.' No one had been able to find exactly what was wrong. 'Cartilage,' they'd told him, 'cartilage or something like it — something that doesn't show up on the x-ray.' Ten years later whatever it is, still gives trouble — and right now an excuse to prevent something happening that shouldn't happen, and perhaps Angie doesn't want to happen either.

'Is it bad?' she asks him. 'Is there anything I can do — get a compress, massage it?'

The exercise off Pulau Tingi — that was what caused it. When the divers had been detected and brought on board, the interrogation had become too realistic, gone too far. The interrogators had started slapping them around and the captured divers had hit back; a fight, a full-scale fight developed and he'd been caught up in it and slammed against a bulkhead, against a door clip...

'Are you sure — absolutely sure? Perhaps a compress — a hot compress.

It wouldn't take a moment, really, it wouldn't.'

'No — no. It eases off — goes away when I'm sitting up, when I'm moving around. Leaning on it — putting weight on it — that's what causes the trouble,' which is true and which he usually keeps to himself because having other people know about his personal aches and pains makes him feel vulnerable and uncertain of himself, embarrassed. He doesn't like lying to her but stretching the truth seems the easiest way out, the simplest way to deal with what's happening — and if he concentrates it might become true, his shoulder might ache... perhaps just a little...

F o u r

John Stuart Mills — *Junior* — there's never been a 'senior' of the same name but Stuart has added the 'junior' because he believes it gives him an advantage, suggests a family of lineage and distinction. John Stuart Mills is trying to sell a car. So far, after more than an hour of waiting, there have been no enquiries, no customers — not one. If he's going to be successful though, even without customers, he has to look busy.

He takes a large square of white cloth from the vehicle's boot, goes round to the front of the car and leaning over the right-hand headlamp gives the chromium and paint of his red 1975 Triumph Stag a quick polish. Well, it's not really a polish because he's already spent some hours bringing the shine on it as close to perfection as possible. Nevertheless he moves the cloth across the gleaming paintwork with what he hopes will represent a modest but not inconspicuous flourish, a flourish designed to attract attention and at the same time convey a suggestion of care, of quality — the 'class' of the vehicle.

It's a Saturday in early autumn, the kind of Saturday which promotes optimism — offers temporary relief from rain, wind, the approaching winter — draws people out into the open air and encourages them to spend more money than they can afford. Stuart (he prefers to be called Stuart), despite so far having failed to make a sale, is enjoying himself. The car he's polishing stands with forty or so other vehicles on the upper floor of a car park, no more than three blocks from the motorway. The cars are lined up around the perimeter of the car park and in two neat rows across its centre. All of them, with one or two exceptions, have been tidied up and their owners are leaning over engines, tinkering with carburettors and fan belts, talking to possible purchasers or simply sitting in their cars waiting for customers to appear.

Stuart likes being seen and he enjoys being out in the sunshine. A neatly printed notice attached to the windshield of his car announces it's origin, year of manufacture, mileage, and the price he's seeking. When he's finished polishing the front of the car, he returns the cloth he's been using to the glove box and begins a slow perambulation around the car park. He does this because it allows him to make a comparison of the prices his rivals are asking, it gives would-be purchasers an opportunity to appraise his own offering without the embarrassment of feeling they're being watched by the seller, and it gives him the chance to check up on other people who like himself, attend car fares on a regular basis.

Recently he's attended a course on the art of selling (*How to Make a Sale Without Really Trying*), and he knows from the course that well-presented goods often sell themselves. An effective salesperson, he's been told, has faith in himself. Stuart has faith in himself, and therefore — and he believes it — he's an effective salesman. He's also been told an effective salesperson has to know that failure to sell isn't always the salesperson's fault. Sometimes the customer isn't a customer — merely somebody who's wasting his time and the salesperson's as well; and there are people — there really are people who can't be persuaded to make a purchase, even when they're being offered exactly what they need and can afford to buy.

It's the kind of philosophy Stuart has always subscribed to — and a principle that's readily transferable to other situations. When things go wrong, it's not because of any lack of ability on his part, but because his motives are misunderstood, because his virtues and the excellence of what he does aren't fully appreciated — because there's a lack of faith in his vision and judgement, in the wisdom of what he says.

He walks round the car park twice. His initial circuit tells him the autumn sun is having an effect and people are beginning to buy. His second circuit confirms that the price he's placed on his vehicle is marginally less than others might ask and therefore he has a good chance of making a sale. Sometimes he stops to talk to one of the other vendors or to examine a vehicle more closely. Occasionally he's mistaken for a buyer. His easy appearance and apparently relaxed manner conceal the watchful eye he's keeping on the car he's trying to sell.

Stuart specializes in Triumphs because he likes them — because Triumphs, as he frequently tells himself and anyone else willing to listen, have a distinction not available in lesser cars. He likes the polished wood around the instrument panel and under the windows. He likes them because they have six cylinders and his father has told him (and in this case, he believes what his father has said) six-cylinder engines last longer and give a smoother and quieter ride. The first car he'd owned (they were still talking to each other at the time, and his father had helped him buy it) was a Ford — a Cortina more than fifteen years old. He'd liked that too, until the ring gear began to give trouble. And then (again on his father's advice), he bought a Honda Civic which turned out to be largely composed of chicken wire, fibreglass and copious quantities of rust. After that he moved to Triumphs — British cars — partly because of what his father had told him and partly because they were relatively inexpensive and he'd read a feature article on them in *Classic Cars*.

By the time he's completed his second circuit of the car park, his car is under inspection. The driver's door is open and a child (a pre-schooler), is standing just inside it pushing her fingers into the upholstery — into the hole he'd thought he'd successfully concealed under the seat cover. Fortunately her parents, a slim young woman in her early twenties and a heavy-looking man much older than she is, haven't noticed what their child is doing. They're looking at the headlamps and the paint work, admiring the high polish he's given the vehicle.

'I've always liked Triumphs,' he tells them, moving over to the car and placing himself between the two adults and what their child is doing. 'It's knowing the body work is solid enough to take a knock and stand up to it.' He leans on the door pushing it in a few centimetres so that the child is forced to relinquish the attention she's been giving to the upholstery and retreat to safer ground. 'Yes,' he says, opening the door again with a flourish 'you can recognise the quality of a Triumph just by looking at the way it's put together — by the sound the doors make when you close them.' He closes the door, opens it again, and repeats the operation several times. He's oiled the hinges and lock on the driver's side, and tightened the lock plate. It doesn't necessarily result in the exact sound he's after, but it always improves the way a door opens and shuts and impresses a potential buyer.

'It's not just any kind of car,' he tells them, 'it's a classic, a quality car — old enough to be distinguished but not so old it's going to need expensive maintenance.' He identifies the moment they've arrived at as critical — the point at which the potential buyer begins to show interest, or gives up and walks away. 'Take a closer look — take a close look at it,' he says, 'cars are all different — there's always something new to be learnt from them.'

They inspect the car in some detail. The man opens the hood and peers underneath. (Stuart knows how impressive the engine looks — he's had it steam-cleaned and as soon as it was dry, splashed a little paint over the engine cover and the engine block.) The woman checks out the interior. While they're looking and much to Stuart's relief, the child wanders off towards the next vehicle — a buckled nineteen fifties Ford with a missing hub cap.

'A Stag,' says the would-be purchaser. There's an encouraging note of appreciation in his voice. 'A Stag 1976 — Mark 3 — one owner and 56,000 on the clock?' Stuart knows the inaccuracy of the figures, knows from the

41

car's registration papers there have been several owners, that it was manufactured a year earlier than 1976, that its mileage is considerably greater than what's shown on the odometer. Nevertheless, he neither confirms nor denies the information he's been offered. 'Not easy to find,' he tells his prospective purchaser, 'not many of them around.'

He goes to the other side of the car. 'Get inside,' he suggests, 'have a closer look, take the driver's seat — get the feel of it.'

They sit inside and admire the woodwork; woodwork which has been polished until it gleams not plum-red like the outside of the car, but a rich, golden yellow. 'Switch it on,' Stuart encourages, following up his earlier suggestions. Because it's still warm, the engine starts immediately while the thick layer of felt he's placed under the floor coverings reduces any discordant sounds it makes to little more than a distant and pleasant hum.

Despite appearances however, Stuart's Triumph isn't all or anything near what it ought to be. A hundred kilometres south of the city where he'd expected a bargain, he'd been assured and convinced that the local garage was operated by a mechanical genius who'd miraculously taken the engine to pieces and restored it to almost new condition. The vendor hadn't appeared overly bright, and had shown him a receipt and a job sheet that confirmed the work had been carried out. After he'd paid for it (a ridiculously low price!) and driven the car back to the city, he'd realised his mistake. It wasn't what had been done that was the problem; it was what hadn't been done — and that was almost everything! Strangely, when he looked for the job sheet and receipt for the repairs he'd been told about, they weren't in the glove box where he'd expected to find them; consequently there wasn't any evidence with which to challenge the vendor's claims, and Stuart wasn't prepared to spend the kind of money that would be required to dismantle the engine and give it the new piston rings, the re-bore and valve grind it needed.

Stuart's ignorance is forgivable. He isn't an engineer and he's not a licensed motor vehicle dealer, he's a carpet salesman who buys and sells cars on the side — but he doesn't expect to remain in such menial occupations. His father's employment as an army officer and his own three painful years in the Navy have convinced him he's cut out for better things and that someday, sometime, things will indeed be better.

'Rev it up a bit,' Stuart advises, 'rev up the engine so you can hear how it sounds.' His client puts his foot on the pedal and the engine responds with a powerful and satisfying roar.

'There,' says Stuart, 'listen to it.' He gets out of the car and helps the woman and her child into the back seat. 'Four cylinder vehicles — Fords, Hondas — imported second-hand cars — none of them have a sound like that.' His voice is confident, cheerful and considering how thin his body is, surprisingly deep. 'Would you like to try it out — go for a spin?' He fastens his seat belt and turns his head to ensure that the woman has fastened hers and that of the child. 'Safety,' he says, 'safety's important when you have children.'

The purchaser, as Stuart hopes the driver will become, the purchaser handles the car (*fully automatic, factory mags, hard top, excellent condition, only 56,000 miles*) expertly but with the slight hesitancy and the additional care usually necessary in driving an unfamiliar vehicle. Occasionally his foot reaches for a clutch that isn't there and from time to time he slips the gear lever from 'drive' into first, and back again. Stuart can see he's afraid of putting the car into reverse by mistake — of making a fool of himself. He watches what the man's doing with his feet and his hands, watches the way he's using the brakes and indicating the directions he's turning the car in — and he tries to catch glimpses of his face — to get some idea of his emotions — of what he's thinking and feeling.

Stuart's client steers the car up Broadway and eases it into Parnell Road. An unseasonal shimmer of heat rises from the roadway suggesting El Nino is still holding off and that the coming winter might not be as severe as the doom and gloom merchants predict. A few minutes later they turn west into The Drive, and then north into Stanley Street — the long way round — which in terms of a possible sale seems encouraging. He listens, trying to detect the shudder and grind he knows the engine emits and the slight rattle the exhaust usually makes. He can hear them faintly in the background if he listens carefully, but hopes they're not audible to anyone else — to people who don't know what to listen for.

'Six cylinders,' says the driver, 'it makes a difference.'

'Quality and performance,' Stuart assures him, encouraged enough to believe they're talking the same language.

'I don't like *old* cars!' The child is leaning forward between the bucket seats in the front of the vehicle. She licks an ice cream which has appeared miraculously from nowhere. A large part of it obscures her chin, an equal quantity drips over the handle of the brake lever and onto the upholstery beneath and around it. Stuart hasn't previously noticed the ice cream and even if he had noticed it, doubts if he could have done anything about it. 'The seats are too hard and I don't like them!' the child complains.

Before either he or anyone else can realise what he's doing, he takes the child's sodden ice cream cone from her, winds the window down and throws the dripping mess out onto the roadway. The woman pulls the child onto the back seat next to her and re-attaches the safety harness she's escaped from.

'I'm terribly sorry. Mr... er...'

'Mills,' he smiles at her, 'Mills — but you can call me Stuart.' He takes out his handkerchief and cleans up as much as he can of the ice cream that's dripped onto his cuff and the upholstery beside him. He does it carefully, trying to give no indication of the distaste he feels. Criticism of a client's child, directly or by implication, is the worst of the many mistakes a salesman can make — it's the quickest and easiest route to losing a sale.

'Such dear little things,' the woman says, and then repeats it a little more loudly in case he hasn't heard, 'and so astute, Mr Mills, aren't they?' She turns towards the child, 'But sometimes we're a little bit messy — aren't we, darling — just a little bit messy?'

'They grow out of it,' Stuart informs her. He's never been fond of children but it isn't an occasion suited to the expression of his personal feelings and it's true, children do grow out of things — at least, sooner or later most of them grow out of things.

'It drives well,' the driver announces, manoeuvering from Beach Road into Customs Street. The heavier traffic and the last two kilometres or so he's covered, have given him confidence. 'And the suspension's not bad either,' he adds, as if he's forgotten he's the potential purchaser and shouldn't be offering such comments.

'Sporty — tons of pick up. Worth the money — every cent of it.' Stuart comes back at him, remembering from his course in salesmanship that favourable remarks from a client virtually guarantee a sale.

The driver, who might or might not have heard the first part of what Stuart has said, pushes his foot down and thus applies more force to the accelerator. The lights at the intersection of Queen and Customs Streets loom rapidly closer, turn green to orange, and then to red. 'A good place to test the brakes,' the driver calls out to them and then, 'Now!' he shouts suddenly, glancing quickly towards the back seat, 'Hold on!' Stuart braces himself. The car leaps forward and before he's ready for it, squeals to a halt within a few centimetres of the double line. The child in the back wails prodigiously.

'Be quiet!' the woman admonishes her. 'There's nothing to be afraid of! Daddy's a good driver — a very good driver. He knows what he's doing and you're perfectly safe!'

'I don't like him! I don't like him — he's nasty!' the child wails at her. 'He's a nasty man... a very nasty man... he took my ice cream... the nasty man took my ice cream and threw it away... why did he throw it away, Mummy?'

F i v e

Despite his former marriage and the two or three relationships he's had since it finished, Harry has never been successful with women. His failure rankles, it rankles because he's attracted to women and likes them — because he likes to think well of himself and thinking well of himself isn't possible when he's failing in an area that's important, in an area most men seem to have no difficulty with. Inevitably, the women he's most interested in always elude him: they're already married or if they're not married, they're engaged, living with someone, or too busy with their careers or political movements to be bothered with long term relationships.

Increasingly he's begun to wonder whether the problem lies with him rather than them — at least, when he looks at it objectively, it's not reasonable to believe all of the women he's met and made tentative approaches to, have something wrong with them. The laws of probability suggest otherwise — that there's something wrong with him, with Harry Houghton, something about him that discourages them, puts them off. What he has to do, is identify the 'something' and take remedial action — do whatever's necessary to overcome the problem — take counselling, join an encounter group, change his life-style.

He thinks about it while he puts away the cups he's washed and the tray he's retrieved from the bedroom. He's showered and dressed but Angie is still in the bedroom where he left her almost an hour ago. So far and even though he's suggested it's time to get moving, she's shown no interest in getting up and departing for wherever it is she belongs, or to do whatever it is she does on Saturdays. Sometimes he wonders what attractive, single women like Angie do with themselves in their free time, and for a moment he sees her in a one-bedroom apartment vacuuming carpets, tidying up the living room, tossing things into an automatic washing machine, deciding what to wear for a night out or dinner in town. He sees her in an office immaculately and stylishly dressed, working on a report she has to finish by Monday, dashing off a letter, getting ready for the ski slopes or checking the gear she'll need for a trip to the mountains.

It's absurd! He's been married and knows enough about women to be aware that what he's imagining, isn't the way things are — it's the way television and the glossy magazines have persuaded him they are. He knows what women do on Saturdays because he's seen them doing it — and he knows what they look like while they're doing it because he's seen that as well. The problem is that he likes women and misses them when there are none around, and that's when he begins forgetting the realities and starts inventing things.

Sometimes he's surprised at what he thinks about. A lot of the time it has nothing to do with the real world: it's fantasy — he invents it. He's read somewhere that people fantasise eighty per cent of the time and that most of their fantasies are about sex — about the opposite sex or the same sex, about having sex, wanting to have sex, or not having it. And here he is doing exactly the same thing as everyone else! The absurdity is there's an example of exactly the kind of woman he fantasises about in the next room, in the bedroom — a woman he can even now hear getting up, moving around the room, opening the wardrobe doors, and all he's doing is washing the dishes!

He thinks about it and stares across the sink towards the gum tree he's going to have to consult his neighbour over. He stares at the gum tree and at a starling perched on one of the lower branches. It's trying to pull off a tendril of bark when it's autumn and there are four months of winter yet to come. He watches the starling with its tendril of bark and thinks about other equally crazy things — the things people do to each other for no reason at all. 'Nothing makes sense,' was the way Tony Poindexter put it. They were alone and locked in the kind of late night collective misery people experience when they live and work together and don't have any choice about who they drink with.

As he remembers, Poindexter was drunk or very close to it, and talking about women. But Poindexter usually talked about women — was one of those men who seldom stopped talking about them. 'Nothing makes sense,' Poindexter told him toying with the stem of his wine glass and looking towards the wardroom fireplace — watching the last flickerings of the fire that had kept them warm all evening.

'It depends,' he remembers responding although at the time he hadn't understood, and still doesn't understand, what they were talking about, 'it depends on the circumstances. If you're interested in what you're doing, you don't care whether it makes sense or not.'

'You know,' Tony went on, 'The last time I had to go down to Defence Headquarters, I took the car... drove there. Had some leave... stopped off half way... at *Irirangi*. Expected Bill and Margaret to be there. Nice guy,

Bill, served with him once...' He stares into the fire, twisting the stem of his glass as if he's about to break it. 'Wanted to talk with him... didn't phone beforehand. He wasn't there, but Margaret was... Margaret was there.' He lapses into silence.

'It seems like that sometimes,' says Harry who hasn't been listening properly. He too stares into the fireplace where a burnt-out log, glowing a little more brightly than the remnants of other logs around it, is about to collapse under its own weight. 'Sometimes the service makes things seem like that... as if they don't make sense. You just keep doing the things you have to do and when you've finished, go back to the beginning and start all over again. You're supposed to do things that way... then when you have to do them quickly... when they count for something... you're so used to doing what you're doing, you don't have to think about it...'

Poindexter takes their glasses over to the bar and refills them, both of them. 'Margaret was here last week,' he tells Harry, 'here in Auckland.'

He comes back to his chair in front of the fireplace and stares into the dying embers. 'Funny — it's funny about women. You just can't tell how they'll take things — what they'll do. Men — maybe men are the same... sometimes you don't really know what you're doing yourself.'

'We do what the service expects us to — and the way we're supposed to do it,' Harry explains, 'keep going until we can do everything without thinking about it. Then, when we're really good at what they pay us to do and we want to go on doing it because it's not as difficult as it used to be, time's up — we have to quit, make way for someone else...'

'And then, after you've spent a few hours with Margaret it doesn't make much difference who you've been with... You get into your car and drive off... and then there's these traffic lights. You put on the brakes and stop the car, and there's another woman on the pedestrian crossing. You look at her and she knows you're looking at her, knows why you're looking at her... and you know why you're looking at her and you've just left Margaret... It doesn't make sense.' He gets up and waves towards the door. 'A game of snooker?' he says. 'What about a game of snooker before we call it a night?'

Harry still thinks about Tony, just as he thinks about almost everything else that's happened which he hasn't enjoyed. Right now as he stares through his kitchen window at the gum tree that's slowly strangling his drains and which sooner or later he's going to have to do something about, he wonders what Tony would have done about Angie. But then, is there any sense in wondering? He can guess — and he guesses Tony would have done whatever it was that suited Tony best.

They retrieve the snooker balls from the pockets where earlier players have left them. Tony racks up the reds and locates the full assemblage precisely at that point on the table where it's supposed to go. He lifts the frame, leaving the reds in a neat, triangular formation and then puts out the colours: green on the left, brown in the middle and yellow next to it — blue, pink and the black along the centre of the table. He moves quickly, displaying the expertise and confidence of long practice and easy familiarity. He takes a cue from the rack, runs a hand along it, and holding it up to the light sights along it checking for irregularities — warp, distortion, twist — and then chalks the tip.

'A dollar each way?' Harry suggests.

'Five dollars, or better still — make a real game of it — say, ten dollars? You can't get anything much with less than that — not even a couple of drinks.' They settle for ten which, on Harry's part is sheer folly because he's never been a particularly good player and doesn't expect to win.

They toss for it and Tony opens the game. He places the white a little to the right of centre on the baulk line, draws back the cue, sights and with the smoothest of movements sends the cue ball up the table. It moves at little more than a snail's pace, barely touches the most distant of the right-hand reds, bounces off the back cushion, strikes the right-hand cushion and rolls up to the top of the table where it stops a little back from the yellow. He steps away from the table, places the butt end of his cue on the floor and inspects his handiwork. This first shot, although he has a more than average amount of alcohol in his system, is a statement of his expertise and the strategy he intends to follow — and equally a statement concerning his attitude to the world and the way he believes Harry and he should relate to each other. Harry inspects the result of Tony's opening shot. The lie of the ball isn't encouraging.

The white can't be fired directly at any of the reds but will have to be deflected from one of the side cushions. He has to choose between a vigorous and haphazard stroke which will disintegrate the assemblage of reds, a precision shot which will take out the one loose red at the far corner of the assemblage, or a double cushion manoeuvre which will leave the cue ball in direct contact with the base of the reds and make it difficult for his opponent to play without infringement and a four-point penalty. He likes the idea of Tony having to chalk up a penalty score before the game has made any real progress.

'Margaret,' he says lining up his cue and speculating on the pattern of trajectories and double triangles shaping themselves in his head, 'does Margaret play snooker?' It's a stupid question — no less stupid than the one raised over dinner by the British exchange officer who'd arrived two days ago. 'Missiles,' he'd asked the gunnery officer in a lazy, upper-class drawl, 'Missiles, guns old chap, missiles — what's all this about missiles?'

The corners of his mouth tighten, but otherwise Tony ignores the question. 'Don't scatter them, take the easy shot,' he advises. Harry interprets this as a reflection on his skill — a statement that Tony is more experienced and more knowledgeable than he is. There's the further implication that all things being equal — or as in this case, unequal — he should let himself be guided by an opponent who's as good a fellow as he's likely to meet, and who's doing all he can to help.

He draws back his cue, sights and lets it slide over his knuckles. The ball moves forward, deflects from the side cushion, goes to the top of the table and comes in behind the general mass of the reds where it makes a slight clicking sound and releases two balls. They roll a short distance to the right and stop within a centimetre or so of each other. He steps back from the table more than pleased with himself. It's not what he intended, but it's the next best and he's left Tony a difficult shot — one which he should find impossible to do anything with. It seems, and he should have raised the subject earlier, a suitable time to talk about John Stuart Mills.

'Mills,' he says. 'He's not up to it — not doing much of a job.'

Tony is the officer responsible for Mills' being there — being in the service. It was Tony who confirmed the initial report, which described Stuart as, 'not impressive as a candidate — but has suitable qualifications — the right background.' Harry assumed (and still assumes) that 'the right background' was a reference to Stuart's father's rank in the Army.

'Margaret doesn't play, but she likes the game — she likes to watch,' Tony tells him, moving towards the bottom of the table and examining the cue ball. He leans over the table until his eyes are almost level with it and sights from the right hand pocket to the nearest red and back to the white again. He gives an impression of great concentration, an impression that there's every chance of his potting the outer of the two reds. Harry doesn't think it possible — particularly in view of the slight swaying of Tony's body. He'd have to strike the inner of the two reds first, which would scatter the main group, and employ the cannon-effect of his first contact to drive the second ball towards the pocket.

Harry stares at the gum tree outside his kitchen window and thinks about Tony and his opinion that 'nothing makes any sense', and for the moment the connection between the two seems tenuous, beyond his grasp. The starling is still pulling at the tendril of bark, or maybe it's a second or a third tendril in view of his having been watching the bird without having noticed what it's been doing. But there has to be a common factor just as there's a common factor between Tony talking about Margaret and what he said about the woman at the traffic lights.

Logic tells him he's thinking about Tony and Margaret because Angie is still in his bedroom and he's done nothing about it, whereas if it were Tony here instead of himself… Trying not to think about what Tony might or might not do if he were here in his place, Harry runs warm water into the sink and rinses it out with the dish mop — not the best nor the most efficient way of dealing with sinks, but his usual way of handling the problem. Outside the window the starling takes off trailing a tendril of bark from its beak while the gold braid on Tony's sleeve, the cue he's holding, move in a blur of russet and gold across the green baize of the snooker table.

'How's that!' The white has barely touched the outer of the two reds. It moves almost imperceptibly towards the left-hand side of the table and stays there, hard against the cushion. 'It's snooker, the way it ought to be played: you make it difficult for me — I make it difficult for you', Tony tells him as he moves away from the table. There's triumph in his voice, and cruelty in his eyes and in the tight line of his lips.

Harry examines the lie of the table. He doesn't like it and he doesn't like the kind of game that's developing — a game designed not so much for the enjoyment of the players as to ensure one or the other of them is defeated — and humiliated by defeat. There's only the one shot available and he can see that if he takes it, breaks up the reds, Tony will take charge of the game and he'll be left trailing behind and at a psychological disadvantage — a disadvantage he knows Tony will extend beyond the snooker table and out into their professional and social life. If he's going to lose, he has to be a graceful loser, but he knows Tony won't allow that to happen. Therefore if he loses he'll have to balance things up later and he's not sure how to do it…

He bends over the table arching his left hand slightly and making as flat a bridge as he can. A strong and determined thrust of his cue breaks up and scatters the reds. Two of them fall into pockets — one in the centre pocket and the other in the corner pocket opposite him. He lines up for his second shot and the pink rolls across the table and disappears. Tony retrieves it and returns it to the table. The present turn of events isn't what he expected. The reds were easy enough — a matter of chance and statistics. The pink was more difficult, and taking into account their several hours of drinking and his normal standard of play, he should have missed it. The reds gave him the opportunity, and luck did the rest.

'Another red,' Tony suggests, 'another red, and then the blue — it's easier than the black.'

Harry doesn't like it — he doesn't like being told what to do — he's never liked it. And it's not in the spirit of snooker — not how people are supposed to play the game. He takes his next shot — a red near the centre of the table. If he sinks it, he can move up and try for either the green or the brown. The white moves away, strikes the red, but too wide to be effective.

'You should have tried for the blue,' Tony tells him. 'Never take a difficult shot when there's an easier one available.'

'Margaret,' says Harry, stepping back from the table, 'are Bill and Margaret still in Auckland?' He's not interested in Bill or Margaret even if he's worked with Bill on several occasions. He doesn't know either of them very well but if his opponent wants to play rough, then he can play rough as well. Tony doesn't answer. He puts down the glass he's been drinking from, chalks the tip of his cue and moves up to the other end of the table.

Tony turns and looks at him. He draws back his cue, levels it and jabs it forwards two or three times testing his aim and the amount of thrust the shot will require. 'Watch this!' Tony tells him. The cue ball flashes across the baize. The nearest red strikes the middle pocket with a solid thunk and disappears. The blue follows it. The side and bottom Tony has given the white, brings it off the cushion and stops it in perfect alignment for a second red and then the black. He takes the black twice before he misses a shot and steps back from the table.

'That's it — that's what you'd call a bishop's panic,' Tony tells him with considerably more than modest satisfaction, and then adds in explanation, 'it's supposed to put the fear of God into you — scare hell out of you!' Harry brings his opponent's score up to date on the marker board: twenty-two points — fifteen ahead. He's never heard of a bishop's panic and isn't sure whether it's the name of a specific break in snooker, or something Tony's invented. He doesn't like the phrase but he acknowledges (unwillingly) the efficiency of Tony's play, the increasing gap between their two scores, and the difficulty he's going to have in catching up.

S i x

Harry drives over the bridge — the biggest apart from Golden Gate and the Sydney Harbour bridge he's ever been over. He drives in the outer lane. He prefers the outer lane even though he can remember Tony Poindexter's warning: 'the engineers may have done their sums properly, but they're last-minute additions — the outer lanes weren't put in place until the city's leaders realised the traffic loadings had been underestimated. If one thing can be underestimated, then so can another. They just hang out over the water as if nothing's holding them there, as if there's nothing holding them up, and maybe some day they'll fall off — metal fatigue, something like that.' Poindexter was as good with maths as he was with a billiard cue; it was out of character for him to show lack of faith in things that could be calculated accurately and in advance.

Harry remembers arguing with Tony about it — trying to show it wasn't logical to believe the engineers hadn't done their work properly. 'Logical!' Tony had been adamant. 'Of course, it is — everybody makes mistakes. And when the experts make mistakes, then there's less likelihood of anyone uncovering them and a greater need for the rest of us to be more careful.' Harry drives over the bridge wondering whether Tony was right. It's one of the recollections he can't get out of his head, and in this case it's reinforced by his noticing every time he crosses the bridge that the extensions are fixed at different heights in comparison with the main carriageway.

As he drives towards the top of the bridge, he can see the difference — the outer carriageways are definitely out of alignment with the rest of the bridge and with each other. Engineers allow for different rates of expansion and contraction in metal, but he's sure such large differences aren't included in their allowances, and he's certain the same differences are there every time he crosses the harbour. He's certain there's been a mistake but he tells himself as he usually does, that it can't be important — that if it was important, it would long ago have become public knowledge and any repairs that might have been necessary, would have already been carried out.

Momentarily Harry glances away from the road in front of him towards the long sweep of the water below and on towards the inner Gulf — from Westhaven to North Head, from Rangitoto to Motutapu and Motuihe. Smudges of haze and a sprinkle of sails on the water contrast with the blue below the bridge and the immensity of the waterway extending eastward to the distant horizon. When he reaches the top, he checks he's not too close to the vehicle in front, that no one's tail-gating him, and allows himself a quick, panoramic sweep. The girders of the upper section of the bridge obscure some of the view but the arch of the sky, the curve and reach of the world around him make him feel part of everything, that he belongs to it — and then he has to look away from it, concentrate on what he's doing. He reaches towards the dash and switches on the radio.

Someone's talking politics. He recognises the voice, but can't put a name to it. 'Market forces,' says the voice, 'the Government believes in market forces — that if an economy is left to itself — employment, inflation, interest rates, the national debt — they balance out...' Harry's heard it before, everybody's heard it before but he guesses people on radio have to talk about something — it's what they're paid for — what they're there for...

'But isn't that what you believe — the kind of thing you're hoping for when you say there needs to be a universal minimum wage, an official handout for everyone? Isn't it the same thing, Richard — you expect investment and industrial development to pay for everything, to solve everything?' The interviewer's voice is warm, friendly — flirtatious. 'We can call you Richard can't we — you don't mind if we call you Richard?'

'No, of course not, but in a post-industrial society — and that's what we're talking about — in a post-industrial society unemployment isn't temporary — something that appears and goes away. For a lot of people it's permanent and unless something different is done, the good times have gone forever. A universal minimum wage isn't a handout but a necessity — it allows people to use unemployment constructively.'

'Then you accept what the Government says: a self-regulating market creates a pool of unemployed workers — a self-regulating pool which keeps wages at a level that's sustainable?'

'The Government wouldn't say so, but it's what industry and business-people want — what The Round Table wants. They want it because economists have convinced them they need it — that a competitive world works better, more efficiently when there's enough unemployment to keep the price of labour under control. It's what they've been saying about Europe — the current recession in Europe. It was said on this programme only two days ago — on your programme, Jacquie.'

'Of course, Richard.' She's still warm and enthusiastic but briefly there's a tetchiness, a hesitancy in her voice. 'The business of talk-back radio is to spread ideas around, let everyone exchange views... that's what we're here for... we don't hide things. We're here to let people have their say — exchange ideas with each other...' A pause — and then a bubble of laughter. 'Politicians as well as economists — politicians as well economists, Richard!'

'The economist on your show — the economist you interviewed said countries in Europe will recover more quickly if they exploit the availability of cheap labour in China and South East Asia... the unemployed... '

'No-no, I don't think that's what he was saying... just a moment, Richard...'

Politics, Harry thinks, politics screw things up. Nobody — not even the Government knows what it ought to be doing... whether to sell electricity and keep selling it until the hydro-dams run dry... whether to have ships for the Navy built in Australia... how much of the work will be done locally... privatise the health system... raise student fees... and far more important, how many visas will the embassy in Beijing issue in the next three months... and damn!

There's a Porsche almost on top of him... a battered van in front. He slows... has to keep a safe distance from the van... but the Porsche — the Porsche is so close he can't see all of it in his rear-view mirror. What he has do, is get into the right-hand lane... but there's too much traffic... he won't be able to manage it until the traffic clears... until there's a gap ahead of him...

'Now, Richard, getting back to your argument, nobody was talking about exploiting... taking advantage of the unemployed. What the economist... what Johnson said, was that countries making the best use of surplus labour in South East Asia, would recover more quickly than those which didn't. He said it was a matter of economics... and we have to agree on the terms we're using... on what we're talking about. We have to agree...' significant pause, 'we have to agree, don't we, Richard? The economy... we need to agree, don't we, if we're going to make any progress...' Brief silence and then laughter from Jacquie and her guest.

'And we have to agree on the difference between the *unemployed* and the *jobless*,' Richard comes in, 'they're not the same thing, Jacquie... not the same thing at all.'

'Of course,' it's Richard talking, 'of course they're not the same thing. Some of the most inventive and creative people could be classified as having been jobless — Coleridge and Darwin — Darwin perhaps throughout most of his life… and there was Byron. I don't think he ever had a job, well not a real job, but with his writing and *everything else…*' emphasis on the 'everything else' and a hint of mirth from Jacquie, '… nobody would say Byron didn't keep himself fully occupied…'

Although he's sure he knows Richard's voice, Harry can't place him. But he gives Jacquie's guest top marks for style… the ease with which he can take up a difficult point and turn it to advantage: the way he's dealing with 'jobless' and 'unemployed'.

Motuihe, Motutapu and most of the harbour have passed out of range. Harry has come off the bridge and is moving along the St Mary's Bay section of the motorway. His speed is touching eighty and the van he's following reduces his view of the roadway to no more than ten to fifteen metres. Immediately behind, the Porsche is almost on top of him. If he doesn't do something, in another minute or so he'll have it sliding up his tail pipe. He can't increase speed without imposing the same threat on the van ahead of him, and he's so close to it he can't get into the next lane without taking its right-hand tail light with him. Saturday morning, he tells himself. In theory there shouldn't be so much traffic about, but it's his bad luck to be caught between two of the least desirable elements of whatever happens to be on the road.

'It's like religion,' Richard says. 'Once you believe in something — in economic theory — you stop being rational — aren't willing to listen to anyone except yourself… or whatever guru it is who's become the flavour of the month. The Chicago school's no different. It has its economic theory — its tablets of stone — and nothing, not even the harsh reality of unemployment and the increasing crime rate, nothing will make any difference to the people who believe in it.'

Harry tries not to listen. He won't admit it, but he's angry with himself and he's angry with the Porsche behind him. Something has to be done — he has to do something. He switches on his parking lights and eases back on the accelerator. The driver of the car behind might think he's applied his brakes and there's a danger of collision. His car drops back from the van in front of it while the vehicle behind looms closer — so close he expects to hear a crunch of metal, feel the jolt of impact — but nothing happens. He reduces speed still further… but gradually, to give the Porsche a chance to take evasive action. The car he drives is twelve years old and isn't in good condition but he doesn't want it damaged… doesn't want to risk his no-claim bonus.

'What would you do about it, Richard... about the economy... the unemployed... if you had the opportunity...' more laughter from the radio. 'What would you do about the jobless...'

When he thinks the motorway's clear enough, Harry puts his foot down... not too much, but enough to encourage the driver behind him (heavy jowled, he notices, and balding) to take the bait. At first and for a short period, nothing happens. And then Harry slows his car a little in order to put distance between himself and the van. His reward for the manoeuvre is a blast of horn from behind. He likes what he hears, holds his speed for a moment and then gives his car full acceleration.

'It's not a question of the jobless, Jacquie, it's more a matter of philosophy... of political philosophy...'

The van leaps towards him. It appears he's going to hit it but he knows it's unlikely. He turns his wheel to the right. The car lurches sideways and swerves towards the right-hand lane. He passes the rear of the van — closely — so closely he's almost certain he's hit it. The sound he hears though, is coming from behind him and he can see in his rear-view mirror the Porsche has driven into the van and both vehicles are slowing down, pulling towards the side of the motorway...

'And before we bring our callers onto the line, perhaps you'd like to tell us about your own philosophy... your *political* philosophy, Richard. People want to know — people really want to know more about the Alliance — what the Alliance stands for. Perhaps you could tell us something about it, let people know where you stand, what the Alliance stands for — what it might do in the present situation...'

Harry keeps an eye on the scene behind him for as long as it remains in view. He knows he shouldn't have done what he's done — and yet there's a sense in which he hasn't done anything at all, a sense in which the driver of the Porsche alone is responsible. It's not his car but the Porsche which has run into the van... and if both vehicles were travelling at nearly the same speed, there's no chance of anyone having been hurt and the damage can't be great.

'Winston has a question for you, Richard,' he hears over the radio, 'Winston... are you there... we can't hear you, Winston...'

Harry slows at the lights and drives into Fanshawe Street. It's one of the city's drearier thoroughfares — a street separating the down-town area from the waterfront and containing nothing to boast of except a string of tired and dilapidated buildings that are either empty or being used by Chinese importers as temporary warehouses. They remind him of the things that have happened in his own life, of his failed marriage and the business he and Frank operate — the business which is rapidly going the same way as his marriage — of his naval service and the dreary, broken-down Pacific seaports he's visited and remembers vaguely as in a hazy dream. And now, there's Angie who's still in his apartment, who's told him she'll leave later — after she's showered and tidied up — there's Angie to add to his list of things that never happened, that won't happen...

He drives along Fanshawe Street and past Victoria Park — both equally uninspiring. The park is an extensive area of grass with plane trees on one side and a sculpture — an over-sized plough-share constructed of railway sleepers — on the other. A viaduct carrying the motorway sweeps over the park and sometimes in summer he's seen cricketers in white flannels tossing a ball around, practising at the nets...

'Politicians...' Winston tells him over his car radio, '... opinion polls put politicians at the bottom of the popularity stakes, on the same level as second-hand car salesmen...'

'Stacking,' Jacquie says, 'according to the papers politicians don't play fair...'

'Not the Alliance,' Richard interrupts her, 'that's not the way the Alliance works. The Alliance was formed to change things... to bring honesty back into politics... give people a fair deal... make politicians accountable...'

'Politicians cheat,' Jacquie informs her radio audience, 'National Party candidates have been stacking selection meetings, loading them up with their supporters, and the Labour Party does it... Look at what happened with Prebble — your name-sake, Richard Prebble — and Auckland Central. And the people they recruit, when it's all over, when the selection's been made, they disappear, fade away, do nothing... is that playing fair... keeping politics clean? What's your view, Richard? How does the Alliance stand on selection meetings...?'

Seven

Harry is still thinking about Angie when he turns into Short Street and drives into the basement of Edmonton House. He doesn't know why it's called Edmonton. Some day if he has the time, he'll find out — but not today because today's Saturday and he's had a rough night. When he's parked, switched off the engine and locked his car, he takes the lift up to the fifth floor.

There aren't many people in the reception area — just one or two Chinese talking to Bridget about the courses the school offers, or maybe passing the time of day. He nods to her and crosses to his office. Along the corridor, he can see the only class that's held at the weekends: Saturday morning's remedial and catch-up session which is reasonably full — as it ought to be because there's no charge for it. It's offered free as an act of goodwill — originally in order to give students an opportunity to catch up if they missed anything, but now to allow newcomers to master the dozen or so phrases necessary for survival during their first weeks in an unfamiliar environment. Not many require this kind of help, but an hour or two extra on Saturday can make a difference.

He and Frank had considered themselves fortunate when they first found the place — two hundred square metres of floor space with a six months' rent holiday, and the lessors paying for the partitioning and redecorating. As they occasionally do when there's a good reason for it, they'd celebrated with a night on the town and it had been rough, but not as rough nor as enjoyable as the previous evening at the American Bar — parts of which he could still remember even if they were a little blurred.

When he reaches his desk, he takes up the paper he's collected on his way through the reception area and glances at the headlines: *Business Bosses control Power Board.* It's a dispute that's been going on for weeks, a dispute he hasn't been very interested in but he notices the Board members are all top businessmen appointed by government. So much for democracy! *The new chairman is also chairman of the NZI Bank and a former chief executive of the National Bank…* He scans the rest of the article. *He and his fellow board members are determined to follow Government policy and convert the Board into a private company... The directors who yesterday removed the former chairman and replaced him with Mr McElroy, represent the top management of the nation's business sector...*

Bridget waves to him through the glass partition and points to the telephone. It's Frank making sure the excesses of the night before haven't made him unfit to attend to business — if any. Usually there's little or nothing to do on Saturdays, but they take it in turns to put in an appearance, 'just in case'.

'Everything okay?' Frank asks him. 'Any faxes? Any students thrown out of their homestays — anyone waiting on the doorstep?'

'No idea,' he says, 'arrived only a moment ago and haven't had time to check. Doesn't seem to be any problem — just a few students hanging out — talking to Bridget in reception.' He stares through the glass in order to make sure they're still there. 'She's looking after them.'

'And the papers? Anything new in the papers?' Frank isn't much of a reader and likes to have things pre-digested for him — and he's getting nervous. Students enrolled in failed language schools have been picketing the embassy in Beijing and asking for their money back, and the immigration authorities are under pressure from China. Beijing wants the Government to do something about it. It worries Harry. Some of the protesters might be their own students and even though he knows there's no reason for it (he and Frank have made refunds whenever they've been asked to), he feels uneasy if he hears anything critical of the education industry.

'No, of course not,' he says, 'not a word,' although he can't be sure of it because he hasn't gone any further than the front page — but then, there's no sense in having Frank call him back every few minutes just because some idiot is playing politics or trying to snatch a little publicity for himself. The main danger is that there might be another of those crazy announcements from Languages South Pacific, which is currently trying to establish a monopoly over the international market and wouldn't hesitate to denigrate non-members... even force them out of business if there were any chance of it.

'It's not just the big headlines, Harry... there are the smaller items... press releases don't always make the front page.'

'I know...' he hunches the receiver into his shoulder and holds it there, 'and right now... I'm looking through the paper to see if there's anything else.' It's awkward, finding your way through a newspaper and trying to talk to someone on the telephone at the same time. God knows why Frank doesn't read the paper for himself! They both like to get away from things... take a day or two off every week... and it's always possible to read the newspapers... to keep in touch. 'There doesn't seem to be anything,' he tells Frank, 'nothing at all.' He goes to the magazine section — not that there's likely to be anything there either, but sometimes feature writers delude themselves, persuade themselves they're investigative reporters and get carried away. 'God, Frank!' he says, 'why don't you get your own damn paper?' Silence from the other end of the line.

'You know why,' the answer comes eventually, 'no one wants to work twenty-four hours a day, seven days a week. It's bad enough looking at newspapers in the office — we don't have to take the job and the newspapers home with us do we? You're not asking me to do that are you?'

'There's something here,' Harry says, 'a short paragraph. The Minister of foreign affairs is going to China. He's to talk with the Chinese Government, discuss what can be done about language schools that have gone wrong, that have gone out of business. He will, quote — investigate the problem and endeavour to restore goodwill between the two countries — unquote.'

It's not only businesses, Harry tells himself, not only language schools that go out of business, are unable to do anything — close down, stop functioning — it's people as well, people like himself. He thinks of Angie back at his apartment, tidying up (she's the kind of person who'll tidy up before she leaves) — he thinks of Angie, of his being there with her all night and his inability to do anything about her, of not even being able to ask for her address, for her telephone number.

'I don't believe it,' says Frank, 'I don't believe it!'

'You have to! If the paper says he's going to China, then that's where he's going and that's what he'll be doing — trying to smooth things over. We trade with China, we send wool to China — and the Minister is going to make sure we keep doing it. It's his job — what he's paid for — and you can't develop a slice of the largest market in the world without maintaining good diplomatic relations.' It's a long speech — and because he hasn't had as much sleep as he'd have liked, putting all those words together makes his head spin.

There's silence — a pained silence at the other end of the line. 'Don't tell me what I already know,' Frank says in a patient, accusatory tone, 'don't give me a lecture, an intelligence report... just the facts, Harry, the facts... nothing more... simply what's happening, what's been said and who said it.'

He likes Frank — he's always liked him — but sometimes Harry feels disappointed with him, angry even.

'The bus drivers,' Harry reminds him in case he's forgotten, 'the bus drivers are still holding out — won't go back to work unless they're given group contracts and a guarantee that their current pay rates are maintained.' He casts his eyes over the article to see if there's anything else he can draw Frank's attention to — that will distract him. 'Neither party,' he tells him, 'neither party will go to arbitration. They're getting nowhere — it's a stalemate.'

'We're not interested in bus drivers, Harry — we're not interested in their employers or what either of them will do! We're not interested in whether a comet — Swift-Turtle or otherwise — will strike the earth in a hundred and forty years from now. What we want to know, Harry, is if there's anything in the paper about passports and rubber stamps, anything that will tell us whether our students are going to get their visas! We want to know what the Embassy in Beijing is doing — when we can expect more students — whether the Minister's visit to China will help balance our books.'

Their telephone conversation goes on, getting nowhere, serving no purpose other than reinforcing their collective interests, reassuring them that they're businessmen engaged in a worthwhile enterprise, doing something useful... that they're behaving constructively, with humour under fire — are actively dealing with a difficult situation... that they're not simply pawns, the helpless victims of politics and international forces, of obscure and complex political ambitions someone will identify some time in the future and write a book about...

E i g h t

Harry is reading the paper and drinking coffee — he drinks too much of it and there's a small, a distant voice inside his head which reminds him that somewhere, someone has told him of the evils of coffee drinking, of the subtle and insidious damage it can do. Or maybe no one's actually told him, maybe he's read it somewhere — perhaps waiting for his car to be tested for a warrant of fitness or last year when he couldn't get rid of his head cold and had to make two separate visits to his local GP. Angie is right, he reads too much, and even if someone's told him of the dangers of drinking coffee, the chances are he's read about it as well, perhaps on one of those endless flights to China.

Bridget who is also drinking coffee, is reading the magazine section of the paper. They're both creatures of habit — he because nothing is predictable and it seems wise to develop and maintain rituals that give protection against the unforeseen, she because she's paid to do things in a routine manner: keep records, maintain files, check registers, plan schedules, construct timetables, organise workloads. One of their habits, the habit he and Bridget share when there are few other people in the office — particularly on Saturday mornings — is to read the paper and take coffee together.

Less obviously, reading the morning paper and taking coffee with Bridget reminds Harry of the calmer and quieter moments of his former marriage — moments he mistakenly believed would last forever, when it seemed nothing momentous would ever happen and there'd always be someone to talk to, to exchange accounts of the day with. It brings back other things as well — some he'd like to remember and others he'd rather forget — particularly the way his children would try to entice him away from the paper for a rough-and-tumble and he'd pretend he wasn't noticing until they were crawling all over him, and there was no longer a choice.

Harry has expected Bridget might talk to him about the events of the previous evening. He's grateful she hasn't — that she appears to have been unaffected by the little sleep she must have had and the alcohol he thinks she might have consumed. He is even more grateful that she hasn't asked him about Angie or when she might have left his flat.

When he's reading the paper, glancing at the headlines or studying the feature articles (Harry likes the feature articles), he often forgets where he is and what's going on around him — even to the point of imagining he's back in the suburban living room from which divorce ignominiously removed him, or in the officers' mess at the naval base idling away time before having to go on duty.

His grandfather used to read the papers even more avidly and swiftly than he does. And because his grandfather had a white moustache and hair with a bald spot in the centre, he's recently fallen into the habit of checking out the colour and durability of his own hair. So far he hasn't detected any change, but because his circumstances have altered so much in the last few years, he no longer has any great faith in the continuity of things — not even in the continuity of his own body. Therefore, when he thinks about his grandfather and about reading, a feeling of sickness comes over him, the same feeling of sickness he's been fighting off since the collapse of his marriage, and accompanying it there's that other feeling — the panic he experienced when his bags were finally packed and it was time to take leave of his children.

'The fax machine — there's something coming through on the fax!' Bridget puts down her part of the paper and looks towards the outer office. 'Would you like me to get it?'

'It could be from the Embassy — from Beijing. Maybe they've begun issuing visas again and we'll have to go out to the airport and pick people up. We could toss for it — which of us goes to the airport!'

He's joking because it's not Bridget who goes — it's Frank or himself. And indeed, there could and should be new students arriving! The last they'd met left China immediately they'd received their visas. They told him they were afraid of last minute cancellations from the Embassy, or a similar action on the part of the Chinese Government and they'd left before it was too late. Shortness of notice concerning new arrivals has sometimes prevented anyone getting out to the airport in time to meet them, and the Immigration Service's paranoia about student disappearances (imaginary, he suspects) is beginning to make him nervous.

From where he sits, he can see Bridget waiting for the machine to stop. Two or three pages have come off it — too many for a simple notice of student flight times. It has to be something else and if it's something else, then it's likely he'll have to deal with it immediately — and that's a nuisance on a Saturday when he hasn't anticipated having to do anything other than read the paper, drink coffee and take a quick glance round the office. Besides, it's not his — it's Frank's turn to go to the airport!

He's still thinking about it and what he might have to do, when Bridget returns from the outer office. 'It's from Wang Lan,' she tells him, 'from Beijing.' And indeed, it's from Miss Wang, as she likes to be called. He remembers her from his last trip to China: a competent business woman in her early thirties — slim, serious, reserved, and wearing a Western-style suit (jacket, white blouse, medium-length skirt) — sensual even, or so he thought from the sinuous way she moved, the way she leaned towards him. Wang Lan's letter is headed *Beijing Overseas Student Centre, Beijing, People's Republic of China*, and is dated for the previous day (Friday 30).

Dear Mr Houghton, it begins, *The situation in Beijing, it is very serious and I am frightened. Two days ago and very late at night, three students come to my house, Mr Chen Li , Mr Sun Wei, and Mr Zhang Xing Jie. They are very angry and say bad words to me. And then they throw things about and break my furniture. One, Mr Chen, has knife and he say if I not do something and get money soon he will hurt me very much.*

As you and Mr Pierce already know, they have not received visa. They say refunds for them have not yet come and have been waiting a long time for you to send money back. If money not come soon, they will hurt me very much and burn house down. They stay in my house more than three hours and make much damage. I not know what to do because they do not believe me when I tell them you send money already. Where is it, they say, where is it, we have not any money yet.

Mr Chen say he knows some schools in your country have been cheating students who not get visas, they have been keeping money and not send it back. It is in the news. Students go to Embassy and ask where money is but get no answer because Embassy say they not know. I tell Mr Chen you already send refunds, but Mr Chen say refunds have not arrived and students very angry. Mr Houghton, I know you and Mr Pierce honest and not cheat. Please send fax very soon so I can show it to Mr Chen and tell him everything all right. Please say in fax where money is and when he will get it. Wang Lan.

'Hell!' is all he can think of, 'Hell!' It's the kind of trouble nobody needs and it's all the more unexpected because they've been meticulous over refunds, have never delayed as much as a day in arranging bank drafts, writing covering letters and posting them off. And they've processed more than a hundred and twenty of them in the last three months — more than half a million dollars that could have stayed in the country if the Embassy had done its job, if the immigration division hadn't lost its nerve, if the Government hadn't encouraged Chinese students to apply for visas and then after long periods of delay turned their applications down keeping of course, their application fees.

It made no sense. Language schools relying on students from Europe or Japan, from Taiwan or Indonesia, weren't having the same difficulties. But maybe — and he wants to be fair — maybe it's only the way things appear to be, maybe he isn't getting the whole picture. And yet — yet the media seems to be on the side of the Government, and keeps attacking the schools instead of the root cause — the change in Government policy. He's even been attacked himself, described as, 'Harry Houghton, the ex-naval officer who took up a directorship... seized his opportunity!' And while all this is happening, while it's going on — events he'd rather not know about — he sits in his office reading the paper, thinking about Angie, pretending to work when he has neither the desire nor enthusiasm for it. What he has to do, though — and quickly — is get a reply off to Wang Lan.

Bridget puts a file into his hand. 'The Beijing Student Centre — Wang Lan's file,' she tells him. He opens it and looks at the last two documents in the folder. One of them is his letter to Miss Wang. *I have given your request for refunds to Mr Pierce*, it says, *and he will prepare the covering letters, obtain bankdrafts and forward them to your clients.* The last document is a list of student names attached to a handwritten note from Frank, confirming all necessary action as complete. He can see from the date when the drafts were posted and that they should have reached Beijing two to three weeks ago.

'Do you think they got them?' he asks Bridget, indicating the list in front of him, but she's already back at the filing cabinet.

'We'll have to check the receipts — the receipts from the post office,' she tells him. 'But it's all right. I posted the cheques myself — and I remember posting them. Chen,' she calls out to him, 'Chen Li... Sun Wei... Zhang Xing... Here they are.' She pulls their folders out and gives them to him. 'Enrolment forms, medical insurance contracts, and photocopies of the bankdrafts and postal receipts — all present and correct!' Harry recognises the last few words as a phrase she's picked up from Frank — it's not anything that was used in the Navy.

He remembers Wang Lan's letter and her request for refunds but despite Frank's note, he can't recall who organised the bank drafts, or posted them. There'd been correspondence over it — there'd been delays in getting copies of the original student acceptance forms and the Embassy's formal notices of refusal. Eventually Wang Lan had sent them the three sets of papers herself. And the Embassy refusals had all been identical — no explanations for not issuing visas, simply a formal regret and a blanket statement of the students having 'failed to meet the necessary criteria'. He can remember discussing the Embassy's letters with Frank — whether they really needed to have copies of them or not — whether the Embassy officials were actually looking at the visa applications or automatically returning them a few weeks after receiving them.

'Of course, they don't decline them automatically,' Frank had told him. 'It would be too obvious and people would guess. And you called on them when you were in Beijing. They told you what the problem was — more applications than they could deal with — logistics — simply a matter of logistics. And that's what the Minister said — he confirmed it, didn't he — that's what he said, wasn't it?'

Yes, the Minister confirmed it — informally of course but indeed, he confirmed it. Harry had been fortunate to be able to speak with him. It had been at the opening of the Technical Institute's new Maritime Studies building. He hadn't expected to be invited but the opportunity had been too good to miss. 'Price isn't it — Mr Price,' the Minister had said. 'Of course, the Ministry's impartial and of course the Embassy is still processing visas...'

'Houghton,' says Harry, 'Harry Houghton — not Price... there's no Price — none at all.' He liked the joke although the Minister didn't notice it and probably wouldn't have understood it if he had. 'Frank Pierce is my business partner — he wrote to you earlier.'

'It's not the Embassy, Mr Houghton, it's the industry — the industry hasn't disciplined itself, honoured its obligations. The industry has used student fees as development capital instead of holding on to them — setting up student trusts. The Embassy's problem is the number of applications it has to deal with — more than five thousand applications at the moment — that's the latest figure. The visa hold-up is the result of the volume of paper the Embassy's dealing with. No-no, Mr Houghton, Government policy hasn't changed... China has a huge population... visa applications from Chinese citizens receive the same consideration as they would from people in any other country...'

'But the Embassy stopped issuing visas for six months after the Tiananmen Square disaster, put a hold on them, and now only a trickle of students is getting through — not enough to keep the industry going.'

'We're sending another officer to Beijing... it will make a difference — speed things up... what the industry has to do, is get its own house in order...' He didn't believe the Minister — he didn't believe him then, and he doesn't believe what the Government's telling him now.

'The immigration officer at the Embassy,' he told Frank, 'Mrs Strickland at the Embassy in Beijing, Mrs Strickland didn't seem convincing. She said the right things, but they sounded like the things people say if they're not telling the truth and hope no one's going to notice they're lying. She said there'd never been a shut-down — just too many applications... but I didn't get past the front office... She didn't want to see anybody — wouldn't talk — wouldn't look directly into your eyes when she was talking... couldn't spare more than a few moments of her time...'

It hadn't been easy getting to see anyone at the Embassy — in fact, it had been down-right difficult in comparison with the accessibility and cooperation of Beijing's government officials. He had telephoned the Embassy as soon as he'd arrived in China, from his room in the Beijing Hotel, the middle building. It was cheaper than the east wing, less depressing than the gloomy, Russian-style, west wing with its guttural European voices and cavernous public rooms, and lacked the pretentious luxury of the Distinguished Guest Building. 'Mrs Strickland,' he'd asked after the clicks and whirrs had vanished from the telephone, 'I'd like to speak to Mrs Strickland — the officer in charge of visa applications.'

'Sorry, sir — Mrs Strickland not available — visa section not able to take calls.'

'Can I call again — later — when she is available?'

'The visa section, it is over-worked and its officers — they give full attention to visa applications. If you wish make application, write to Embassy and wait official documents be forwarded. You should fill in — complete — the forms and return them to visa section.'

'I'm visiting China... I've already corresponded with Mrs Strickland... I wrote to her before I came here and she said she'd be pleased to give me a few minutes of her time. Well, I am here — I'm in China — and I'd like to speak with her.'

'Very sorry, sir, Mrs Strickland busy. Call back later, some other time when not so busy...'

The clicks and whirrs re-asserted themselves, and then the telephone went dead. He was jet-lagged, but he couldn't allow himself lunch until another half-hour was up. A sense of doom and foreboding came over him, of isolation and melancholy that came from the emptiness of the hotel's corridors and the silent passage of the people who looked after linen and restored the guest rooms to their original, unlived-in appearance when travellers departed. And even then, as he stepped into the corridor and caught voices and laughter coming through the partly opened door to the next room, he was unable to shake off a feeling of having been abandoned, of having fallen into some kind of nineteenth century time-warp.

In the corridor he was briefly uncertain as to what he was doing there or what he should be doing. Fredrick — Fredrick Topping who had travelled with him from Melbourne, was in the room across the corridor and he needed only to go and knock on the door in order to have someone to talk to. But he didn't want to talk to Topping, wasn't sure he liked the man. In the lift his uncertainty persisted until after vainly trying to avoid his reflected image in it's floor-to-ceiling mirrors — he stepped out at the ground-floor level and began to explore the hotel's huge, interconnected buildings and endless corridors.

'Well, what do you think — is it enough?' he asks Bridget. She moves round the desk and looks over his shoulder so she can read what he's written. He hopes it's adequate and finds himself thinking of Wang Lan and Bridget in a way he knows he shouldn't be thinking of them. It's a long time (except for his recent experience with Angie) since he's been on anything more than business terms with a woman and Bridget is close enough for him to be aware of her as more than a pleasant and likeable employee.

He'd felt the same about Miss Wang and still recalls how he'd looked at her and she looked back at him in Beijing — a little too long and openly for him to think of it as mere courtesy. He leans uncomfortably sideways in his chair. Bridget is just behind him, slightly to his right and alarmingly close. He can't get up and move away because she'd notice his discomfiture.

They look over what he's written. It's not long — not quite a page — but photocopies of the bank cheques and the registration receipts from the post office will go with it.

Dear Miss Wang, it says, *Thank you for your facsimile message concerning the current situation in Beijing. I am very much distressed at the difficulties you've been having and the danger you seem presently to be in. The refunds for Chen Li, Sun Wei, and Zhang Xing Jie were posted to China as indicated in the attached post office registration receipts. (Photocopies of the bankdrafts are also enclosed.)*

The addresses the registered letters were sent to, are the addresses originally given to us by your three clients. Please note that Chen Li, Sun Wei and Zhang Xing live at the same address although in different apartments. If they haven't yet received their bank drafts, they should enquire at their local post office and if no further information is available, should write to me personally. Tell your clients they should deal with us direct. I am making enquiries through the post office from which the letters were sent and am sure if you show your clients this facsimile and its attachments, they will understand that the delay concerning their refunds

has been caused by the postal authorities and not by you. If you need any
more help, please advise us immediately.

'Didn't you meet Miss Wang when you were in Beijing?' Bridget asks suddenly and as if she knows what he's been thinking.

'Yes,' he says, 'more than once — several different times — and in several different places.'

'Well, isn't the letter too formal... shouldn't it be... friendlier?' She moves closer, leans over his shoulder and reaches for the keyboard so that he has to stand up and step out of her way. 'Look,' she says, 'all you have to do is make the language less formal.' She moves her fingers over the keys changing his 'I am' to 'I'm', 'they have' to 'they've', and 'will not' to 'won't'.

Originally, it was Frank who was supposed to do the marketing and who had made the first of their recruiting trips. And Frank had been spectacularly successful — not because of anything Harry thought of as his having a great capacity for it, but because there'd been people with him who knew what they were doing — Topping who had originally pointed out the Government's enthusiasm for business with China, and Stephen Chan, an expatriate Chinese from Hong Kong who lived in Melbourne and owned a business which specialised in recruiting students for foreign schools and universities. Beijing, Topping had told them, Beijing had come to a recognition that overseas trade was essential for Chinese economic development and that it couldn't be successfully developed without people who had trained and lived in the countries they wished to trade with.

'Okay — okay,' he says when she finishes with the word processor, 'it's better, a lot better.' And it is! Somehow and by the mere changing of a few words here and there, Bridget has managed to get warmth and feeling into what was previously a coldly formal business letter. He should have done it himself — he knows he should have even if for no other reason than the way Wang Lan had looked at him — appraisingly, he thinks, acknowledging both of them as male and female and that given the appropriate circumstances something might have come of it, might have happened between them.

He had met Miss Wang after his initial exploration of the Beijing Hotel — after discovering the Great Hall in the west wing and the unbelievable Fountain of the Hours with its stylised sculptures and multitudinous water jets. Apparently he'd been fortunate to discover the fountain operating — it was usually out of order or for reasons known only to the hotel management, simply switched off, as he'd been told by one of the bystanders. No one appeared to know why such an elaborate and unnecessary item happened to be placed within the confines of a hotel instead of in a public park or in nearby Tiananmen Square. In contrast with the publicly proclaimed principles of the communist state, its existence seemed decadent — insulting to the millions of poverty-stricken Chinese who would never have a chance to see it or even enter the building in which it was housed.

They were waiting for him when he went back to his room. Fredrick had managed to have the door opened and was seated at the small central table with Stephen Chan and three other Chinese. Miss Wang sat separately from the men, towards the side of the room. All of them were drinking tea. Topping made the introductions and, as soon as the courtesies were over, they talked business. 'Very successful,' Chan interpreted for them, 'Mr Pierce's visit last year, very successful. Everyone pleased and would like to continue finding students and making money.' The reference to money had taken him by surprise. He'd have expected more subtlety — a less direct statement of what their business was concerned with. Although they didn't speak it well, the Chinese seemed sufficiently familiar with English to understand what Chan had said. They nodded their agreement while Miss Wang looked at him just that little longer than was necessary — long enough to make him more aware of her than he was of the others.

'Mr Wu say things not so easy now. Many young Chinese want to study overseas and can get enough money — yes, they can get money — but Embassy very slow. Only a few applicants get visas. It is disappointing, very disappointing.'

'Tell Mr Wu this is only a temporary situation, the Government has said it supports the provision of education for overseas students and the Embassy is having difficulties because there have been so many applications — more than it can handle.' Harry was repeating what he'd been told by the immigration authorities, yet he had a feeling that he ought to be more open, more honest, that he should be telling them what he suspected — that the Embassy may have been given instructions to issue no more visas than necessary and if possible, none at all. There was no clear evidence to support the view, yet Mrs Strickland's unwillingness to see him and the tone of the telephone operator's voice — they were the kind of thing that could be expected when something underhand was going on.

'It is what students say.' Mr Wu speaks slowly and with obvious pride in his carefully formulated English. 'The Embassy take long time to answer and sometimes not at all. No visa. Students think Embassy will not give them visas, but keep application fee — make much money.'

Harry takes the teapot and refills their cups. Mr Wu is drinking herbal tea and requires hot water to go with the tea bags supplied by the hotel management. Harry crosses the room and switches on the water jug and stands next to Miss Wang waiting for the water to boil. Topping tells the three Chinese that the Embassy wouldn't be accepting applications unless it intended to process them in accordance with the standard criteria for issuing student visas. 'There wouldn't be any reason to accept applications if they weren't going to process them,' he says, 'and the fees aren't great enough to add up to anything much.' Chan translates in a placating tone with smiles and gesticulations. He takes longer than might be expected.

'It is very difficult,' Miss Wang says while Harry waits for the jug to boil, 'not like when Mr Pierce... how you say... Fran-k Pi-erce?... when Frank Pierce was here.' He notes that although her voice is warm, she doesn't laugh. She shows the modesty and restraint characteristic of business women in China. She sits upright — very straight — and doesn't move her body more than she has to. She looks at him a second time, and again a little longer than necessary. He unplugs the jug and takes it across the room to Mr Wu.

'Mr Houghton will explain,' Chan says. 'He arrive in China today, and knows best his country's policies and how his Government feels. Is that not so, Mr Houghton?' Chan, who usually speaks English perfectly, has relapsed into the style of language employed by the majority of Chinese Harry has met since fastening his seat-belt on the Air China 747 that conveyed him on the second part of his journey — from Melbourne to Beijing. The difficulty is that he doesn't know what his Government's policy is and there are things, such as what happened in Tiananmen Square, nobody — particularly Chinese officials — will talk about.

'It's not that the Government wants to delay issuing visas,' he tells them. 'Over the last year, there have been so many applications that the regular staff at the Embassy is no longer able to deal with them. You know, when an initial enquiry is received a letter has to be sent out with the application forms that have to be filled in, and then when the completed forms have been received, a letter of acknowledgement has to follow and each application has to be processed.' Topping waits for him to go on. Mr Wu stares at him as if he doesn't believe a word of what he's being told.

'The Minister,' Harry tells them, 'I telephoned the Minister before coming to Beijing. The Minister says there have been no changes in the Government's instructions to the Embassy and the additional staff allocated to it should see an increased number of visas issued in the next few weeks.' It was near enough but it wasn't exactly what the Minister had said and he doubted he'd believe it himself if someone were to say it to him, but it was the sense of what he'd been told — and it was all he could tell them.

Stephen Chan translates and for a few minutes, a heated exchange in Chinese ensues. 'Mr Wu,' Chan finally tells him, 'Mr Wu say if there have been as many applications as he thinks, the Embassy must make a very large sum of money in application fees. He says he doesn't think it is a small sum. He believes that if the Government is honest and visas are going to be issued, it is good. If visas not to be issued, then it is not good and young Chinese who wish to study overseas should be told not to make applications.'

Harry assumes an appearance of seriousness and concentration — at least he hopes that's what it looks like. Mr Wu has posed the one question he doesn't want to have imposed on him and thereby impaled him on the horns of a dilemma he would rather not be associated with: if he says the Embassy is honest, he's unlikely to be believed; if he states the opposite then it will be a factor against their doing business together. Everyone stares at him — including Miss Wang. 'The Embassy,' he says slowly and deliberately, 'the Embassy is an agent of Government and Mr Wu, we both have to deal with governments: they are as honest as they have to be — and I'm sure my Government is no more honest or dishonest than yours.'

Mr Wu waves towards Harry and responds in rapid-fire Chinese. 'He says,' Chan tells them, 'he says what Mr Houghton say is very true. That is way governments are.' He lifts his right hand and turns it over sideways, first to the right and then to the left in a rocking motion. 'Governments are so-so, not to be trusted — and Mr Houghton,' he breaks into a smile, 'Mr Wu is very happy with your answer to his question. He says it is… it is very Chinese.' Everyone claps, although quietly, including Miss Wang who smiles not only with genuine amusement and as politely as the others, but more warmly and with prolonged and direct eye contact as well — at least, it's the way Harry interprets what she's doing.

'Do you think it well help at all?' Bridget asks, pulling him back from China and his business dealings with Mr Wu, and then — in view of his lack of awareness of what she's talking about — follows up with another question. 'Do you think the fax we've sent Miss Wang will do any good?' For a moment he's unable to reply: he's still somewhere between his hotel room in Beijing and what's happening in Auckland — between Bridget and Miss Wang, or is it Miss Wang and Angie? 'Will it help at all?' Bridget asks him, this time less patiently.

Somehow it's Angie who's getting in the way of things, who's blotting out China, Bridget, Beijing, Miss Wang — even the fabulous Fountain of the Hours with its water jets, marble unicorns and mythical water beasts and he wonders about her — whether she's left his apartment — where she might be at the moment. And Harry remembers he doesn't have her address or telephone number, that he forgot to ask for them — or did he forget?

But it's ridiculous to think he forgot, because he didn't forget — it never occurred to him that he could ask, that he had a right to ask... but... if he phones his apartment... if he phones now and she's still there, he'll be able to get her telephone number and address before she leaves. That is, if he wants them he'll be able to get her address and telephone number — if she wants to give them to him... but... but then it's unlikely he'd use them, even if she did give them to him.

'Miss Wang,' Bridget asks him, 'the cheques — do you think the fax we've sent will do any good?'

'It depends... it depends what's happened to them... whether they were received... if we made a mistake with the address, if they were stolen, whether they went astray in the post.'

'What if they've received their cheques already — what if the cheques have been cashed and they're trying to get a second payment?'

It's something he doesn't want to think about, that they shouldn't have to deal with; and they shouldn't have to deal with it because they have the documentation — because they can prove the cheques were prepared and despatched. The problem is whether Chen and the others will carry out their threat against Miss Wang — whether they'll harm her. If they've received the cheques and want more than they're entitled to, whatever harm they do, will have to be done in stages — a little at a time — enough to demonstrate they're serious and that only another and immediate payment will stop them. How they respond to the fax, will give an indication of how far they're prepared to go, and yet the longer the situation continues the more dangerous it is for Wang Lan.

What makes it worse is that people are paid so little in China that the money required for study overseas would take the average Chinese a lifetime, if ever, to accumulate. It's the kind of money people would — and do — kill for.

'It's too difficult,' Harry tells her, 'we don't know whether they've received the letters we sent, or what will happen when photocopies of the cheques and postal receipts reach them — and there's nothing more that can be done at the moment — not a bloody thing!' Of course, Bridget is as aware of all this as he is. She's not asking questions because she wants answers but because she feels as badly about what's happening as he does and just as helpless. Beijing is so far away and there's a woman there they've both had dealings with, who could be in serious danger — who might perhaps even be killed.

'Harry, do you think they'd do it — they'd really kill her?' Bridget hasn't been to China, but she knows from the students she's dealt with, she knows from what's been in the papers and as well as he does how desperate people can become, how quickly a difficult situation can escalate into something worse.

It's a question he's already asked himself. From an outsider's point of view, China is a strange and unpredictable country — a place where art, culture and an effective civil service have flourished for more than four thousand years, where however permanent anything seems the situation can change in the flash of an eye, where the endless expanse of Tiananmen Square can suddenly become slippery with blood, where people can and do disappear without trace. He doesn't know whether Wang Lan might actually be in danger of being killed — but it's unlikely, while Chen and his associates think she's essential to their getting their money back. Short of killing her however, they could seriously hurt her — and that's the part neither he nor Frank has any control over.

He turns from Bridget to the windows and looks out towards the car park — towards the trees around the car park, and the harbour. The world is full of light. There is light over the water, fish beneath the water, trees and birds above it, men and women in the streets, yet everywhere — in Africa, in America and Europe, in China — even in his office — things not only go on but they also go wrong, people land in trouble, endure it, get out of it, or go under, take in vast mouthfuls of ocean and drown. And they're doing it for no reason he can think of except that they're human, and while they're doing it they talk to themselves and to each other — say the stupidest things like, 'Perhaps something can be done,' or 'I can't think of a damn thing,' or, 'I don't know what to do about it...'

'Would you like some more coffee?' Bridget asks him. 'Yes,' he says, 'yes,' and stares through the glass panels to the left of his desk at the catch up class along the corridor, and then more fixedly through the windows of his office, out towards the trees, out towards the cranes on the waterfront — towards the harbour, the water itself, and the harbour bridge beyond.

N i n e

It's almost noon when Harry stops in the front car park of the New World Supermarket. The sun is on the meridian and at an elevation of approximately forty four degrees above the horizon. It is due north of his present position — Latitude thirty six degrees fifty point five minutes South, Longitude one hundred and seventy four degrees forty six minutes East. It is significant because it is the time when the sun's meridian altititude can be observed and with appropriate reference to the Nautical Almanac and the Altitude and Azimuth tables, the ship's position calculated. He prefers forenoon and meridian altitude sights because taking them is less unpleasant than going out onto the wing of the bridge in the cold and damp of the night and looking for stars that aren't always there. Today the sky is clear, the wind minimal and it's a good day for taking sights which fortunately, he doesn't have to do because even if he's not too sure of anything else, he already knows, what his latitude and longitude are.

Still glancing at the sun, he gets out of his car and locks the door. It's a stupid thing to do, stare at the sun — and more stupid to think of things like sextant angles and meridian altitudes when there's no need to be doing it. But navigation is one of the things he's continued to think about since leaving the Navy. It involves mathematics and astronomy, science and luck and is thus, still not far removed from astrology which is its near relative and preceded it.

The more he thinks about it, the more reasonable the comparison seems — maybe the astrologers are right, maybe the motions of the stars do affect everyday events. The shift of the tides is driven by the moon, the moon moves round the earth, the earth is held in place by the sun, the sun is a star not very different from other stars — and stars are a major part of the universe and related to everything in it.

The door opens automatically as he reaches the entrance to the supermarket which isn't the largest or the most sophisticated of its kind but is convenient because it stocks everything he needs and is on the route he usually takes between his office and his apartment. He collects a wire shopping basket from the rack just inside the door. (He never uses a trundler because he shops frequently and buys only in small quantities. This saves him the trouble of writing out shopping lists and has considerable advantages. It makes shopping a lesser task than it would be otherwise, reduces the amount of thinking he has to do, fills in what would otherwise be an empty part of the day, and makes him feel he's still an ordinary family man in daily contact with ordinary family people.) He begins his shopping as he usually does, in the left-hand aisle and from the same starting point as everyone else.

The supermarket Harry shops at doesn't have much connection with astrology, but it requires careful navigation. The shelving has been arranged to encourage traffic flow — to take shoppers past every item that's offering — it allows him to think of the passageways he travels, as navigation channels, and the tiered shelves as rocks and headlands separating navigable waterways. Throughout the journey there are hazards: stationary trundlers which have been left to themselves while their owners have departed for other, still invisible bays and roadsteads, or joined up with their fellow shoppers for a moment or two of gossip. Their trundlers resemble merchant ships waiting for the tide, or fishing boats working the shallows in the hope of a quick catch before their rivals return from more richly endowed and therefore more profitable fishing grounds further off-shore. Harry peruses the information he's filed in his head concerning the purchases he needs to make, plots a course and commences to navigate the twists and turns, the hazards which will lead him to open water and eventually safe anchorage beyond the check-out counter.

He doesn't like shopping. Even when he was in the service and still married he disliked it. Sometimes he feels guilty about that, about not liking it, not doing as much of it as he should have, yet many of the men he's known have avoided it completely — and the bulk of their other domestic responsibilities as well. Tony, for example. He can't imagine Tony picking his way through a supermarket. Gardening — he might do a little gardening — but it's unlikely he'd do any shopping.

Nothing is ever as it seems, thinks Harry — not even filling a shopping basket or playing snooker — and certainly not running a business. Yesterday things seemed as if they would go on in no particular direction and without any special meaning forever. Now in addition to keeping a business operating he's worried sick about what might happen in Beijing, what might happen to Wang Lan, and he's angry with himself because he's failed to take any positive step towards contacting Angie. He should have asked Bridget — and he could still ask her by calling her up when he gets back to his apartment. It must have been Bridget who invited Angie to join them at the American Bar. She knows Angie came with them when they left to go to his flat, would know she was still there when everyone else disappeared. Bridget could help, could tell him how he could contact her, give him Angie's address — her telephone number.

And now, picking up a can of Campbell's soup and a packet of Continental pasta and sauce (sour cream and chives) which regrettably, he's not going to be able to share with anyone, he remembers his present troubles are merely a continuation of an older pattern from the past. He could have remained in the Navy another five years, might have picked up a brass hat — become a full commander — if he'd stayed there. He also remembers how bad his last two years were, how difficult they became — and the late-night game of snooker with Tony Poindexter. Tony was trying to tell him something, warn him of the danger he was getting into, of the noose he was putting around his neck. But he hadn't believed him — hadn't taken him seriously.

He knew Tony was losing his cool when there were only a few reds left on the table and the ten-point lead he'd so painstakingly built up, had lasted long enough to suggest he was not only holding his own against Poindexter, but might stay ahead until the colours were put away and the game wrapped up. Tony had sunk a red and missed the black, which rolled towards one of the pockets and stopped no more than a few millimeters from the rim. A nudge — no more than a nudge — and it would drop! Tony is so certain Harry will miss the next red that he hasn't played his cue ball for distance or given it bottom. And now he's left the black sitting there on the edge of a pocket, and one of the three remaining reds in line for the corner pocket, he's feeling uneasy. Yes, he expects Harry to miss because he usually beats him, but it's an easy shot and Harry just might — Harry just might sink it.

Harry chalks his cue and studies the table — not because he feels he needs to — but to prolong the pleasure that comes from such a moment, from knowing Tony who almost always wins and rarely shows sympathy for an opponent, has made a mistake and is facing defeat. 'Not all that easy,' he remembers saying to Tony, and the words are as fresh in his mind as they were at that very moment when he was leaning over the table and lining up for the shot. 'Not all that easy, but with a little care... just a little care... sinkable!' The cue slides over his knuckles and the white rolls forward as if in slow motion, strikes the red, runs down to the end of the table, comes back and positions itself in readiness for the black. 'Not that easy... but sinkable,' he repeats as the red, the ball he's been aiming for, rolls slowly towards the centre pocket and falls with a slight click onto the ball that preceded it.

'Nothing's as easy as you think, and it's usually a damn sight more difficult... like this little problem you have... this problem you have with Mills... with Stuart.'

'A perfect set-up,' Harry tells him, 'perfect for the black — especially if the cue ball comes back to the other side of the table.' It's a custom of the mess that people don't talk about the shots they're making. They're free to support other people's performances and encourage them, but not to denigrate them, and they're not supposed to say anything about what they're doing themselves — perhaps because it could be construed as immodest, damaging to the Navy's view of itself as the silent service. It seems to Harry though, that the present occasion is an exception — that he can allow himself a little licence. Besides, he doesn't like the suggestion that he has a problem. It's not Harry who has the problem, it's Mills who doesn't seem to be making a fist of things, whose students are failing their technical and trade examinations.

'The officer in charge takes the blame, Harry — the guy who's supposed to make sure everyone's doing his stuff. If there's dirt around it's the man in charge who collects it. And dirt sticks, Harry — it sticks and it stays there.'

'What am I doing,' Harry asks, 'that's so bloody... awful?' His cue slides forward. The cue ball hits the black which surprisingly, misses the pocket, comes back from the side cushion and stops a few centimeters from the pink.

Tony's apparent indifference to what's been happening on the table vanishes. 'You're leaning forward,' he says, 'swinging your cue when all that's needed need is a touch... just enough... to set... the ball rolling...'

'Like this!' he says leaning over the table and potting a red. He follows it up with the pink and then the last of the reds. 'The blue,' he says, nominating his next shot, 'the blue's next.' The blue disappears into a side pocket. Harry retrieves it, and returns it to the table while Tony sets himself up for the yellow — not an easy shot when the white's finished up at the other end of the table. 'A kiss...' Tony tells him, '... a kiss... just a touch... that's all it... needs.' His cue slides forward propelling the cue ball towards the yellow which it seems scarcely to contact at all. The yellow rolls across the baize, appears to pause above the pocket and then disappears...

Without any real awareness of what he's been doing, Harry's half-filled the wire basket he picked up as he came into the supermarket, and now stares disconsolately at a display of small items — margarine and cheese. He likes to keep a wedge of cheese in his refrigerator because it allows him to put together a quick snack when he's watching television or reading a book. He doesn't like disrupting whatever it is he's doing simply for food, but at the same time he likes a cup of coffee and a cheese sandwich — the coffee to keep him awake, the sandwich to provide protein and energy. They distract him from what he suspects are his more fundamental needs — needs he's constantly and frustratingly reminded of as he goes about his business at the office, in the city, at the post office, and now at the supermarket.

He chooses a segment of Mainland's Danbo and a wedge of Galaxy blue — the first for the sake of economy, the second because he likes it. Sometimes it takes several minutes to make a selection — usually because he's torn between the need for economy (increasingly so, since his divorce) and a tendency towards committing financial suicide. But it's the things he can't or shouldn't buy and which are too expensive, that bother him most. Blue vein cheese falls into both categories — it's too expensive in his present financial circumstances and because he enjoys it, it's not entirely moral. He follows up on his selection of cheese with tomatoes and a lettuce — low calorie stuff that served with potatoes and meat (preferably steak), and embellished with thousand island dressing, can be superbly satisfying. Most of his meals contain the same ingredients. Of course (and he tells himself this, but not too frequently), if he weren't eating alone, if he were eating with someone else, someone he liked, he'd cook something more elaborate: steak Wellington, filet mignon flambe, vol-au-vent a la Reine, Duchesse potatoes — but no dessert — no pavlova, no peach Melba — perhaps ice cream, if his guest wanted it.

'Excuse me,' he hears from behind him, 'excuse me but do you know if there's any French bread — long French loaves — something like that?'

He turns towards the voice. 'Yes,' he says, 'in the next aisle, near the — near the...' and falls silent.

'Harry!' says the voice, 'Of course it is — it's Harry! What are you doing here, Harry? Is this where you shop — the place you usually come?'

'Yes,' says Harry, 'I stop off on the way back from the office. But you... what about you? I've never seen you here before.'

'I'm getting something for the weekend.' Angie displays her trundler — a trundler prodigiously filled with packets, packages, jars — with kitchen provisions, bathroom items, plastic containers — even two bottles of wine and a garbage disposal bag. 'And I've almost finished — except for the bread.' She looks at Harry's basket. 'That's not much, she says, 'you don't buy very much, do you?'

'I don't need to,' says Harry knowing he's been thinking about Angie most of the morning or at least, even if he hasn't been thinking about her, she's been at the back of his mind most of the time. He looks at Angie and Angie looks back at him. Her eyes are deep green — wide and unblinking — and she's looking at him as if she's waiting for something... perhaps for him to say something.

'You couldn't give me your telephone number,' he asks her, 'your address, could you?' She continues to look at him, soberly, seriously — without answering — without blinking. 'We... we might need it... we might need someone in the office,' (Why couldn't he be more honest?), 'but only part time,' he adds hurriedly. 'You said something about a job, didn't you... that you were looking for a job?' He's embarrassed because he can't remember her asking about a job and even if she wanted one and there were a vacancy, he and Frank are losing money and couldn't afford to take anyone on.

'No — I didn't. I'm a student, remember? I told you I was a student — and I already have a part-time job, but,' she's smiling at him, 'you could show me where the French bread is.' Her refusal (he interprets it as such) is neither encouraging nor discouraging. Her face gives no indication of what she's thinking, but she's smiling and if she's aware that there isn't really a job available, she's not giving any indication of it.

'You buy an enormous amount when you're shopping,' he comments after she's added Camembert and two French sticks to what's already in her trolley.

'Yes,' she says, 'but only when we've run short and need to stock up.'

'Your telephone number,' he suggests, 'if you gave me your telephone number, I could call if anything came up later.'

'Okay — I don't want a job, but if you'd like me to, I'll give you the telephone number.' She takes a note book from her carry-all, turns to a blank page and writes a number and an address on it. When she's finished, she tears the page off, folds it, and pushes the folded page into the top pocket of his jacket. 'There,' she says, 'put it away somewhere safe until you need it.' She's still smiling — he can see she's smiling — even if he doesn't understand it, can't find an explanation for it. But that's the trouble with people who have faces that are unusual, don't fit the norm — their emotions aren't easy to interpret — not that it's ever possible to know exactly what other people are thinking! In some ways, he wishes he could read the minds of others, but the catch is that if he had such an ability, then other people, including Angie, might have it too and would know exactly what was going on inside his head. He's grateful that they can't read each other's minds and that it's unlikely Angie knows what he's thinking.

Outside in the car park it occurs to him that she referred to stocking up when 'we' need to — when 'we' run short. She'd used the first person plural, not the singular and he hadn't checked up on it, hadn't found out who the 'we' were before asking a second time for her telephone number. It could have been the reason she didn't want to give it to him — particularly if she'd guessed that he didn't have a job available and that there wasn't likely to be one in the future. He might have offended her — insulted her — with his clumsy suggestion of a job. And there was Frank. She'd talked with Frank the previous day, and he could have said something about the company's financial circumstances. It wouldn't have taken more than a hint, and Frank's like that — sometimes says more than he should — especially in front of women. Frank likes women and tends to play up to them — he could have said more than he should have.

He puts the two plastic carrying bags with his groceries in them into the boot of his car, gets into the driver's seat and starts the engine. The car park is crowded and it isn't easy to get out and onto the main road. He tries to concentrate on his driving, accelerates for a moment, reaches the main road, brings his car to a halt and waits for a break in the traffic. As soon as the way is clear, he eases the brake off, touches the accelerator and moves across the road so he can make a left turn towards Glenfield and the flat he rents. And then there's the way in which she gave him her address and her telephone number. Yes, when she pushed the slip of paper into his pocket, she'd suggested he keep it safe until he needed it. What did she mean by 'need' and by 'when', for that matter? 'When' implies a specific time, a specific occasion and occasions invariably carry specific events and circumstances with them. Need comes in different shapes and guises. He's confused because he doesn't know what events and circumstances Angie might have had in mind nor, in view of her use of 'we', whether she intended he should use her telephone number at all.

The three words, 'when', 'need, and 'we' keep coming back to him — tumbling over each other in such a confusion that he almost hits the vehicle in front when the traffic signals change. He's at the corner of Tristram Avenue and Wairau Road, opposite the gas station where the motorway empties out into Glenfield. There are two cars between him and the traffic lights and an odd assortment of the usual Saturday traffic behind. He can see the line-up in his rear view mirror: a flat top with household furniture tied down with yellow rope (perhaps a tow rope — he has one very much like it in his boot), a car with a trailer-load of hedge and garden trimmings, and somewhere further back — a massive Chevvie with a boat trailer behind it.

The traffic lights look as if they'll remain red forever. This isn't one of the weekends he sees his children, so he's in no hurry, has nothing particular to do — nowhere particular to go — and he feels badly about what's going on in his head. It's not the way a naval officer (he corrects himself, an ex-naval officer) is supposed to think. What he should be doing, is to acknowledge the ambiguities in what Angie's said, identify the unknowns and the predictables, and then take whatever line of action is necessary to sort them out — it's the service way of doing things. Ideally, the action he takes should advance the situation in his favour — give him the advantage. Unfortunately, he's not sure what the situation is and suspects that if he knew what it was, he'd still be uncertain as to which of the directions it could move in would be desirable or to his advantage — all of which demonstrated the futility of trying to think of such things in military terms.

When he's through the lights and driving towards the turn-off into Ellice, he berates himself for his stupidity — and he has to be stupid after everything that's happened to him previously, has to be stupid to be debating absurd questions of what Angie (or any other woman) might or might not have meant, or what she might be thinking. She's a student — perhaps a graduate student — and almost certainly sees his request for her telephone number as just another of many such inquiries a young and attractive woman has to deal with during the course of a week.

And again, it mightn't be her telephone number she's given him — simply the first series of numerals that came into her head and which she's written down on a piece of paper and pushed into his jacket pocket in order to avoid offending him. If he calls her, it's possible whoever answers the telephone will never have heard of her — and that will be the end of it. And then, perhaps she believes he's asked for her phone number out of politeness — because he thinks it's courteous to ask for it after she's stayed in his apartment and spent the night in his bed. Perhaps she thinks he's afraid of having offended her, thinks he doesn't find her attractive, or should have been more assertive — made advances to her. Or maybe times have changed and people don't expect anything to happen if they've been drinking together and finish up in each other's beds, that it's just a question of somewhere to sleep, of convenience.

It's a difficult to understand things like that if you've been married for the larger part of your adult life — and even more difficult if a lot of those years have been spent in the services. Maybe monks who lose their vocation and go out into the world, have similar problems. There are things about marriage and the armed services that aren't much different from monasteries: all of them involve complex social relationships, ideas of right and proper conduct, and in Harry's experience (with the exception of Tony Poindexter) a surprising lack of interest in women either at home or in foreign ports.

Suddenly he realises he's missed the Ellice Road turn-off and he's still travelling north. The flat-bed truck and the car with the boat trailer are too close for him to swing round — to make a one hundred and eighty degree turn — and even if they weren't so close there's too much traffic on the other side of the road and nowhere he can stop. 'Hell,' he tells himself, 'bloody hell!' He's locked onto his present course and there's nothing he can do except keep moving, keep following the road — not when he thinks about it, that it matters much.

The good part (and there is a good part) is that the rest of the day is free — and is his. If there's nowhere he has to go, nothing he has to do, then he might as well keep driving — go on to Limeburners' Bay where he keeps his boat. He drives past the Cut Hill Garden Centre where in better days he sometimes bought flowers and shrubs, accelerates up the hill and half a kilometre further on turns off towards the Greenhithe Bridge — a part of the road he enjoys. He likes the way it lifts and curves, the green and rolling countryside it passes through. And then he's on the downhill section, descending towards the bridge, sweeping out over the water. Even at the modest speed his vehicle is travelling at and despite its absence of wings, the sensation of lift — of motion and weightlessness — is very close to flying and for the moment he forgets the problems of the office, his feeling of guilt and helplessness over what might or might not happen to Wang Lan, the Beijing embassy's disinterest in student visas, the difficulties he has in dealing with women.

T e n

Harry is working on the engine of his boat — an activity which no longer gives him any great pleasure and which has already depressed his earlier (and temporary) lift of spirit. He likes boats, has always liked them. It was his interest in boats — sailing boats — that originally took him into the Navy. Sometimes however, he regrets ever becoming involved with them. The problem with his boat is the engine — a Yanmar YSE 12 which is fifteen years old — half the age of *Susquat* and all he could afford after the even more ancient diesel that came with the boat fell apart, just as he was leaving the Navy. His boat, old as it is, is the last major item that survives his years in the service and the ups and downs, the alarms and excursions of his marriage. He is very fond of *Susquat* even though over the last two seasons the state of the engine has made it impossible for him to use it. He's fond of it because he's a romantic and has a life-long attachment to the sea — an attachment he's incapable of giving up. The engine is worn out and he lacks the financial resources necessary for its replacement. No matter how long he works at it, or what it is he fixes, something else goes wrong every time he attempts to use the boat. Right now it's the manifold that's the problem.

The engine in its gloomy well beneath the companionway seems to have a morose, brooding quality about it. It crouches, silent and reproachful in front of him, as if it resents the efforts he's making to remedy its shortcomings. He is tapping one of the manifold bolt holes, replacing the thread so that the flange and the new gasket he's had to drive out to Mt Wellington for, can be tightened sufficiently to prevent exhaust gases escaping into the cabin and making it uninhabitable. He turns the tap carefully, gently, but with enough pressure so that it cuts cleanly and accurately through the metal of the engine block. If he works too quickly he'll damage the thread and if he doesn't apply enough pressure he'll get nowhere. The block's been made from cast iron and the vibration and varying temperatures it's experienced for so long have fatigued the metal. He's not sure if this is correct, but it's the only theory he's managed to come up with which explains why the engine block doesn't seem able to hold a thread.

Harry has stripped to the waist and put on a pair of old trousers to avoid ruining the clothes he usually wears. He took off his shirt and changed his trousers immediately he came on board and will try to avoid going up on deck until he's finished the job he's doing and is again properly dressed. Being 'properly dressed' is important to him even though he knows that in objective terms it's meaningless and absurd to worry about appearances. But his clothes have become thin and shabby, and he is himself not in such good condition as he used to be. It's something he shouldn't worry about, he tells himself, especially when other people have genuine and serious problems far worse than his own.

Last time he worked on the engine, it was the lubricating oil return line — a small copper tube that snakes up from the lube oil pump beneath the engine and over the top of the engine block. He isn't as knowledgeable about engines as he pretends he is, and when something goes wrong, he can't always be sure he'll discover the reason for it. It had been like that when the engine had overheated and he'd thought the boat was about to blow up. He'd been trying to get his daughter back to her mother on time. They'd had a great morning sailing — perfect wind and a bright, clear sky — she'd liked the apple turnovers he'd made for lunch and been excited by the old gaff-rigged schooner they'd passed — a 'pirate ship daddy, a pirate ship!' But in the afternoon the wind had changed and with the tide against them as well, he'd pushed the boat too hard.

'It was the smoke,' he tells Georgina who (unexpectedly) does most of the engineering at Westpark marina and is leaning through the hatchway watching what he's doing. He can't afford to hire her, but she's lent him the tap and die set he's using and therefore, he assumes, is interested in what he manages to achieve with it. 'The cabin was full of smoke,' he says, 'and it was pouring out of the hatch so fast that it looked as if the boat was on fire.' It's painful to remember: his daughter's fear, her embarrassment at being late home — but no more than an hour, thanks to the tow he'd been offered — and his ex-wife's snide comments.

'Yes,' Georgina agrees. 'It looks awful, but it's not serious if you turn the engine off early enough — before the rubber hosing melts or there's a fire.' And she'd been right except (and this is something he hasn't told her) he didn't turn the engine off in time and had to replace the hosing — a laborious, time-consuming job that required him to lean over the engine compartment bruising his body, scraping his knuckles, and exhausting his patience. He'd carried out the task furtively and in secret in order to avoid the humiliation and embarrassment of having Georgina find out what had happened.

'It's been roughly treated,' she reminds him. 'Your engine, it's been roughly treated!' she calls out again and more loudly in case he hasn't heard. Harry winces because he doesn't need to be reminded of the kind of treatment the engine must have received prior to his owning it — nor of some of the rougher treatment he's inadvertently inflicted on it himself. When he bought the engine, he'd had it surveyed and reconditioned. What he hadn't known and Marine Services hadn't bothered to tell him, was that the engine was past repair and the best they could do would give it no more than another year to eighteen months of life.

'Someone seems to have worked on the manifold before,' he tells her (two of the bolts are metric and the third's imperial and larger than the others), 'and I'm not very good at this kind of thing.' The last observation is an appeal for help but it elicits no response. Sometimes when he's working on the engine, he wishes Georgina would do the job for him, but he knows it's not going to happen even though they've developed the kind of relationship that would normally produce such a result. Georgina is an engineer — a real engineer — and although she gives no verbal indication of it, her manner makes it clear that even if she were paid for it (and previously Harry's offered to pay her), she wouldn't waste her time on an engine that's so far gone that any repair made on it immediately has to be followed by another.

'Any problems?' Georgina asks, when he's finished with the cutting tool and tested the new thread by inserting one of the bolts he's bought and giving it a few turns. Her interest surprises him because usually when he talks to her about his engine, she shrugs derisively or suggests he get another one — 'new or second-hand,' she tells him, 'sometimes second-hand's almost as good.'

And yes, of course there are problems — there are always problems, although he's not going to admit it — and he guesses Georgina has them just as he does, just as everybody has. In Georgina's case, they're not easy to identify because she prefers to talk about things rather than people. It's what men are supposed to do — especially men who work with machines and mechanical equipment. They aren't supposed to have interests beyond the practical aspects of life and even if they bore everybody to death, that's all they're supposed to talk about. And engineers, he remembers from his service days, engineers are less inclined to talk about themselves than most people. You can live and work in the same ship with them and never find out anything about them. Even now, as an ex-serviceman, he still has difficulties talking about personal matters — which isn't really much different from the engineers.

'Nothing to worry about — except the manifold's going to finish up with bolts of different sizes — no problem unless they're put back in the wrong places...'

'You need another donkey,' Georgina reminds him, 'a good two-cylinder job, something reliable... an engine you can trust.'

He likes the idea — the thought of being able to take the boat out and have the motor start when he needs it, knowing he won't have to waste good sailing time stripped to the waist, bruised and aching, trying to coax life from an engine so close to extinction that it's immoral — cruel — to ask anything more of it. And there are other advantages: being able to share a day or two's sailing with people he likes, people like Angie — maybe Angie herself (yes, he'd like to see more of Angie) — and even if it's for no more than a day, forgetting the marriage that came unstuck, whether it's Frank's turn to go out to the airport, what's going on in China, an economic situation that's thrown ten percent of the population out of work and isn't likely to provide any additional jobs in the future.

'It shouldn't have happened,' he says, pasting sticky, blue sealant round the exhaust exit, the manifold he has to bolt to it and the gasket that goes between them. No, it shouldn't have happened. Angie shouldn't have stayed at his apartment. She should have gone home (wherever home is) — Angie should have gone when Frank and Bridget — when the politician did. If she'd gone home he wouldn't have found her next to him the next morning, wouldn't still be thinking about her, wouldn't have exchanged more than a polite 'hello' with her in the supermarket, wouldn't have been thinking about her in the way he's been thinking about her, wouldn't have asked for her telephone number...

'But what else can you expect?' Georgina asks him. She's made herself comfortable — settled into the cockpit as if she's going to stay there until the job's finished. 'It's worn out. If you spent the price of a new car on it, you'd have the same problems next year, or the year after. If you don't believe it, get another opinion. Salinger's would give it to you — Denny Salinger would tell you if you asked him.'

'No-no, I'm not talking about the engine — it's unemployment, the economy. I'm talking about what's happened to the economy — what wouldn't have happened if the politicians had acted earlier, if they'd developed other markets when the British went into the Common Market.' He puts the gasket and manifold back where they belong and screws the first of the three bolts into place. He takes the last two turns on each of them slowly and carefully so that he doesn't damage the threads.

'Politics, Harry! You're talking politics! Why can't you talk about the weather — something sensible — the way everyone else does?'

'The weather then,' he tells her, 'it's less painful!'

Now that he's finished with the manifold, he puts the cover back over the engine compartment, replaces the companion ladder, puts the tools he's been using back in the carry-all and stows them under the starboard bunk where they're usually kept. Next, he pumps water into the sink, squirts in a generous quantity of yellow detergent, and washes the grease from his hands and black streaks of engine oil from his chest and arms. While he's washing, Georgina comes down into the cabin, goes over to the starboard settee, sits down and continues to watch what he's doing. She doesn't usually come into the cabin, but the way things have been happening lately no one's been doing what they usually do, he reminds himself, and anything's possible.

'A new engine.' he says for the sake of conversation. 'It's not easy to decide whether to throw another bucket of money into this one, get another, what kind to buy, or how to get the money to pay for it.' He squirts more detergent into the sink, pumps water on top of it, scrubs everything clean (the sides and bottom) and rinses it out.

'Rum,' Georgina asks him, 'you wouldn't have any rum aboard?'

'Rum?' he says, surprised. 'You'd like some rum?' He takes two glasses from the locker above the chart table and lifts out the bottle he keeps next to them. Georgina holds the glass he gives her up to the light so she can see the colour and quality of what Harry has put into it. 'Good stuff,' she says, 'but not as good as the kind you get in the Navy.'

Harry doesn't tell her that he seldom drank the stuff when he was in the Navy, that he doesn't like it very much — that officers didn't get a rum ration and that the custom's no longer observed. They drink without speaking while Georgina looks round the cabin examining the mahogany panelling and shelves in the way boating people do when they're aboard a boat they're not familiar with.

Harry doesn't want to think about the Navy. His naval service is over, gone, finished, done with, and he can't change anything, can't make the last two years of it any different from what they were. And that game of snooker with Tony Poindexter. It had been like so many other things that ought to have worked out but didn't — like the things it should be possible to anticipate, but people seldom do. He swallows some of his rum and watches Georgina do the same with hers. Drinking rum with Georgina isn't a situation he's familiar with. She seems curiously distant — curiously foreign — just as the interior of the boat, which he knows with the same exactness of detail as he knows his face in the shaving mirror, has suddenly become foreign. Yet he recognises, as he always has, its odour of dampness and ropes, of wet wood and old paint — the old familiar odours of boats and boat sheds he first encountered when he was still an adolescent.

But then there'd been the newness of the experience — the first time he went into a boat shed — a recognition that it was important, and later a realisation that it had become permanently locked into his memory so that even now it comes back to him as if he were standing in the doorway of the same shed looking at skiffs and dinghies inside their wire cages and watching people at work on the landing — sanding, polishing, busy with paint and varnish — getting their boats ready for the summer. The landing was a wooden platform built on a framework of railway iron — a platform hanging out over the water with a long ramp extending from it so boats could be launched and recovered at any level of the tide. Later when he was more familiar with the place, he used to lean over the balustrade when the tide was in, watching fish (small ones, no larger than minnows) or trying to guess how long the shingle and the concrete blocks into which the railway iron disappeared, had been there.

'A Volvo,' he tells Georgina, 'a Volvo Penta — eighteen horsepower — would do it.' He turns round, reaches into the locker behind him and takes out a folder which he places on the table and opens. It contains quotations from suppliers and brightly printed brochures giving details of the various engines they offer. '"The Volvo Penta",' he reads from one of the brochures, '"two-cylinder, four-stroke, direct-injected marine diesel with reverse gear." An S drive. That's what would do the job — get rid of the V and provide more space in the cabin,' he tells her. He wonders if Angie knows anything about engines — or if she doesn't know about them, whether she'd be interested in the difference between V and S drives, rates of fuel consumption, injection systems, gear and propeller shaft ratios, power outputs…

'I don't think so,' says Georgina, putting her glass down and leaning back. 'The S-drive has a rubber seal to keep the water out. It doesn't have the guts the straight shaft and direct drive have — and it's aluminium — won't stand up to off-shore cruising, the higher salinity — water temperatures in the tropics… electrolysis…'

She's told him the same thing before and because she's repeating it, he guesses it's not engines Georgina wants to talk about. If it had been engines, she wouldn't have come into the cabin — she'd have leaned over the companionway for no more than a few minutes before going back to whichever of the thousand and one boats in the marina she's working on.

Sometimes Harry wonders whether other people have the same sense of unreality he experiences and is experiencing at the moment, whether Georgina has it — a feeling of being cut off — removed from things. Even when he's talking about Volvo Pentas (a subject that matters to him) it's as if the words are coming from a distance, from a long way off, while the glossy photographs in the brochures he and Georgina are examining assume a peculiar appearance, an appearance as of great age, and move in and out of focus as if their existence was merely partial and at any moment they could vanish. And it's not the rum, he knows it's not the rum because he hasn't drunk enough of it...

Georgina is still talking engines: 'Parts,' she says, 'parts and repairs are another consideration. It's better to have something that doesn't cost too much to maintain...' While she talks she gazes into the distance. It's a habit she has of not looking directly at him when she's talking. It's a habit that makes Harry worry about himself — that makes him afraid Georgina doesn't look at him because she doesn't want to embarrass him, doesn't want to let him know she knows how ignorant he is and how terrible it is that he should be so ignorant of things that traditionally men are supposed to be expert in. He fears also that she has a considerable degree of contempt for his engine and a dislike of developing any form of hands on, intimate relationship with such dilapidated, clapped-out machinery.

'Reliability,' Georgina continues, 'an engine has to be reliable. When you need to use it — when you really need to use it — it has to be reliable. You can't have it tripping over itself when there's a forty-knot off-shore gale blowing you and your boat onto a lee shore — when the anchor's beginning to drag, your sails aren't self-furling and the headsail you want is still in the sail locker.'

Harry pours more rum, not because he wants any himself, but to encourage Georgina — to help her get round to whatever it is she's trying to get round to. 'Lee shores,' he says turning the conversation away from engines, 'everyone talks about lee shores, but not many get caught on them. Good sailors know about the weather... they listen to forecasts... they watch out for it...'

'Yes,' says Georgina, 'there's something I want to ask you... something I want to ask you about.'

'The weather?' Harry says, 'You want to ask me about the weather?'

'Well, not exactly the weather.' Georgina puts down her glass, stands up, turns towards one of the cabin windows and peers through it at the boat in the next berth — peers at it as intently as if she were a broker attempting to put a price on its elegant, gel-coated, glass-reinforced hull. 'It's my daughter,' she says, 'I'm worried about my daughter... about what she's up to... what's going on... what the hell she's doing...' Harry doesn't know what to say to her.

'I think it ought to be the Volvo Penta,' he says trying to keep things impersonal and because he's still thinking about engines, and doesn't want Georgina to remember what he's said or — when she thinks about it later — to work out how short of money he is. 'It costs more but it's easier on fuel than the Yanmar...'

90

'This guy my daughter's interested in — I want to ask you about him.'

'I didn't know you had a daughter — didn't know you were married.' Harry has never thought of Georgina as having a daughter. The owner of *Karamea* once told him that Georgina had spent half her life working in a foundry and the rest of it on an oil tanker sailing between the Gulf states, South America and the West Indies. And certainly, he hasn't thought of her as the kind of person who cleans up after work and goes home to cook dinner for her family.

'I don't like him — the guy she's going with. There's something about him — something about what he says and the way he says it...'

'You want to talk about your daughter. . . you really want to talk about her?' Harry is surprised and flattered by it. He's never thought of himself as the kind of man women would consider suitable to discuss their daughters with — well, not since his divorce. Before his divorce perhaps — but not since.

'Yes, I need someone else's opinion... need another opinion... have to decide what to do... what to do about him.'

'But I don't know the guy, I've never met him and probably I've never heard of him.'

'He's twenty-eight... twenty-nine... could be older... he'd have been in the Navy when you were — well, some of the time. Stuart Mills... says he was a lieutenant... that he's in the reserves.' Somewhere along the marina an engine thumps over for a moment and then fires up. Georgina has turned away from the window and is looking towards him with an appearance of expectancy — even of anxiety. 'He drives different kinds of cars — owns a car business.'

Harry doesn't like what he's hearing. Daughters are daughters, he reminds himself and if they're old enough to go out with people of Stuart's age, it won't be more than a year to eighteen months before they'll do exactly what they like whether their mothers want them to or otherwise. The part he doesn't like — the part he'd rather not hear about is John Stuart Mills — that it's Mills who's involved with Georgina's daughter.

'I don't know any car salesmen,' he tells her. 'I don't know anyone who sells cars.'

'A sporty dresser... wears a reefer jacket with gilt buttons... buttons with anchors on them... Thin, very thin, with a slightly hoarse voice.'

Harry hears the click of billiard balls, sees Tony bending over a snooker table in full mess kit — black bow tie, stiff shirt front, mess jacket with gold lace, voice slightly blurred by alcohol — not that he recalls ever having seen Tony drunk — but he used to get as far as the blurred vision stage himself and maybe it's the way he's seeing and hearing things that makes him think Tony's speech is blurred.

'You're riding him too hard,' Poindexter tells him. He slides one of the two brass markers along the tally board, adding eight more points to his total score. 'They say it's a personality thing — you have it in for him — won't leave him alone... The last report you wrote —' Tony walks to the end of the table and takes up the chalk, 'your last report recommended holding back confirmation of appointment another six months.' He chalks the tip of his cue slowly, absentmindedly as if he's thinking of something else. 'The Commodore doesn't like it. He hasn't looked on it very favourably. No one else thinks a delay is necessary... they say you're imagining things.'

Somewhere outside an outboard adds its metallic whir to the thump of the diesel. 'Yes,' Harry tells Georgina, 'John Stuart Mills — that's the guy — Stuart Mills!'

Harry hears the click of billiard balls on the snooker table, sees Tony Poindexter bending over it, getting ready for a shot at the black. 'You're making a mess of it, Harry,' he hears Tony telling him, ' — you're making one hell of a mess of things.'

'Power,' he remembers Tony telling him, 'leverage... getting an edge... an advantage... that's what it's about.' They were working at it, each of them trying to get as many points as possible out of the colours still on the table. 'And it's the same with snooker and billiards — they're not just games, they're another version of it — politics and power. And what goes on between people, between the sexes — it's exactly the same... power and politics...'

Typical, Harry tells himself, the kind of thing Poindexter could be expected to say — correct, and yet at the same time incorrect, depending on the point of view and who's expressing it. He thinks about what Tony's saying and the relative merit, the value of such things... about Air Vice Marshal... it was a long time ago and he can't remember the man's name. He's forgotten it... the Air Vice Marshal (what a hell of a title, like a long handled shovel with a two centimetre blade!)... it comes back to him... Gill!... yes, that was it! Air Vice Marshal Gill... describing the South East Asia Treaty Organisation as the corner-stone of national defence — three months before it went out of existence!

Tony leans forward, trying to get a better view of the table. 'Mao Zedong said it... power grows out of the barrel of a gun...' He extends his cue across the baize and sights along it, checking the angle it makes with the side cushion. 'But it's what's behind the gun that makes the difference — politics

— the political aim. You have to have a strategy and tactics to back it up, you have make sure the cue has force behind it — enough weight to keep the white going, get the target ball to the pocket. A little too much,' he leans forward lining up on the white, 'a little too much and you overshoot — the ball goes go off the table — not enough and it doesn't reach the pocket.'

Harry steps back out of Tony's line of sight. He hopes for, but doesn't expect one of these two outcomes from his opponent's next shot. 'Power,' says Tony, 'it's power and the way you use it, knowing what it's for, and the intent — that's what Mao would have said — the intent to use it that makes the difference.'

And practice, Harry reminds himself — a little ability and a lot of practice. Tony however, never seems to practice — simply keeps on doing, keeps repeating the things he's good at and avoids everything else. It convinces other people (and Tony as well) — it convinces people he's good at everything and saves him the trouble of expending energy on the things he's not and never will be any good at.

Tony leans over the table, draws his head back until it acquires the slightly crazy appearance billiards and snooker players are forced to adopt, and sights along the cue. Harry watches what's happening, locks the scene in his head freezing it as if it's one of a series of stills taken for a cinema advertisement: Tony's head and shoulders, the green baize, the light from the lamps above it… He freezes it — the entire scene — and adds it to the already extensive collection of such images he carries inside his head: his father telling him to avoid the mistakes he's made himself, naval officers in full kit at a formal mess function, the spin of a ball moving towards a bat (a ball he knows he will and does in fact, miss), a boat pursuing its own individual and remarkably private life under sail…

The faint click of snooker balls striking each other pulls his attention back to the billiard table. 'They'll get you for it, Harry,' Tony tells him watching the blue glide towards the near end of the table, the white wend its way along the baize and down to the far cushion, come off it and roll back at a slow and ever decreasing pace until it finally settles behind and within touching distance of the black. 'You can't treat a guy the way you've been treating Mills and hope to get away with it.' He straightens up and steps back from the table. 'And it makes no difference what you write in your report — what you say about him. An officer can get away with almost any damn thing except smashing up naval property or getting into a fist fight — and Mills has done neither of those things, not one of them…'

'Mills,' says Georgina, 'that's the man's name… says he left the Navy because his uncle died and he inherited enough money to start a business…

enough to get into the car business. He says he's always liked cars — good quality, slightly conservative cars — but drove an MG while he was in the Navy because it was sporty and good for his image.'

'I don't remember the car, but I remember Mills.'

'They met at a party — one of those parties kids go to. She — my daughter — didn't get back until about two in the morning, wouldn't say where she'd been or what she'd been doing...'

The boat rocks gently in the wake of the outboard fastened to the transom of the security officer's aluminium dinghy. He'd be doing his rounds about now — checking the security of the marina. That's the advantage, of Westpark, he reminds himself — apart from the cheapness of the berths the security's good, there are very few break-ins and nothing much is ever stolen. The disadvantage is that it takes a hell of a long time to get to North Head — to get out of the harbour and into the Gulf.

'I keep asking... and her father — if he was still alive... her father would keep asking... but she won't talk about it — won't talk about him... says she's not a child and doesn't have to say anything if she doesn't want to. But she's not very bright, Harry... she's my daughter but she's not very bright... and he's too old and too experienced for her... not that a few years make much difference... I just don't like the look of him, don't trust him, don't like the way he talks, what he says. It's as if... as if there's something not quite right about him... that he's not who he says he is, that he's putting on an act...'

E l e v e n

Harry's father is dead, very dead, but they still have unfinished business with each other. And because the business is unfinished, Harry sometimes talks to his father. 'You bastard,' he says, 'you bastard!' Usually he doesn't say anything more than this — because it seems enough and he knows that his father isn't going to hear what he says anyway. Sometimes he says a great deal more — things like: 'Whatever you did, you bastard, you did it for you, for yourself, and I don't blame you, nobody would blame you because you weren't doing anything much different from what almost everybody else does — except you did it all so bloody badly!' And mostly, even on his worst days, the days when he has a desperate need to say things to his father, these few sentences seem enough.

Today he's talking to his father because Georgina has spoken with him at length and in mother talk — even if it was about her daughter she was speaking, rather than anything that concerns Harry personally. But what Georgina has said and the manner in which she's said it, remind him that everybody has parents, that he himself has them, dead though they might be — and that he sometimes addresses them (and his father in particular) as if they were still alive. Georgina is the opposite of what Harry's parents were, Georgina is a good woman and her daughter is almost certainly a good kid. Yet good people can be handicapped by their goodness — it sets them at a disadvantage, makes them vulnerable, and in their lack of familiarity with political manoeuverings, with the processes of government, and with people who break into houses and smash furniture and other property — people who forge documents or lie habitually — they have no defences. He suspects that this is the case with Georgina and her daughter and fears he may not have helped a hell of a lot.

Of course, he's told Georgina he used to know Stuart Mills and he's told her something of his history as well — but perhaps he should have told her more. He's tried to be fair, to acknowledge to himself that Mills could have changed: people do change, they do reform, and Mills could be one of them. He could own a second-hand car business exactly as he's said he does, he might have inherited money, he might (unlikely as it is) be in the naval reserves — and being older than Georgina's daughter isn't morally wrong nor an offence against the law. In his own case and although it worries him, Angie is younger than he is (younger than he'd like her to be) but it hasn't stopped him thinking and wanting to do something about her — asking for her telephone number — hasn't stopped him intending to contact her again or wanting to see more of her. The problem is that he has to balance being fair to Mills against being fair to Georgina, has to offer due warning — if warning is needed — before anything serious happens.

He's still thinking about Georgina and her daughter, when he reaches his apartment and drives into the carport. He has daughters himself — two daughters — and, in spite of their existence and the existence of their mother, despite what experience he does have of women, he acknowledges the problems he has in relating to them. Sometimes he puts it down to attending a single-sex school and having no sisters — to not having experienced everyday contact with women until his marriage when he didn't seem able to get the formula right (if there were a formula or if it could be got right!). Whatever the aetiology of it, he's nervous of women, he's unable to make a reasonable estimate as to what they think or what they're feeling. Usually, it makes no difference: things happen, events and circumstances work themselves out. But it's the events and circumstances that don't work out that cause him problems. He wonders whether he'll see Angie again and if he does, how he'll behave and what might happen.

He's still wondering how he ought to behave with Angie when he reaches the door of his apartment and, carrying his two bags of groceries, pushes his key into the lock and opens the door. He should have noticed — it's early evening and dusk is coming down — he should have noticed as he walked up from the carport that the lights in his apartment were on. Angie (it couldn't have been anyone else) Angie must have switched on the lights in the morning before she left the apartment and forgotten to turn them off. He closes the door and moves across the hallway into the kitchen. The light above the sink is on and there's a smell of cooking — an appetising smell of cooking — filling the room. 'Don't touch it — don't touch anything!' It's a woman's voice. He puts his groceries on the kitchen bench and turns towards the voice.

Angie is standing in the doorway with the light from the living room behind her. She is dressed in a black track suit with a white slash across it and wears running shoes. Her skin seems paler, her hair more luxurious than it was earlier and, because of the light behind it, brighter than it was when he saw her in the supermarket. 'It's a surprise,' she tells him, moving across the room and inspecting the oven. 'The dinner's cooking and you're not to touch anything — it's chicken and needs another half hour in the oven before it's ready.' She busies herself with the pots and pans on the stove and does something to the microwave. 'But we're going for a run first,' she says, turning her head towards him. 'And I know you're a runner because your running gear's in the bedroom.' She checks the timer above the oven. 'It's no good sitting down to dinner, unless you've developed an appetite for it.' He's surprised and she sees he's surprised. 'I've put your things out — you don't have to look for them. They're on the bed — track suit, socks, shoes. When you've put them on, we're going for a run.'

A few minutes later — before he can work out what's happened or how it's come about — Angie is keeping pace with him and he's running at a quiet jog, confused and pleased, along darkening streets. There's still a hint of colour in the west: the last touch of the vanished sun. The air's pleasantly cool, there's a rustling of leaves from hedges and trees, and an odour of pine needles (which he's always liked) drifting towards them as they move along the grass verge of the footpath that climbs up towards Glenvale Park.

'I don't understand it,' he says, 'I don't understand how you got into the apartment.'

'Came back... to cook dinner.' Her speech comes in the short synchronised bursts runners use to match their breathing and stride. 'Locked the front door... and took the key from the back. You left it there... you shouldn't have. People who want to break in... can do things with keys left in locks... long, thin pliers pushed in... just a quick twist and the door's open. When you come back everything's gone... clothes, television set, radio, disc player... there's nothing left... nothing movable. You can't trust anyone... should be more careful.'

Even while she's running and has to match her phrasing to her breathing, her voice is pleasantly musical, precisely modulated. He seldom listens to voices properly — to what the wordless part of a voice is saying — and now, as Angie runs with him towards the park and he matches his stride to hers, he likes what he's hearing. She's told him how she got back into his apartment, but he still doesn't understand why she's done it, why she should be cooking dinner and going for a run with him as if they have a close and continuing relationship when they hardly know each other — and worse, he's not sure how to talk to her about such things.

'No one's ever broken in and taken anything,' he says, 'but I know people it's happened to.'

They reach Glenvale Park, push through the turn-stile and begin moving across the rough grass towards the far side. They're following the circuit he usually takes, a wide loop through the park and back to his apartment. He's gone the same way so often that he knows how to extend or shorten the distance to match the time available and that they'll get back to their starting point just inside the half-hour Angie has specified. Now and again white blobs appear out of the darkness or move reluctantly out of their way. 'Sheep,' he tells her. 'They use sheep to keep the grass down — it's cheaper than paying someone to cut it.'

They reach the other side of the park and begin a left-hand sweep along the curve of Glenvale Crescent, a sweep which will take them up to the main road and then to the downhill section of the run. The slight northerly they're leaning against, is pleasantly cool now he's developed a sweat and Harry, pleased and puzzled as he is at having Angie with him, can't understand why he's telling her about how the people who look after the park keep the grass under control — discussing irrelevancies such as how to protect himself against theft when they should be talking about the reasons for her coming back to his apartment and cooking dinner for him. Perhaps she doesn't know how mystified he is, that there's so much he doesn't understand — things like how Stuart Mills got to be the kind of person he is, what caused Tony Poindexter to do what he did, whether the fax he sent to Beijing will prevent anything serious happening to Wang Lan, if the newly acquired agent in Korea will pull the business out of the financial disaster it seems to be moving towards, how often he sees his children...

'How long do we climb for?' She asks him, moving with a smooth, easy pace that suggests she's serious about what she's organised him into and runs to a regular schedule.

'Five to six minutes,' he tells her. 'A little more... uphill work... and then...' he's not as fit as he'd like to be, and breaks off to catch his breath, '... and then there's a flat section... the rest of it's downhill.'

Somehow as they climb up to the flat section of the run, he suspects what he should have done was to come out into the open with it and ask her what she was doing, why she'd given him her telephone number when she knew she was going to go back to his apartment and that he'd find her there. And yet although he can only guess at her motives, he knows his own — why he didn't ask: she'd set out to excite his curiosity, and he'd been afraid if he challenged her, she'd change her mind. It was a fatal weakness — indulging his personal hopes and wishes when he should be keeping his feelings out of things and fronting up to them, when he should confront them, deal with them directly.

Recently, he's been reading Saul Bellow's *Henderson the Rain King*, and his vacillation and lack of decisiveness make him feel a little like Bellow's protagonist — not really in touch with anything — someone who has unexpected and sudden swings of mood that take him from introspective passivity into doing things that keep turning out wrong. It's the same with the business he's developed with Frank. It started out fine, but increasingly the evidence suggests it's not going to be a success — and like Henderson he's going (if he hasn't done so already) to leave things until it's too late. He should quit the whole deal now, get out of it, and yet if that's what he does, he leaves Frank with the mess, Wang Lan up to her eyebrows in angry students, the immigration authorities and the Government (as they're going to be no matter what he does) victorious and safely secure in the falsity of their international image.

He's read *Henderson the Rain King* before but he's enjoying it more and grows more appreciative of it every time he opens it. Rightfully, it doesn't belong to him. It was lent to him after his marriage collapsed — for reasons (another mystery) he still hasn't identified. Perhaps the donor as she seems to have become — perhaps Jennifer recognised his difficulties and thought the book would help him. Initially he'd flicked through the pages looking at an occasional sentence and trying to unravel the mystery of why she'd lent it to him. And then he'd put it conspicuously on one of his three bookshelves to remind himself to return it after a decent interval had elapsed. The difficulty was that the language was too dense to get into properly; it was like some kind of thicket in the Africa it dealt with, and yet once he'd taken the book down from the shelf and begun to read it, its multi-branched foliage and clutching thorns grabbed hold of him so fast he was unable to get out of it again — which was why he was reading it for the third or maybe the fourth time.

But he hadn't gone into the thicket directly, that is, he hadn't gone straight to the path at the beginning and entered where he was supposed to. He'd ignored it, skirted round it, passed it hundreds of times without doing anything about it — second shelf from the top, third book on the left... And when he did begin reading it, he began two-thirds of the way through — not because he'd decided to read the book or to begin at that point, but because that was where it fell open when he took it down from the shelf two years after he'd been given it, and found himself in the thicket...

He's still thinking of *The Rain King* when they reach the top of the run and begin to move along the flat section — along the main road towards the downhill stretch. 'It's better,' he tells her, perspiration trickling down his face and soaking his singlet, but his breathing more comfortable because the going's easier, 'it's better if you don't start at the beginning... if you dive in anywhere...'

She's ahead of him, but drops back when he speaks to her. 'What's better,' she says, 'what is it — that's better — if you don't start at the beginning?'

'Books... reading books, or anything else... anything at all. It's better to start things wherever you happen to be, not to bother going back to the beginning or looking for... for a conventional starting place.'

He sees the principle applies to almost everything, and particularly to what he's doing at the moment — running with Angie. Whatever's happening between them hasn't begun at the beginning, but wherever they happened to be — and so it was with *The Rain King*. He'd begun reading it at the point where Henderson is making friends with King Dahfu and admiring 'the beauty of his person'. It was an observation Harry had found disconcerting until he realised Henderson wasn't admiring Dahfu for any of the reasons he might have expected him to, but out of a sense of dislocation — a feeling of estrangement in terms of the everyday world; he was admiring him out of respect for the man himself and for his ability to fit perfectly into his surroundings and at the same time uncompromisingly preserve his individuality and distance.

'I don't follow it... what you're saying.' They're now on the downhill stretch and the running's easier. 'Why is it better... not to start... at the beginning?'

'It's better because... it's not the way things usually start... because most things don't start at the beginning... they only appear to. We think they begin at the beginning because we put them into a time frame... cut them up into chunks.' He's not sure he's said exactly what he meant to say, but it's as near as he can get to it.

'I'm not sure... I don't get it.' She slows while she thinks about it. 'We started this run at the beginning... didn't we... and we'll finish it at the end?'

'No.' he says, and it seems simple enough although he doesn't understand it completely and has a feeling there might be an inconsistency in it somewhere, 'we didn't start at the beginning... we started from where... from where we happened to be... and when we finish... it will only appear... we're back where we were before.' Harry can't specifically recall reading it in *The Rain King*, but it's the kind of answer Dahfu might have given Henderson, and which Henderson would then have spent a day and a half reflecting on — and another day and a half arguing with himself or the King about. In the world of King Dahfu where everything is clear, it is also and at the same time surprisingly and perplexingly opaque.

'Let's make a race of it!' Angie calls out.

The end of the run — it's starting point, middle, or whatever Dahfu might have persuaded Henderson it was — is almost in sight. Angie increases her pace and begins to move away from him. He lengthens his stride in order to catch up and the last two hundred metres become a race. When they reach the house they're both breathing heavily and their running gear is soaked with sweat. Harry is even a little unsteady on his feet. He usually doesn't put as much effort into it as this and he's feeling the effects and further, he's not going to confess it even though Angie seems in much the same condition as he is. She leans against him, throws her arms round his body and gasps for breath. 'It's too much!' she tells him. 'It's too much! Do you always run as fast as that?'

'No,' he says, 'I was trying to stop you getting too far ahead.' He can feel the heat of her body — her sweat — the rapidity of her heart beat and the pleasurable sensation of being close to her. He hasn't been so close to anyone since the night he and Frank went out on the town, but then it wasn't anyone he wanted to be with — no one he cared about. It hadn't been an Angie — someone he might have wanted to take home. It's a closeness he would have liked to have experienced the previous evening — that he very nearly — that he almost did experience.

'I was trying to stop you catching up... to stay in front!' she tells him. Harry has grave doubts that this is the truth — but true or otherwise it has advantages. Her breathing slows and begins to return to normal. Sadly (from Harry's point of view) she steps away from him.

'Dinner,' she says, immediately they're inside the apartment, 'I have to look at the dinner. Take a shower, Harry, and I'll see if the dinner's all right.' She goes into the kitchen, checks the oven, and switches on the microwave and the two pots on the top of the stove.

'It's really my job,' he tells her, 'what the host should be doing.'

'Not this time.' She pushes him towards the door. 'I did the shopping and worked out the menu — and I'm cooking the dinner. What you have to do, is get cleaned up and properly dressed.'

Everything she says sounds logical but isn't. It's the kind of thing Dahfu might have said to Henderson — what he might have said out of concern for Henderson's comfort and well-being. He thinks about it and the different ways in which people behave — about his ex-wife and what she'd said when he'd finally given up and was leaving. 'Good riddance,' she'd called after him, 'good riddance, and don't come back!' He still wonders whether her anger came from a primitive and private animosity towards him, or was the result of his taking so long to make up his mind that it affected her relationship with the other guy — the one she was getting rid of him for.

It's mysterious, he says to himself, once he's under the shower and soaping himself, it's a mystery! Why is it that when things have changed so much, when they're so different from the way they were previously, when they're so very different and enjoyable — why does he think of his ex-wife, of the least pleasant moments he's experienced? But then again, as King Dahfu might have said, even if things are different it's a mistake to believe they're enjoyable. Enjoyment is subjective, it requires a value judgement and belongs in the same category as beginnings and endings. And Dahfu might have been correct because it wasn't the end of his marriage when he left. There were still so many problems relating to it (painting to do, plumbing to fix, money to be paid... and paid) that 'good riddance, and don't come back' could have meant something else — the middle rather than the end...

'You aren't offended are you?' Angie pushes back the glass door of the shower and looks at him quizzically. 'You aren't offended?' she asks, stepping in and closing the door. 'You don't mind sharing your shower with the cook, do you?' She takes the soap from him and begins rubbing it over his shoulders. Her hands touch him lightly, caressingly. 'You don't really mind, do you?'

There's a bantering tone to her voice, but he's uncertain whether she's referring to how she's come back to his flat or to the smooth and easy way she's sliding the soap over his body. And then without his knowing how she does it in such a confined space, she's moved round behind him and is working on his back. 'Backs are easier,' she tells him, 'there's more to do but they're flatter and there's nothing much to get in the way.' As if to demonstrate what she means, she slides the soap round to the front again and moves it across his lower abdomen. He feels her stomach, her breasts against his back, his rigidity (it may be imagination), and the rigidity of her nipples just below his shoulder blades.

'We don't know each other,' he says as the soaping continues, 'we don't know each other all that well.'

When she's finished with his back (she seems to have taken very little time at all, and far less than he would have liked her to) she moves round to the front and stands so close to him that he feels the smoothness of her skin against his stomach and chest — and is able to confirm his guess about her nipples. 'No, we don't know each other very well,' she says, 'but we're working on it... we're getting to know each other.' She gives the soap back to him. 'Your turn,' she says moving away from him, 'your turn to do some of the work!' Her mouth touches his — apologetically, he suspects — a quick brush of the lips as light as the wings of a butterfly, but the soap is going every which way and getting into so many different places at once that he can't be sure of it, can't be sure it's actually happening...

'Is this,' Angie asks him, 'is this where we were before?' She's in front of him, her body arched towards him and because she's shorter than he is, looking up at him.

'I don't know... I really don't know where we are,' he says uncertain whether she's talking about the parts of her he's soaping, the bits that are in physical contact with him, where she thinks she was when she woke in his apartment, or whatever it is that might or might not be developing between them. He doesn't know, and anyway it's absurd to think he knows.

And increasingly and in the best of circumstances he doesn't always know where he is or what he's doing either — and he certainly doesn't know where Angie is, what she's doing, or where she's coming from. He doesn't know why she's taking a shower with him, whether he asked her to spend the night in his apartment, why she gave him her telephone number, went for a run with him — why she's cooking his dinner. She hasn't told him and he doubts she's going to...

'The towels,' she asks when they've finished soaping each other and have rinsed themselves, 'where are the towels kept?'

He points to the wash basin and the cupboard under it. 'In there,' he tells her, 'you'll find them in the cupboard under the basin — on the top shelf.'

She slides the door open and steps out of the shower — her hips, her square shoulders and thinner waist distorted by the glass panels of the shower box, by the haze and steam that drifts round her. Women are the most beautiful creatures in the universe, he reminds himself, and Angie is more beautiful than most. He dislikes thinking it, (because of the attitudes so many people have, isn't sure he's allowed to think it) — he dislikes it because it reminds him of things he doesn't want to be reminded of: the way women are still treated as advertising accessories, consumable items — the way Tony Poindexter used to think of them...

'Getting to the front... staying there... being a winner,' he remembers Tony telling him as he moved round the table, 'that's what it's about... power... leverage... having an edge... an advantage.' They were trying to do the best they could with what was left — each of them trying to get as many points as possible out of the colours that were still on the table. 'And it's the same with snooker and billiards,' Tony persisted, 'they're not... just... games... they're another version of it... of politics and power. What goes on between people, between the sexes... it's exactly the same... power and politics... politics and power.'

Harry remembers it, remembers exactly what Tony said as if it had been tape recorded and the tape were being played back and forth in front of him — remembers it as if someone were still thinking about it, as if it were being considered for use in evidence against him. He turns off the shower, steps out of the shower box, and takes a clean dry towel from the cupboard under the hand basin. Tony had been right about what the Navy might or might not allow its personnel to get away with. It was people's attitudes that made a difference, affected outcomes — Tony's attitude, the attitude of the service. Recently there had been a newspaper report on attitudes in the Navy — something about a survey on the attitudes of naval personnel. It was last November — yes, that was it — last November. The Navy had surveyed the attitudes of its personnel towards 'unprofessional behaviour such as sexual misconduct'. The survey was undertaken, he remembers, drying himself, 'for Navy use only'.

It's a ritual he enjoys, taking a shower, towelling himself. And he's enjoying it now, the brusque dryness of the cloth, the remembered dampness of the shower itself, and during and immediately after his run with Angie, the trickle of sweat over his chest and back — the feeling of relief when the run was finished. 'Unprofessional conduct,' he says, towelling himself — and then he says it a second time and a little more loudly, letting the words reverberate from the walls of the bathroom, repeat themselves again in his head. They could mean almost anything, words like that could mean almost anything: Tony's relationship to Margaret, Angie and what's been happening between the two of them — what he's been thinking about over the last twenty-four hours — their being in the shower together...

T w e l v e

'For Christ sake!' Stuart is nervous because being nervous is his usual disposition, and because he's not sure that what he's saying is convincing or that Bridget or Richard will be convinced. 'They're going to do you,' he says while Richard looks at him unemotionally and without any sympathy. 'They're going to do you because you're not necessary. None of us are necessary. We're expendable.' In addition to selling cars and carpets, and to pursuing Georgina's daughter, Stuart is keenly interested in politics — not because he has any special gift for it, but because it's another possibility which just might work out — which might make up for the way things turned out in the past.

Richard is drawing small, precise, interlocking triangles on the scratch pad he's taken from his pocket and is balancing precariously on his knee. He suspects neither Richard nor Bridget believes him. Both of them know Stuart hasn't been in the party very long and neither of them really trusts him.

'Winners and losers,' says Stuart. 'The Executive sees the electorate as winnable but they think we'd lose it — that you'd lose it, that I'd lose it, Colin would lose it. They want an outsider — someone with a higher profile — who might have a better chance.'

Neither Bridget nor Richard responds. They know Colin has been excluded from the present meeting and that Stuart wants to keep him out of it and gain their support for himself or, if he can't gain their support, to make sure Colin doesn't get it. 'The Party Executive thinks Colin will get the nod — and they don't want it to happen,' Stuart tells them. While the Executive mightn't want it, Stuart doesn't want it either. He's found it difficult to get the seven signatures needed to validate his nomination and Colin's been working against him behind the scenes.

'What if he doesn't — what if it's one of us who gets the nod?' Richard begins drawing wide, swirling lines that weave in and out between the triangles, linking them more tightly together and into the body of a loosely constructed ball — not unlike a ball of string but with a streak of lightening and curious and sharply pointed metal objects projecting from it suggesting it could be something from outer space — and dangerous.

'Richard's better known than you are — and better known than Colin.' Bridget is defensive. She doesn't like Stuart. She's tried to warn Richard against him — that is, on the increasingly frequent occasions when he's invited her to have coffee with him, she's tried to warn him — but he hasn't believed her and he doesn't seem to believe her now. 'You're too hard on him,' Richard has said to her, 'we don't know much about him, and in a democracy people are presumed innocent until they're proven guilty.' He talks like that — he talks like it too much — which Bridget puts down to the expensive single-sex school his parents forced him to attend before he became sufficiently himself to offer any opposition.

'They want someone from outside the electorate — outside the Party even. That's what they say. They want someone with a national reputation — who's well known and a woman.They say it takes a woman to beat a woman...'

'We asked around,' Bridget tells him. 'We tried people in Wellington. Richard tried... said he'd withdraw in favour of a woman if there was a woman available. And the Executive chairman — Gilbert phoned from here, from this room... long distance...' She points to the telephone on the other side of the desk, the desk next to Richard. 'Richard paid for the calls.'

'They don't want him.' Stuart takes out a packet of cigarettes and a book of matches, looks for an ashtray, and puts them away again. 'Colin... the Executive doesn't want him. They think he'll win the selection... and if he wins... They say he can't be trusted because he tried to do a deal with Labour... The Executive wants a special meeting — wants him out of the race.'

Richard's pencil begins a second group of interlocking triangles. Apart from these jottings and the almost imperceptible change of pace in his voice, he seems calm and at ease, emits the soothing phrases and displays the relaxed body-language he was taught by the private tutor his mother hired for him.

Bridget leans forward. 'Control of the selection process is the responsibility of the electorate — of party members in the electorate. The Executive endorses the candidate... it isn't supposed to intervene... but if there was a woman candidate, if there really was a woman...'

'They want talk about it — they want us to ask the electorate to re-open nominations. There's a letter...' Stuart takes an envelope from his pocket. 'It says here,' he shows them the single typewritten sheet he takes out of the envelope, 'it says there's a meeting called for Sunday — in the afternoon.'

'Nominations closed four weeks ago,' Bridget says with finality in her voice, 'and the selection's tomorrow — the selection meeting's on Sunday!'

'It says here,' Stuart reads it out to them, '*Re the special meeting called by the convenor prior to Sunday's scheduled selection...*'

Richard's pencil stops moving.

'That's what it says.' Stuart is enjoying his role as key player. '*This isn't a local problem,*' he continues, '*it has ramifications for all members of the Alliance and for the Party itself, and needs to be resolved as quickly and as amicably as possible.*'

'*There's a real concern expressed by our Alliance partners that the choice of candidates in such a key seat isn't wide enough. There's a real possibility that as matters stand the candidate selected may not get the endorsement of the Alliance — with serious problems resulting.*'

'What problems?' Bridget breaks in. 'What problems is he talking about?'

'*Should the local group at this meeting,*' Stuart continues, '*should the local group choose not to re-open nominations — or re-open them and still choose one of the existing candidates, local party members are assured of one hundred percent support from the Executive, and from the Party's Alliance councillors.*'

'*Without an electorate-wide meeting taking place, we will not have done our best to resolve what is much more than a local issue — leaving the Party exposed at a national level.*' And then there are the details about discussing the proposal,' Stuart points out, 'about starting the selection meeting half an hour later than scheduled in order to allow enough time for it... '

'One hundred percent support from the Executive!' Bridget's response is exactly what Stuart has hoped for. 'What do they mean by saying they'll give us one hundred percent support if they're threatening not to endorse whoever it is who's selected!'

Richard looks up from his scratch pad. 'I've not been contacted about it — about re-opening nominations.'

'It'll be in your mailbox,' Stuart tells him, 'there'll be a notice in your mailbox.'

'Call Gilbert,' Bridget suggests.' You ought to call Gilbert.'

'Coffee,' Stuart suggests, 'maybe we should have some coffee.'

'Do we have to — shouldn't we get on with what we're supposed to be doing?' This is the second time Richard's invited her home and she's still hoping for something more than a political discussion. It's a large room with untidy book cases, a word processor on a make-shift desk, three comfortable chairs with a coffee table, and a battered desk constructed of a wood she doesn't recognise. The top of the desk is cluttered with paper and writing materials. She glares at Stuart while Richard begins making coffee at a bench set up with the equipment for it in the corner.

'Why don't they want Colin? What's wrong with him?' she asks when Richard has finished what he's been doing with the hot water jug and the coffee cups.

'It says here,' Stuart takes two spoonfuls of sugar and waves the milk away, 'it says here... there are problems.'

'What problems,' Richard wants to know, 'what are these problems you're talking about?'

Stuart studies the paper in front of him. He knows what he'll say, but believes studied silences and a slow, deliberate manner lend greater importance to things. 'There's a reason,' he tells them, 'there's a reason for what's in this letter. The Executive has found someone who has the profile they're looking for... they've found someone they think has a better chance.'

'You've said it before.' Richard is impatient. 'You said Gilbert wanted someone from outside the electorate...'

'He said there was no need to re-open nominations if people didn't want to,' Bridget tells them. 'He wanted to extend the date — everyone knows he wanted to extend the closing date — but there wasn't anyone else interested in standing. He said we hadn't allowed enough time... the selection process needed more refinement... But he accepted the decision of the group, the decision of the electorate. He said he didn't want to close any options off until every eventuality had been considered, but he'd go along with what everyone decided.'

'No he didn't.' Richard hasn't touched his coffee. He's drawing a third group of triangles and circles. 'It might have seemed he accepted the decision of the group, but he didn't — he didn't say he accepted it.'

'The letter — the letter's quite clear,' Stuart reminds them.

'It isn't clear — it doesn't say anyone's dissatisfied with the present nominees. It doesn't say they want someone from outside the electorate, that they'd prefer a woman — it says more consideration should be given to the selection process — that's all it says.'

'I've been talking to some of the Executive,' Stuart tells them, 'They say that if Colin wins the nomination he won't get the endorsement of the Alliance.'

'Who said it? If you don't tell us who you've been talking to, there's no way of knowing whether it's an official view or merely opinion.'

'Gilbert — I was talking to Gilbert. He says the Executive wants nominations re-opened.'

Bridget collects the cups and puts them back next to the hot-water jug. She spends too much time doing things like that — collecting cups — and dislikes herself because of it.

'Gilbert signed it — the letter — I talked to him about it. He says they don't want Colin — they don't want him because — well, everyone knows why they don't want him.'

'No,' Richard corrects him, 'everyone doesn't know why they don't want Colin. I don't know why they don't want him, Bridget doesn't know — and there are others who don't know either.' He draws three triangles of different sizes and decorates the spaces around them with five-pointed stars. The trick is to draw each of the stars with a single, fluid movement that starts and finishes at the same point.

'Well,' Stuart says, 'Colin's recruited people — brought people into the Party — his family and friends. He's recruited people he knows will support him, he's stacked the electorate with people who don't live in it... the last paragraph says it quite clearly. It's signed by Gilbert and shows what the Executive thinks.'

Richard's pencil is poised over his scratch pad. 'You've recruited new members too, haven't you, Stuart? Didn't you recruit new party members fairly recently?'

'No, it's not the same — it's not the same as Colin's been doing.' Stuart seems nervous. 'They live in the electorate. The people I've recruited live in the electorate and they have the right to vote for anybody they want to vote for. They'll decide for themselves.'

Richard draws hearts and flowers linked by a sword and a dagger. He's not as good at these as he is with stars and lightening flashes, but recently he's been extending his range.

'Someone said Claudia was interested in being a candidate — that she'd put her name forward if anyone wanted her,' Bridget breaks in, 'but only if she's invited.'

'The electorate,' Stuart tells them, 'if the electorate decides to re-open nominations there'll have to be a delay... there won't be enough time for the campaign... to get voters solidly behind the candidate...'

Stuart's pleased with himself. Things seem to be working out the way he wants them to. And he's pleased because of the contrast between what's happening now and what happened in the Navy. This time he has the winning hand: he's better at things than he used to be, there's no Harry Houghton around and he's managed to get Bridget and Richard confused. Like most members of the Party, they believe people come first — they believe people and the environment matter. But it's not the way the world operates. Real politicians work the system for their own advantage, they don't let principles stop them doing what they want to do, achieving what they want to achieve. Real politicians know what they're doing and where they're going, and they get on with things.

T h i r t e e n

In his soft leather shoes with thick spongy soles (brothel creepers his service colleagues called them), grey slacks and a white shirt Harry feels uncomfortable. It's not the clothes he's wearing that make him uncomfortable, it's Angie — her being in his flat and his awareness she's there, that already she's important to him. The familiar and well-known things around him — his furniture and books, the three paintings he bought as a job lot at one of Webb's auctions, his seventeenth century horse pistol (the one memento of his long-dead grandfather he still possesses) — have suddenly become foreign to him, assumed an unfamiliarity that makes him feel they no longer belong to him.

It's the feeling he sometimes had when he was overseas in foreign countries (Korea, Thailand, Japan), when languages he didn't know confused the meaning of things, smudged their significance, distorted situations and events and prevented him from understanding exactly what was going on — from recognising who was who and what was what. And it's the same with Angie, with having her here in his apartment. He's confused by it and not sure of what's happening — not sure of the kind of behaviour she expects from him.

He can hear her moving about the kitchen, doing things with the dinner — the dinner she's about to bring out and put on the table. Several dishes, she said. She's prepared several dishes and he knows from the way she's set out the plates, knives, forks, spoons — the glasses — that it's not going to be the kind of dinner he usually prepares for himself, that it's to be special — a special dinner — and he still doesn't know why she's doing it, doesn't know exactly what to say to her about it or how to say it. And he wonders about Frank — how he'd behave in a similar situation — Frank who's also spent twenty years in one of the services and come out of it damaged just as everyone else who serves in an organisation devoted to violence and death and to threats of violence, comes out of it damaged. But then, perhaps Frank's made a better recovery than most: his marriage hasn't fallen apart — it still exists — and when a marriage survives then there's a sense in which the two parties to the marriage may have done better than survive; and there's the possibility — a distinct possibility — Frank himself may have made a complete recovery.

'Soup?' Angie asks him. 'Soup and garlic bread?' She puts soup in front of him, sits down at the table, and offers him the cane basket he bought at the mixed stationery and hardware shop next to the New World supermarket where they met earlier in the day.

'Do you like it?' she asks as he takes a piece of the bread which, now that he's touching it, he recognises has been heated to a delicious golden brown in the oven, is crisp and hot to the touch, gives off a tempting and attractive aroma of yeast and garlic and he surmises, is probably moist, heavy with butter, and equally delicious inside.

'The bread,' she repeats her question, 'do you like it?' and then adds as if to prevent any delusions he might have concerning her expertise in the kitchen, 'It's the kind that comes already prepared and you finish it off at home in the oven.'

'Yes,' he says, and bites into it, 'yes! and the basket — where did you find it?' He knows he's handling the situation badly. 'I lost the basket,' he tells her, 'bought it at the place next to the supermarket, put it away somewhere and couldn't find it.'

He's being too formal — things aren't going the way he'd like them to, not according to plan, if there is a plan — and whatever it is that's happening, it isn't anything he's prepared himself for or anticipated. And again — for a second time — he sees her in the shower: her breasts, hips, the shape of her buttocks, the curve of her thighs. What he's seeing disturbs him. It disturbs him because although the image he sees is uniquely Angie, it's close to other images — images presented in cheap movies and equally cheap magazines, the images men construct when they want to see what they want to see, the fictions they put together in such a way that they no longer represent people: Angie in the shower, Angie sitting at the table asking whether he likes the dinner she's cooked, Angie who's come back to his apartment without his asking her to.

'The soup,' she says brightly — watching him, waiting for his response — so brightly that he senses her underlying nervousness, 'the soup's made from mussels. You take some mussels, cook them, and put them into the food processor — or chop them up as small as possible...' He takes her comment on chopping up the mussels as a concession to the limitations of his kitchen equipment, to his not having a food processor. 'And then you put them in a pot with onions and a little garlic — onions cooked in a few drops of oil to bring out the flavour...'

'The wine,' he responds trying to cover his ignorance of soup making and the absence of a food processor, 'would you like me to open the wine?' She's brought a champenoise in from the kitchen — Selak's — chilled, and with a film of condensation on it. He peels back the foil and unscrews the wire cage which holds the stopper in place. Cork, not plastic — God! He's thinking like some character from fiction, a worn-out James Bond! And even if he doesn't own a food processor, he can still recognise it when somebody has gone to the trouble of selecting a good wine — one of the more enjoyable wines he can no longer afford to buy himself.

'Yes,' she says as he fills her glass, 'you add tomato paste while the mussels are still in the blender or if there's no blender, put the mussels in the pot and add the paste afterwards — stir it in with a dollop of soya sauce and a splash of white wine.' She tastes the soup as if to reassure herself it's come out as well as might be expected. 'Sugar,' she tells him, 'usually it needs sugar to counteract the vinegar you put in to bring out the flavour — I forgot to tell you about the vinegar.'

'Great,' he says, lifting his glass and toasting her, 'it's great and you — you're even greater!' She's wearing a silk blouse with loose sleeves and corduroy trousers — white on black — not what he'd have expected, but stylish and attractive. 'And I like what you're wearing. 'It's,' he's not sure he ought to be saying it, 'it's... inviting.'

'It's supposed to be,' she tells him. 'Isn't that what clothes are for — why people dress for dinner — to be inviting?'

'The recipe,' he says, pretending not to understand and hoping to conceal it, 'your recipe for soup — you'll have to let me write the recipe down so I don't forget it.'

'They're important — clothes are important — they contribute to conversation, let people know how you feel about yourself — what you think about the people you're with — whether you're... interested...' Her emphasis on 'interested' confuses him. If she's dressed as she says to be inviting, then what kind of 'inviting' is she talking about, what is he supposed to do about it — or is he supposed to do anything at all?

'Women like men to know when they're interested,' she says, sitting straight — very straight — almost primly upright in her chair and looking at him wide-eyed and without expression. 'And they like them to know,' she continues, 'they like the men they're with to know whether they're available or not...'

'The recipe for the soup,' he says to her again, confused at the direction the conversation seems to be taking and bewildered — bewildered because she's pushing things faster that he wants her to and because of the fragility he senses underneath her brusque and practical, her business-like manner.

'I already have a boyfriend,' she says even more unexpectedly, and the word — the single word — 'boyfriend', hurts when he knows it shouldn't. It hurts because he has no claim over her, met her only twenty-four hours ago, hardly knows her at all. And then, when the short, sharp pain lessens, he's puzzled by it — he's puzzled because it's not a word in current usage, that's used very much and can't work out what it is she's saying to him. He looks at her across the table, at her red hair now recovered from the dampness of the shower and at her pale, elongated face. He tries to imagine what her boyfriend might be like — somebody the proper age for her — young, fair-haired, or dark perhaps. He would definitely have to be one or the other. She's not the kind of woman who'd be interested in anything in between — in the colourless, the nondescript.

She takes another piece of the garlic bread and sips her wine. 'Yes,' she tells him, 'once you've added the tomato paste to the mussels, you bring them to the boil and let them simmer. Then you dice up another onion, crunch up some garlic and add them to the mixture — both of them — together with half a glass of white wine, a shake or two of black pepper. Really — it's like politics but simpler and more enjoyable — partly a matter of procedure, and partly a matter of judgement. I'll write it down for you later, if you like.'

Sometimes Angie talks as if they've known each other for years, sometimes as if they've just been introduced and they're chatting aimlessly at a cocktail party. Too many things are happening too quickly — too many things he can't deal with. The worst of them is that he no longer sees much of his children — and then there are other problems: Wang Lan in Beijing, and at the school the problem of student numbers, of whether the business will survive, of Angie telling him she has a boyfriend (whatever that means), of his personal life or lack of it, the worn out engine in his boat, and another of those crazy letters that have nothing to do with anything he wants to know about — which arrived two days ago from the same anonymous writer of three weeks earlier. And the letter — the letter keeps coming back to him, takes up more space in his head than it ought, more than he wants it to.

Dear Harry, the second letter began, *You will of course, forgive me for communicating with you again and so soon, but unsettling events have overtaken me and I do not know how to deal with them other than through writing to you.*

Since returning here I have corresponded with a number of people I saw while I was away. As I told you, I see few people — and the outcome of not seeing people is far too frequently loneliness, cold, an empty belly and getting into situations of the sort most people would not want to know about. Not only is it a question of suffering but a sort of ratification of original despair (original sin?), the same sense of impossibility you experience when you're seven or eight years old and totally powerless. It has become very clear to me that states of mind, like depression, don't just 'happen' to us — that we create them like almost all other events in our lives. Therefore two weeks ago I refused to accept the depression and sorrow that so easily manifest themselves and left here, willing myself, forcing myself to visit people I used to know.

I stayed for five days with my good friend Dr (theological) Bigelow and attended his Christian College over Easter for its religious celebrations. I am a disciplined man — get up at six each morning and take long walks. I am simple in my eating habits and in everything else of little trouble to anyone. However, when I went up to the kitchen sink at Dr Bigelow's house to help with the dishes, his good wife told me to 'get out of the road'. I remembered that it is the mind that makes good or ill, that makes us wretched, happy, rich or poor and, not liking what she said, got 'out of the road'. Of course, you didn't know I had friends, or friends in such good social standing. I also have a wife who lives in Fairhaven. I went to stay with my wife and two sons and hoped to stop a few weeks with them but each day was a continual harping on my weaknesses, my personal state and the various ways in which I offend.

'You get up too early. Try not to play your classical music first thing in the morning. You use the milk and there's never enough for a cup of tea or to give to the pussy cat. You leave the bathroom a mess and the bath mat very wet. You're always washing your clothes and use up the washing powder...' And so it went on... 'Don't make phone calls — particularly toll calls — and when are you going to pay back the thirty dollars I lent you for the fee Dr Bigelow wanted from you for attending the Easter celebrations?'

I didn't have the money — didn't have any money at all and asked her for two dollars to put my clothes through one of the drying machines at the corner dairy. She didn't give it to me — told me she had a perfectly good machine herself and I could use that if I left it clean or didn't break it, and I should have brought enough clothes with me so that I wasn't washing and drying things all the time. I walked to town every day (I like walking). Then she said I had to leave because her rich old friends Karl and Gloria were coming from Denmark to stay a month or two, and she needed the beds.

Of course, there was plenty of space — she had settees and blankets, sleeping bags and she could have told me I could stay as long as I liked, that I was no trouble to anyone... but I could see I was an embarrassment *to her. I left and went over to the Shore — to stay with Blanche Whitehead who wanted me to paint her house and garden fence. I worked for four days without stopping — I worked really hard. She said she would pay me for it and I hoped she'd give me at least a hundred, but I left without her offering me breakfast or a cup of tea, and she never gave me a cent on my leaving.*

I walked all the way to the city-centre and hitch-hiked over the harbour bridge, worn out and thinking of God. All I had was a return ticket and not a penny, so after sleeping out I took the bus the next morning and returned here. Forty-five dollars arrived today from Mrs Whitehead for four days' labour — what an insult! — with a note to say she forgot to pay me. Nobody forgets things like that! It's just that she didn't have the face to offer only forty-five dollars for four days' labour, and if she had offered it I would have declined and told her to buy herself something. So she cleverly sent it, knowing I wouldn't be able to make the insulting gesture of returning it by post.

I hoped to stay at least five to six weeks and then come and spend an hour or two with you — drink a glass of wine, talk — but then, I had no way of obtaining accommodation with Dr Bigelow or my wife. There didn't seem much point because if I'd phoned you and told you what was happening, you might have thought it was just another sob story — just another bum pulling out all the stops...

Now, the real difference between those who succeed and those who fail, isn't one of money, but their life experiences and what they choose to do with the resources they have. I wrote letters of appreciation to Dr Bigelow and Blanche Whitehead and my wife for their kindnesses to me and now seek other patterns of thought that will create strengthening bonds for my spirit. like — like writing poetry. I write a little poetry and perhaps some day I will send you some of it.

Again, there was no signature and as Harry recalls, not much of a valediction — merely a conventional wish for his good health and an assurance of another letter some time in the future. The first of the two letters, he remembers, annoyed him, although he hadn't realised it at the time — annoyed him because it was unsolicited, from someone he didn't know, who appeared to lack any sense of dignity and pride. He now wonders whether he should have felt so condemnatory of it and whether indeed, there wasn't a kind of pride in it — a dignity that comes from recognising the limits of personal endurance and not being afraid to state those limits. It was that or something like it. The alternative is that the two letters are part of a softening up process designed towards taking advantage of him, conning something out of him, or in some other way taking advantage of him.

If they represent a preliminary move towards a confidence scam, then he would feel a horrible sense of disappointment (not that he would wish on anyone the difficulties of his correspondent) — he would feel disappointed because in a peculiar way he can't analyse, he's looking forward to a third letter and to further insights into the tribulations of the anonymous writer; besides, there's always the possibility that eventually a name and address will appear and he'll be able to do something to help — send money (well, perhaps not send money!) — put the guy in touch with an organisation that looks after people with such terrible problems. But only if there really is someone desperately in need of help, if the letters are genuine!

'You're not listening!' Angie has put down her spoon and is waiting for him to finish his soup. 'Businessmen and politicians,' she tells him, 'none of you ever listen, you're always trying to take short cuts, to work out how to get rich quickly — how to become millionaires by next Wednesday!'

'It's delicious!' he tells her — and it is, 'the soup's delicious — if there's any left, could I have more of it?'

'You didn't know I'd be here,' she says a little later, 'you didn't know I'd be here when you came back to your apartment. You thought I'd be gone — that you'd seen the last of me.' Very little expression shows on her face: her pale skin (paler, almost translucent in the light of the candles), the long face, the spread of her hair give no indication of what she's thinking. But there's amusement in her voice, a suggestion she's knows more about him than he knows about her — is way out in front because he's not observant enough, hasn't been able to work out what she's doing.

'Of course I did — of course I knew you'd be here.' He hadn't, of course he hadn't, but he's as good at games as she is — well, it's possible he is. 'When we were at the supermarket — I worked it out when we were at the supermarket.' And as he says it, he wishes indeed, he'd worked it out, just as he wishes he'd met Angie much earlier — had known her long ago and been able to think about her during the long loneliness of watches at sea, been able to write to her, talk to her through good times and bad...

'You didn't Harry, you didn't really work it out,' she suggests. 'There were clues. You could have checked up on the telephone number, but you didn't look at it — and you could have guessed when you saw me at the supermarket. It isn't the usual place I do my shopping.'

She was right, he'd missed the clues when he should have recognised them — picked up on them then — guessed from her having stayed the previous night that there was more to what was happening than a matter of somewhere to sleep. There had to be more to it because she isn't a woman who doesn't care where or with whom she sleeps. She knows who she is, what she's doing and why she does it. He doesn't know enough about women, that's the problem — he doesn't know enough about women and therefore hasn't been able to work out what's going on, and come to think of it he isn't too sure even now of what's happening!

'Well, aren't you going to ask me about the telephone number?'

'I haven't looked at it, haven't had the time,' he tells her (which is true), and it's turned out — it's turned out there's no need to, well, not right now, not when she's sitting opposite him at the same table and they're having dinner together. But he doubts she believes him. She's leaning towards him, looking at him with that strange wide-eyed stare which worries him, which appears to be habitual to her — which is is uniquely her own. The top of her blouse is undone and it's impossible not to notice the lift and curve of her breasts, the depth of the valley between. There's something about the position of her body, the sound of her voice that suggests she intends him to see what he's seeing — that the blouse she's wearing and her posture have been designed to ensure he sees it.

'You need to be more observant, Harry,' she says, 'you need to be more in touch with what's going on around you — you have to stop thinking about the things that are happening in your head and look more closely at what's in front of you. You have to take notice of it... really notice it.' She looks at him intently for a moment, and then pushing her chair back, collects the soup plates, places one on top of the other and takes them out to the kitchen. 'How do you like your potatoes,' she calls to him, 'with or without butter? You can have them either way — with cottage cheese — or with both.'

'Cheese,' he calls back to her, 'they're better with cheese — and butter...' He likes cheese but he's been trying to avoid it, as well as butter and potatoes. It's not that he feels any desperate need to reduce his carbohydrate and fat intake, but that he's been imposing a restriction in diet on himself, perhaps as a punishment for drinking too much and too often, and out of fear that some time in the future — and sadly, the not too distant future — he is going to have to watch his waistline.

'There,' she says when she's returned from the kitchen, 'it's not cordon bleu — nothing as fancy as the soup was.'

She's put dinner and two smaller plates on each side of the table. In the centre are serving dishes — one with chicken sliced and ready to serve, two containing mixed vegetables — baked potatoes and kumara filled with sour cream and a cheese mix — and a fourth containing lettuce, tomatoes, onions and capsicum. 'That's the side salad,' she says, pointing to the lettuce. 'Add thousand island dressing if you want to, and the little jug — that's chicken and mushroom gravy — a speciality of the house!'

117

'Wine,' he suggests, when their plates have been filled and they've begun eating, 'a little more wine?' He refills her glass and and tops up his own, a little surprised (and agreeably) at his moderation.

'Tell me about yourself,' she says leaning across the table. Her blue — no, he corrects himself — her green eyes stare straight at him, seemingly even larger and brighter than before. 'Tell me about yourself,' she says, putting her knife on the plate in front of her as an indication that she's waiting for him to begin, waiting for him to 'tell' her 'about' himself.

He doesn't know what to say or whether he wants to say anything at all, whether she'd want to know about the state of their business (the business Frank and he have put so much time and effort into), about Wang Lan and the danger she's in, whether she'd be interested in what happened when he was in the Navy — in John Stuart Mills — in Tony and the game of snooker which despite its no longer having any relevance, still wakes him at night in a cold sweat, or comes back when there's no reason why it should and he least wants it to. And then there's his boat and that damned engine, the question of whether he'll ever be able to use it again, get out onto the Gulf and experience the perfection of things, the balance of wind against tide — feel the boat moving towards whatever it moves towards. And that damn awful and endless game of snooker which is beginning — is beginning again — the way it always does when he isn't thinking and doesn't want to think about it...

Tony steps out of the way so Harry can see more clearly the lie of the table and the difficulty of the shot he has to make. The cue ball sits behind the black and he has no choice except to play for the blue. 'Not easy,' Tony tells him, his voice almost expressionless, but with hint of pleasure, of triumph in it, 'not easy at all. You'll have to come off the cushion and give it a little side — bottom even — if you're going to stop it following on and into the pocket.' Tony isn't usually as helpful as this but then his suggestions aren't meant to be helpful. And this time they're designed to tell him that he's losing and that if he misses, it will take unusual luck on his part or a major mistake on Tony's to get back into a winning position.

At the same time as he's playing snooker with Tony Poindexter, Harry watches himself, sees himself sitting opposite Angie, trying to work out what to say to her. He sees her blue-green eyes staring at him, waiting for him to answer. He sees the litheness of her body, the energy in the way she sits, waiting for something — something she expects from him, that she expects him to give her or if not give, to at least offer so she'll have a chance to think about it, consider it. She knows she has a right of refusal — that they both have rights — a right to say nothing, hold back, withdraw, move in opposite directions, and she knows that if he does hold back, he's establishing boundaries, imposing limits, setting rules. And for the moment — just for the moment — he can see the freshness, the newness of things, the possibilities of the world as she might be seeing them from her side of the table — not exactly the way she sees or experiences them, but the way she might be seeing them, the way people sometimes do see them when the past isn't complicated enough to get in the way of the present or obscure the future — the way he might once have seen them himself.

Angie stares at him, she stares at him waiting for him to say whatever it is she wants him to say — willing him to say it.

'It depends,' he tells her, 'it depends...' and he doesn't know where to begin, what to start with...

'Now that you've got me here,' she says, suddenly changing the direction of her question, 'now that you've got me here, what are you going to do with me? You're supposed to do something, aren't you? Once you've managed to get a woman into your apartment and you're having dinner, drinking wine with her, you're supposed to do something — at least, once the dinner's over and the wine's finished you're supposed to, aren't you?' She leans back so that her red hair moves beyond the reach of the light of the candles and turns dark, almost black.

'But I didn't get you here, I didn't bring you,' he tells her. 'You brought yourself... and I didn't ask you to stay last night... I didn't ask you back — to come back a second time...'

'No,' she says, 'but you wanted my number — you asked for my telephone number. And it's the same thing, very close to the same thing.'

There's an affectionate, teasing quality in her voice which unnerves him — it's not what he's been expecting (if he's been expecting anything at all), and it makes him uneasy because she's not sticking to the rules — well, the rules as he knows them — not behaving the way women are supposed to behave, the way women he's tried to 'chat up' (without any great success) have behaved, the way his ex-wife behaved. She's supposed to wait for him to make the moves — to suggest the moves if he's not actually making them or lacks the courage. Well, it's what he understands she's supposed to do, or perhaps things have reversed themselves over the past few years — maybe he's forgotten how things are supposed to happen — or maybe she's older and more experienced than she looks, than he's imagined she is.

'You aren't as young as I thought you were,' he tells her, trying to change the conversation — to conceal his embarrassment. 'I thought you weren't much more than in your early twenties, but you don't behave as if you are and sometimes — sometimes you look much older.' Perhaps it's the shape of her face or the pallor of her skin; things like that make it difficult to determine what people are thinking, what they're feeling.

'I'm not really as young as all that,' she says. 'I just look younger. My mother says I've always been old... that I was born old! It's the hair and the face — the shape of my face. And... and... I've done a lot of things... a lot more than most people have... that Bridget doesn't know about'. For no reason he can think of, she's trying to change the subject again, to move the conversation somewhere else. 'Bridget told me about you and Frank — and the mess you're in,' she tells him. 'Bridget says it's not that you're bad businessmen, that you're making mistakes — it's politics — what the Government's doing...'

Suddenly Harry feels he's the intruder, not Angie, that it's he who's stayed the previous night in her apartment, bought wine and come back a second time and now because he's the guest, she's getting round to exercising the host's privilege of directing the conversation, of deciding what happens next, where things will lead to — or whether they'll lead anywhere at all. He feels detached, distant, that he shouldn't be sitting opposite her — as if he's lost his identity and the accustomed familiarity of the walls and furniture, the plates he's eating from, the utensils he's eating with, have disappeared — as if he were a stranger to himself as much as he is to the situation.

'Yes — Bridget says there are better ways — you might have found better ways of doing things like... like joining the Private Language Schools Group — is that what it's called? You could have used its marketing network. Bridget says a combined marketing strategy works better — is more effective — and you shouldn't have tried to go it alone, relied on China as your sole market... or believed what the Government said. Perhaps you could have brought in more capital, somebody who could provide money but didn't want to be involved in the operation — a sleeping partner...'

'Richard,' he suggests, steering her away from what he ought or ought not be doing, from how he and Frank should be operating their business, 'Richard and Bridget seem to know each other. Last night they left together — I think they did — when the party finished.' And now he thinks about it, he realises Richard of the American Bar and the night before, must be the same Richard who was on talk-back radio earlier in the day. 'Is Bridget — are they both interested in politics?'

He hasn't thought of Bridget and politics because the things she usually talks about at the office are stationery, telephone calls, classes and classroom equipment — the day-to-day operation of the business — rarely what she does outside working hours. And then when Angie answers him, her voice comes from a great distance, from a long way off, and a picture forms in his mind giving him an independent, a third-party view of them sitting at the table finishing the chicken and the salad. She's leaning towards him, a fork in her hand, talking about Richard and politics, about Bridget, how Bridget told her about Frank and the business — told her about Harry — how Bridget called her up so she'd be able to join them at the American Bar, could meet them there.

'What does he do — what does Richard do apart from politics?' Harry asks her. 'He has to do something — has to to earn a living. Politicians don't get paid unless they've been elected to Parliament or they're full-time party officials.'

'They're both into politics. That's how they met, how she met Richard. They're in the Green Party and want to change the world...' Angie takes some of the salad from the bowl, puts it onto her plate and adds thousand island dressing. 'You should eat more of it,' she tells him. 'People who eat lettuce and tomato — stuff like that — have better complexions, healthier skins. It's the trace elements, the vitamins.' She stabs the salad with her fork and lifts out a wedge of tomato and a slice of cucumber. 'And the wine,' she says, 'wine sharpens the flavour — brings it out so it's cleaner, clearer... particularly when the wine's as fresh and fruity as this is.'

'Not while I'm driving,' he tells her. It's a joke he's heard somewhere but doesn't properly understand. He collects the plates, the knives and forks that are no longer wanted, and takes everything except the salad out to the kitchen. He would have preferred not to have bothered with tidying up, to leave everything on the table and spend the time looking at Angie, the play of light on her hair, the small movements of her face and hands — how she sits and moves, the colour of her hair — the clothes she wears. It's peculiar the way people look when they're right there in front of you and often it's different from how you think they look, the way they appear in photographs. Photographs cut something out — one of the physical dimensions, the time continuum — which is why photographs are so often poor likenesses — why people like Angie who don't conform to conventional ideas of how women should look can't be caught in a photograph. If he had to choose between Angie or a photograph, he'd choose Angie every time.

Fourteen

Stuart is waiting for the milk to be collected, not milk for himself, but the milk which in the morning Georgina will put on Sandra's breakfast cereal — perhaps on her own as well — and which Georgina will drink even if Sandra doesn't, with the strong, hot tea she's been addicted to since she started work with her husband (now a long time dead of a heart attack) at the St Mary's Bay Ship and Foundry Company. The milk Stuart is waiting to see collected is contained in two standard-sized cartons placed in the lower part of Georgina's letter box earlier in the evening by her milk vendor. He's not certain because he hasn't been able to look closely enough to be certain of it, but he suspects when he thinks about it, that it's trim milk, that it has to be trim milk considering Georgina is overweight and given to frequent comments on how slim Sandra is, and how people have to watch their weight early if they want to avoid losing their looks and risking heart problems later.

Stuart knows the milk is in the box because he saw it there just as he was leaving after he took Sandra home an hour earlier. He also saw that someone had left Georgina's car at the top of the drive and adjacent to the steps leading up to the front of the house. The car was still unlocked. Stuart has since checked the door and knows the keys are still in the ignition switch — which is very careless and unlike the kind of behaviour that's expected of someone as careful of her possessions as Sandra's mother is. But then there's the possibility that it wasn't Georgina but her brother (he's unemployed and sometimes borrows her car) who might have left it there. It could have happened in the earlier part of the evening while there was still light. Perhaps whoever was responsible for the oversight had taken a quick trip to the local shopping centre before dinner and had been in too much of a hurry to put the car in the garage or lock it up. Whatever the case, somebody has left Georgina's car in a most vulnerable position. It could be stolen — anyone could steal it — and she should have been told about it.

Stuart has no interest in Georgina's car as such. It is, although almost new, a relatively commonplace vehicle lacking the special features and extra fittings which would make it more interesting than others of its kind. While the simplicity of the vehicle makes it more readily disposable 'as is' and therefore attractive to a car thief, the same quality makes it uninteresting to Stuart who is presently sitting in his own car — a plum-red Stag convertible — which he's parked in the shadows on the opposite side of the road and about fifty metres from where Georgina lives. He isn't a car thief, Stuart reminds himself — he doesn't steal cars. He buys and sometimes sells them on the side. There's no licence required for buying and selling a car and, in any case, he's not actually trading in them: anybody can buy a second-hand vehicle, drive it round for a while and then decide the colour's unsuitable, the upholstery's not as good as was originally thought, or it doesn't hold the road well — and sell it again.

While he waits for the milk to be collected, Stuart takes out a cigarette and lights it, using the cigarette lighter in the dash. He likes smoking. It steadies his hands and it helps to pass the time when he's not doing anything much — like he's not doing much at the moment, and yet still has time enough to change his mind if he feels like not going through with it. And then, it's merely an accident that he's here at all — an accident that began earlier and is an indirect outcome of his talking with Richard and Bridget, of his being involved in politics.

At the same time as Angie was finishing the salad and Harry was stacking the dishes and attending to the coffee grinder, Stuart was getting himself invited to dinner. That is, because no one seemed inclined to invite him, he'd invited himself — and Sandra as well. He had suggested when Richard was drawing the conversation to an end that it was getting late — too late for him to go home and prepare anything for himself — and there seemed 'little sense in going anywhere else', well, not when Richard and Bridget were themselves probably going to have something to eat fairly soon. 'And anyway,' he'd added after Richard's natural courtesy and surprise had prevented an immediate refusal, 'if the three of us are going to eat here, you won't mind if I use your phone, if I call Sandra? You won't mind, will you?'

'Sandra?' Richard asks, suspiciously and confused by the sad and melancholy tone in Stuart's voice.

'Sandra,' Stuart tells him sadly, 'Sandra is a friend of the family. Nobody does anything for her. She lives and eats alone. I promised her mother — her parents are divorced — it's she who's a friend of the family — I promised her mother I'd keep an eye on her...'

'I don't see there's much harm in a phone call,' Richard defends himself.

'It might make her — it might make Sandra happy,' Stuart suggests.

'We have to help people.' Richard answers, as Stuart moves over to the phone and out of earshot. 'We have to help people — because it's what we ought to do... and because... because some time or another we might need other people's help ourselves.'

'Not Stuart's help,' Bridget glances towards the telephone and whispers back to him, 'not help from Stuart!'

'But I thought you liked him — you and Angie were friends of his?'

Bridget shakes her head. 'No,' she whispers again, quickly, 'no one knows very much about him. We met — Angie and I met him at the last conference — the last Party conference. She knows him better than I do. He's Angie's friend more than mine — and I don't like him! There's something... something about him...' She gestures towards the telephone. Stuart has stopped talking and is putting the receiver back onto its cradle.

'There,' he tells them, 'it's fixed. Sandra says she'll join us. All I have to do is go round and pick her up.'

It won't take more than a minute or two, he tells them, there'll be no real delay and by the time he's back with Sandra (he knows they'll like her), he's sure they'll have dinner ready — they're so good at everything. The four of them will be able to sit down to something together and have a really great social occasion. And it *will* be a great occasion — it will give him (but he doesn't tell them this), it will give him an opportunity to consolidate his relationship with Richard and then, once Richard recognises that he doesn't stand any real chance of gaining the candidature, to persuade him and perhaps Bridget to work towards his own selection as the party candidate.

Stuart enjoys eating meals he doesn't have to prepare himself. And in this case the meal is particularly enjoyable. The food, simple as it is, has cost him nothing while the wine which Richard suggested they open, 'because dinner without wine is hardly a dinner at all,' cost him the same. And it's good wine — something Richard must have had given to him or which he's bought to impress Bridget with. Sitting opposite Bridget while Richard puts the dishes he's prepared onto the table, Stuart feels very pleased with himself. Recently (and surprisingly) he's become a member of the party's policy committee and is thus moving closer towards the inner circle. This, together with the frequent telephone calls he puts through to the more senior members of the party and the visits he makes (uninvited) to their homes, is an increasing assurance of his chances of becoming the candidate.

He also believes he has a good chance of persuading Richard and Bridget that once he's selected, their political interests would best be served through their joining his electoral team (successful candidates always have a strong electoral team!). He's not quite sure how it would benefit them — and doesn't much care whether it does or not. In fact, it's a mystery to him as to why people work so hard in support of political candidates when there's nothing in it for them personally — when they receive no financial reward and giving the candidate the kind of support that's needed, makes it impossible for them to be nominated as candidates themselves.

It's unfortunate that he's had to lie about Sandra. He prefers to avoid lying unless it's really necessary — yet sometimes it is a necessity. Richard and Bridget are the kind of people who might be a little prudish, disapprove of a man of his intelligence and sophistication having a relationship with someone like Sandra — someone who's not very bright. They'd probably go on about it the way her mother does when Sandra does something particularly stupid, or question his intellectual ability when he's not about, argue over whether he should or shouldn't be involved in politics — and that wouldn't help very much. But he likes Sandra even if she doesn't talk a great deal. She's shy — she's socially reticent — and she likes being with a man who's been in the Navy, who wears a reefer jacket with the gold wire and and a naval crown on the pocket, who drives expensive (in Sandra's opinion) cars — who gives her the opportunity of having dinner with Richard and Bridget and listening to them talk. It's something to impress her with — and he wants her to be impressed.

'It's always the same,' Stuart tells them, unaware of the irony in what he's saying and and trying to make pleasant noises which will encourage everyone to relax and enjoy themselves. 'Politics are always the same. It's not a matter of being wanted, sought after, being asked to participate, but a question of having to fight your way in and when you're there, when you're a part of it and the pressure's building up, of having to go on fighting — of having to watch your back — identifying who are your friends and who are your enemies and treating them accordingly.'

Stuart leans over and helps Sandra to food from the dishes Richard has put on the table. The two larger bowls contain rice and mixed vegetables which look as if they've recently been pan-fried but in fact have been reheated in the micro-wave Richard is still learning how to use. The reason there's enough for all of them is that Richard is usually in too much of a hurry to do much cooking, and has overcome the logistics of supply and demand — of meal preparation — by preparing more than he needs, storing some of it in the refrigerator and reheating it later. It allows him to reduce the time he needs to spend on inessentials to a minimum, and employ what's saved for more important, more pressing matters — usually politics, increasingly Bridget, but on this occasion, the not so desirable activity of providing Stuart and Sandra with dinner.

'Yes', Stuart tells them, 'most people don't want to be involved in a large political party — they don't want more people in it than necessary — in fact, the fewer the better… unless, of course they're willing to pay their dues, do the leg work, and keep out of the way.'

It's a long speech, longer than anything he usually makes, but he's trying to be impressive. He puts down the bowl with rice in it, and offers the other to Bridget so she can help herself to vegetables. He's already filled Sandra's plate and she's begun eating in the American way — with the fork upside down in her right hand — which she's told Stuart is more sophisticated than the conventional method. (It's one of the few ways she has of annoying her mother and getting away with it.)

She's strangely clumsy and spills a little food on the table in front of her as she takes it from the plate. Her clumsiness is one of the things Stuart dislikes about her but which he's prepared to endure on account of her having no brothers or sisters and there being, as she's told him, no mortgage on the house her mother owns — and because (and he doesn't like to admit it) he likes her for herself. 'No,' she's said when he's asked her about it, 'they were careful about money,' ('they' being her mother and deceased father). 'And now she (Georgina) pays cash for everything — doesn't like writing cheques or owing anything.'

'It's only when a party's properly established, when it's well represented in Parliament and its top officials have become cabinet ministers and feel safe, that it can encourage a big membership. Once that's happened, rank and file members are no longer a threat and the hierarchy needs as many paid-up party members as they can get. And it's an advantage to the party if the newer members quarrel amongst themselves, expend their energy competing for lower echelon positions outside parliament.'

He hopes he sounds impressive. Occasionally he reads up on a subject he's interested in and tries to memorise a sentence here, a phrase there — something he might have an opportunity to use before he forgets it. It's one of the few things of any value that he learnt during his year at the university. Anybody could have seen the lecturers didn't properly understand or remember most of the things they were talking about — names, dates, places — well, not for long. Sooner or later almost all of it vanished from their minds unless they were constantly re-reading, reviewing, revising it. They managed to get away with reputations for erudition and vast knowledge, not because they really knew anything, but because the things they talked about happened to be whatever they had to teach and were boning up on at any given moment. Most of the time they weren't remembering anything: they wrote it down and taught from their notes. If they were assigned new teaching areas, they soon forgot whatever it was they'd been working on earlier and became experts in something else — usually what their colleagues expected of them and if possible a new and esoteric theory they'd be envied for.

Stuart waits for Richard or Bridget to respond, but neither of them answers. Richard stares into the distance. Bridget sips her wine and stares at Richard. 'They need as big a membership as they can get in order to maintain credibility — a party that's been in business for a while has to attract supporters or the voters lose faith in its ability to deliver.' He's talking like a university lecturer or a book — one or the other, and neither of them very good; he knows he's talking that way and doesn't like himself for it, but usually it impresses people.

'My mother votes National,' Sandra breaks in. 'She says it's the party that looks after people who look after themselves and doesn't give money to bludgers.' She forks more rice into her mouth. 'My mother says the Alliance is like the Values Party back in the seventies — it won't last more than a year or two. And anyway, she doesn't vote very often. My mother says it doesn't make much difference who you vote for. If things are bad, politicians make them worse, and if politicians make things worse there's no sense in voting at all...'

Sitting in his car and waiting for Georgina to collect the milk, Stuart thinks of Sandra's part in the conversation. He's still embarrassed by it two hours after he's taken her home and seen her safely up the steps and into the house where her mother, as usual, opened the door and let them in. He'd intended to impress Sandra, not to have her join in the conversation and make both of them look ridiculous, but it hadn't worked out the way he'd wanted it to. He wasn't careful enough. He should have remembered that the first principle of political success — he read it in one of the books he picked up at the conference two months' earlier — he should have remembered that the most important principle is to work everything out in advance, even to the point of anticipating random and therefore uncontrollable events and being ready to deal with them when they occur. 'The price of success is eternal vigilance,' that's what the book said — something like that — but most people couldn't tell if a quotation was accurate or otherwise. If it wasn't, it didn't matter because they'd think they were hearing a clever variation of it or if it were very, very wrong, they'd think they were hearing a sophisticated and subtle reference to something they didn't know about.

Another principle was always to tell the truth — or more precisely, to remain so close to it that no one could tell the difference. This was where politicians usually fouled up. They didn't realise straight-out lies could be found out, while something not quite the truth but very close to it was far more difficult to prove wrong. That was the mistake he'd made in the Navy. He hadn't lied — not really, not in fact — not to start with. It had been the interviewer's fault. 'Looking for a job with the training group,' the interviewing officer had asked him, 'want to be a training officer — take a short cut into the wardroom — is that it?' He'd laughed but the laughter had sounded artificial, unconvincing.

It was an impressive interview which, he presumed, was what it was supposed to be in order to encourage recruits who at the last moment (it did happen) might prove unwilling to give up their freedom and submit to the discipline of the service and the whims and foibles of their superiors. But the Navy was well-experienced in such matters and implied without saying it, that every recruit had an equally splendid opportunity of reaching commissioned rank and with a little hard work, of becoming a flag officer. The interviewer himself was a commander — as he pointed out. He wore a uniform with gold braid on its sleeves, brass buttons down the front, and a colourful and exciting strip of medal ribbons. He was tall, lean, and cleanly shaven unlike his assistant (a short, rotund petty officer with a well-trimmed moustache and a red beard — the full set, as Stuart learned later) who did the paperwork and appeared incredibly efficient. The commander spoke with a brusque British accent which made Stuart think of him as experienced and well-travelled — not that at the time he knew a great deal about such things.

'Yes,' Stuart responded in a passingly similar accent to the commander's, having decided that if that was how naval officers spoke and there was a possibility of his becoming one, he might as well get started on it right away, 'yes... training. I'd like to go into the training side of things... the training division...'

'And you've been teaching — you've had two years teaching service in a secondary school? A university man — educated and properly qualified?' In addition to his noticeably British accent, the commander spoke in a series of short, sharp phrases, presumably designed to convey the bluff, no-nonsense image of a practical and down-to-the-sea-in-ships, deck officer.

'Yes,' Stuart agreed quickly, remembering that while he'd only been to university for a year, this had been enough for him to get a temporary job in a local grammar school. In that sense and to that extent, he was qualified. He didn't say anything about his father's influence, that the principal gave him the job because he knew his father and had been in the army with him, that before the teaching job Stuart had given up on the university because his grades were too poor to justify further full-time study. His health, he'd told his father — who had believed him — it was his health. He'd been having trouble with his health and needed a break. He hadn't the courage to say how poor his grades were during the year and that he'd failed his examinations. His father had agreed that a year or two away from the university would do him good, would allow him to go back later when he was older and his health had improved.

'Highly technical, the Navy. Needs people who know what they're doing, people well up in physics and applied science.' The commander looked at him as if sizing him up, as if estimating whether he was sufficiently a man of the world to take a rough, seamanly joke. 'It's not like it used to be,' he continued having decided in the affirmative, 'the Navy's all turbines and electronics these days — that kind of thing.' He pauses, allowing a slight smile to come to his lips. 'Cocked hats and telescopes, wooden ships and iron men — rum, bum, baccy and the lash — they've gone forever! And a good thing too!' Although Stuart isn't aware of it, he's added the last remark as protection — in case he's misjudged his man.

'Simpson's rule,' the commander comes at him suddenly, perhaps to confirm Stuart's knowledge of applied mathematics and at the same time demonstrate the little he can remember of it and might have had trouble with himself. 'Tell me about Simpson's rule.'

Fortunately, Stuart is acquainted with Simpson's rule — partly because he's been forced to study it at secondary school (where he didn't understand it), partly because he's renewed his acquaintanceship with it during his year at the university and finally, because (and although he still doesn't fully understand it) he's recently had to teach it. 'Simpson's rule,' he repeats in the curiously throaty voice that's normal to him, perhaps on account of an unusually large larynx, but intensified on this occasion because he's nervous. 'It's a formula,' he begins, and then corrects himself, 'two formulae for calculating.... for calculating the area... under... within curvilinear boundaries.' The last few words come out at a slight rush as if he's suddenly remembered what's required and he's afraid of forgetting it.

'Quite — quite so!' the commander comes back hurriedly, 'Exactly!'

It had been the same with any other questions he might have asked concerning qualifications, and the discussion had rapidly turned towards the safer subject of his father's occupation and the relative merits of naval as compared with other forms of military service. Stuart had assumed on account of the formal letter he'd received some weeks later, that his background and experience were all in order and everything was satisfactory. It wasn't until he'd reported for duty and taken up his initial appointment that he discovered from *The Navy List* that he'd been credited with a university degree in science. Of course, he didn't have one and by then he'd come to realise that for the appointment he'd received (a direct entry commission) some kind of academic qualification was necessary. It seemed best to say nothing — and that was exactly what he did. And everything would have been all right if the officer whose charge he was placed under had been as easy to please as the recruiter — if it hadn't been for Harry.

The Navy is no longer one of the things Stuart likes thinking about but then, he's never liked thinking about anything unpleasant, especially things that go wrong or become difficult. . . like. . . like not being able to get on the good side of Sandra's mother. She should be pleased about his interest in her daughter. Georgina ought to be pleased. It isn't as if Sandra's attractive to everyone or that anyone else is interested in her. There isn't a string of prospective suitors lined up panting after her. And he's interested, genuinely interested in Sandra — he really likes her — and given time, he'll be able to make something out of her.

Georgina should be pleased because it's not just Sandra he's interested in — it's Georgina as well. He'd make Georgina a first rate son-in-law, he'd be able to help her with the business. In a managerial capacity of course! Widows who have taken over their husband's businesses need a practical, common-sense type of man to look after things for them. But then, it isn't much of a business — really just a one man (one woman, he reminds himself) — a one woman organisation — except when things get to be busy and Georgina has to hire one or two temporaries to help out. What's needed, is a manager who will build the business up — advertise, expand, negotiate, take on more people, develop the retail side...

Stuart stares into the darkness, takes a second cigarette from his pack and again lights it using the cigarette lighter from the dashboard. There's a book of matches in his pocket but he wants to avoid the flash and flare it would produce and the risk of absent-mindedly tossing the dead match through the car window. He's determined not to leave clues, not to give anyone a chance of identifying him. The thought reminds him of the butt from his previous cigarette. He can't remember whether he threw it out onto the roadway or put it into the ash tray and for a moment or two rummages inside the tray until he finds it, and can reassure himself that he hasn't made such an elementary blunder.

Yes, he tells himself, Georgina is in some ways a bit like her daughter, not over bright but with a measure of the common-sense Sandra seems to have missed out on, and she's a hard worker — the kind of woman who's really good at her job, who keeps at things until they're finished. All she needs to build up her business, to develop it into a major enterprise, is a manager with flair and drive, with a sense of purpose. People like Georgina take time to adjust to new ideas — they need to be led up to them, to be persuaded, convinced of the advantages they can't see for themselves.

Besides, if Georgina has managed to pay off the mortgage on her house and the bank overdraft her husband had on the business, she's almost certain to have saved a little money as well, and money's what's needed in politics as well as in business — not much, but enough to get things moving.

What she needs is to be convinced that a bright and intelligent son-in-law, someone with ambition and drive, can do as much for her business as she can herself. Stuart knows he has the ability — knows that given a chance, he could really do something with his life. So far, he hasn't had the opportunity. It wasn't from lack of effort he didn't do as well at the university as he might have — and he's taken a few papers by correspondence since then. It was just that... there was never enough time... and he couldn't get on top of things before the examinations. And the Navy — it had been the interviewing officer's fault in thinking he had a degree when he didn't. After that, he'd had to pretend he held one — and it would have been all right if Harry hadn't been so uptight about it when things started to go wrong. And then there was the business with the sword. He never did get the hang of it — and it had been humiliating when the Chief Gunnery Instructor had been ordered to give him extra sword drill and had marched him backwards and forwards in front of everybody. It wasn't his fault officers had to carry such out-dated equipment and wave it about on the parade ground...

And it's his father's fault he has to sell carpets and deal in second-hand cars... all that pushing around, spying... telling him what to do and how to do it. At least his father doesn't know what happened in the Navy (well, not yet) and he's not likely to find out if he can do something worth while, something impressive, if things can be worked out with Georgina. And it shouldn't take long, not if he goes about it the right way, convinces her John Stuart Mills is a true and reliable friend, the one person who cares about her daughter's well-being — who will help her in good and bad times, in times of good fortune and moments of pain. What he has to do, is convince Georgina he's a great guy, a guy worth having around and the car, Georgina's car is the answer — is the key to the problem.

Fifteen

Harry, like Stuart and Richard, like Frank and Wang Lan — and to a lesser degree, Bridget — Harry also has his problems and the most serious of them is Angie. She's still with him, still in his apartment, still keeping him in a state of uncertainty — of bewilderment and suspense — not the kind of suspense that comes from inviting someone back to your apartment for dinner and waiting to find out if anything might happen afterwards, or from asking someone in after a show and changing your mind, wondering whether or not it's possible to prevent anything from happening. Harry's always found women difficult and Angie seems more difficult than most. It's as if she operates from a different set of principles from everyone else, on a different frequency, maintains a different time-scale, and although he can recognise this is what she's doing, he's unable to locate the frequency, to tune into it. She makes him feel he's still back somewhere in the past, on the wireless, while she's switched to frequency modulation.

The result is he's divided between wanting to know what kind of person she is and not wanting to know at all. And perhaps, it would be better if he didn't know. Knowledge is power, but there's excitement and safety in ignorance, the excitement of expectation, of discoveries yet to be made, islands beyond the horizon, continents yet to be reached and explored — and the psychological safety of always being the traveller, of not coming to the end of things, of not being committed to anyone or anything.

There's something about her he can't recognise, that perhaps he doesn't want to recognise — and it's not just her appearance, the way she leans across the table, not just her eyes or the spread of her hair, the shape of her body under the white blouse and black corduroy trousers — there's more to it than that. It's something to do with the importance of things. Most people don't know what's important from one moment to the next, not when they've no idea of where they've come from or where they're going to — when they're locked into the middle of things. They need to see them from the outside, they need to see them whole, which is what he's not good at — at least he suspects he's not good at it.

'It's a special dinner,' she tells him, 'a special dinner and a kind of celebration — that's why I've done the cooking, gone to all this trouble. It's because it's a celebration.'

'I'm divorced,' he tells her. 'I'm a father and I'm not very good with women.'

'It's a celebration — to celebrate that I've decided to move in for a while, stay a few days.' She stares across the table at him. Her eyes are steady, unblinking, her back straight — so straight that her white blouse and the candle-lit pallor of her face make her appear primly proper — Victorian even.

'I'm divorced and people who are divorced make a mess of things. If they hadn't made a mess of things, they wouldn't be divorced — they'd be back with their families, washing the dishes, painting the house, taking the kids out at the weekend.'

'The telephone number I gave you — you didn't look at it!' she accuses him.

'People who are divorced don't have a history. All the years they've spent creating a family, putting a family together, working for their kids, planning, building up assets... they disappear... everything disappears...'

'The telephone number, Harry — you didn't look at the telephone number.'

'It's not as if anyone's died.' He's heard what she's said but he can't put his mind to it, can't stop saying whatever it is he's going to say. It's as if he's become some kind of an ancient mariner and has to talk to somebody — recount his story — well, part of it. 'No,' he tells her, 'it's not as if anyone's died — there isn't a memorial, a gravestone, somewhere you can go to on Sunday and leave flowers, say a prayer and know the finality of things. The people you care about still exist, but they're changing, or they've disappeared and you can't talk to them — there's no one to talk to...'

'Harry,' she says, 'there is someone to talk to — right now, there's someone here in front of you. There's me — we can talk to each other.' He stares at her fixedly — as if he's both aware of her being there and yet is uncertain, can't be sure of it.

'You're not listening, Harry — you didn't hear what I said. The telephone number — you should have looked at the telephone number. Go and get it, please Harry, go and get it — get it now and look at it — really look at it!'

'OK,' Harry gets up from the table. He shouldn't, he informs himself, he shouldn't just get up and do what Angie tells him — particularly when it's such a small matter and interrupts the rapport they've been developing — but then (and he thinks it's true) she's surprisingly vulnerable — and imperious when she wants to be! And because he's an ex-navalman, he has to remember that the customs and manners of the service are no longer appropriate — that he no longer lives in an organisation where men and women give and receive orders. It's a world where people listen to each other, co-operate with and behave courteously towards each other. But because human behaviour is usually habitual, sometimes he makes mistakes and the way things are, the formally polite manners of the military are no longer popular (perhaps never were) and can easily be mistaken for arrogance and pretence. Sometimes, it's better to forget the habits of the past (even to forget the past itself) — the things he wants or doesn't want — and just do what other people expect.

But then, Angie confuses him. The two of them seem to have very different points of view. He tries to tell her something about himself so that if she's interested, if she's developing a real interest in him, she'll have a better idea of the person she's dealing with — and while he's telling her about himself, he hopes in return she'll talk about the things that have happened to her, what sort of person she is. Instead, she talks about telephone numbers and celebrations when sadly, there isn't anything to celebrate — when in his case it's been a long time since anything's happened that's worth celebrating. And worst of all, he can't remember where he put her telephone number.

In the bedroom, he sits down and thinks about it. He can afford the time because Angie is finishing her dessert and when she's done that, there's still the wine — almost two thirds of the second bottle left. He drinks too much, he knows he drinks too much — not usually so much that he has hangovers in the morning, but enough to deaden some of the pain, dull the senses, reduce the emptiness, the hollow feeling in the pit of his stomach. It's why he's had to put the two photographs of his children onto the top shelf of his wardrobe where he can't see them any more and bury his ex-wife's photograph in the bottom drawer of his bureau with stuff he doesn't use. Angie's telephone number — where the hell did he put her telephone number! He takes out the clothes he was wearing when he returned to the apartment earlier and begins a systematic search through the pockets.

While Angie finishes the dessert and refills her glass, and Harry looks for her lost telephone number, Stuart continues to sit in his car studying Georgina's house and waiting for Georgina to come out and collect the milk (or to send Sandra out if she's not going to do it herself). Stuart's eyes have become adjusted to the increased darkness, the almost but not quite complete dark that comes when the faint and elusive glow of the moon's last quarter has been swallowed up by thickening cloud and the street lamps are slowly becoming obscured by a thin but persistent rain that makes him feel how alone he is — that he's always been alone and there's been so little he's been able to do about it.

He knows he's going to steal Georgina's car — well, not exactly steal it. Stealing means taking and using it for financial advantage — changing the plates, erasing the engine and chassis numbers, either disposing of it in going order or cutting it up and selling the parts. What he intends to do is to take it away and hide it — nothing as final as rolling it off a wharf into the harbour — simply hiding it where it won't be noticed and no one will find it. He's waiting for Georgina to collect the milk so that when he removes the car, neither she nor Sandra will see it's gone until they get up the next morning. The longer there is between the car's disappearance and their noticing it's gone, the more unlikely it will be that anyone will discover where it's gone to or who took it. And his task will be easier, much easier, if when Georgina comes out for the milk, she doesn't notice the car's unlocked and the key's in the ignition. If she doesn't notice it and doesn't go to the trouble of putting the vehicle into the garage, Stuart's task will be simple — 'a piece of cake', as they used to say in the war films he liked to watch before he took up politics — when he had the time...

That's the problem with politics — the enormous amount of time that's required for meetings and more meetings. And he has to attend all of them or as many as he can get himself invited to: meetings at the national and local levels, policy meetings, the regional and national conferences, the networkers' and the executive's meetings — the informal meetings he has to arrange himself if he's to get the support he needs to be selected. Stuart prefers the informal meetings even though they're more time-consuming, He prefers them because they're usually small (one to one or perhaps to two or three), because there are no formalities and it's easier to persuade people into co-operation individually than in groups, and he prefers them because he's always the central figure, in a better position to control things.

Politics are the reason he has to be careful about Sandra's mother and the car. There's no room for mistake. But then, he's the last person anyone would suspect of stealing Georgina's car. People don't steal cars from the widowed mother of someone they're going out with — might even marry. The most likely suspects are professional car thieves, local gang members — drunks on the way home from a party. And the motive — there has to be a motive that makes sense — which is why no one's going to suspect him, why it's safe to take Georgina's car and dump it. And it doesn't matter if it's recovered or not, whether Georgina gets it back or doesn't. The car will of course be insured and by the time she's got it back or given up on it, she'll be grateful to him. She'll be grateful because he will have lent her a much better car and neither she nor Sandra will have suffered any inconvenience.

Yes, Sandra — he thinks of Sandra as well as Georgina and the car. He knows she's not very bright and not very attractive, but he could teach her — he could teach her everything she needed to know and eventually she'd become attractive and no one would realise what she'd been like before, everyone would think she'd always been attractive and interesting...

'You're... you're... not supposed to be doing that,' Angie says. 'I read it... I... I saw it in a magazine... in *Time* magazine. It said United States naval personnel aren't allowed to do that... that kind of thing.'

'What kind of thing?' Harry is occupied — so much so that he doesn't properly understand what she's saying, and because the specific nature of the activity he's engaged in requires his full attention and precludes coherent verbal communication. In any case, he seriously doubts she either wants him to stop, or has any interest in a reply. 'What... kind of thing?' he asks her. 'What is it naval personnel aren't allowed to do?'

'What... what... you're doing!' Angie is breathing heavily. For the last few minutes she's been breathing very heavily indeed. From time to time she pauses to throw back her head and gasp for air — just as she has only a moment ago. Rivulets of sweat wash over her breasts, across her stomach, down her thighs. 'That — that kind of thing you're doing right now. What you're not... supposed to be doing... what you're doing now!'

'But I'm not in the United States Navy — I'm not in any navy at all and you wanted me to do it — isn't it what you wanted me to do, what you were hoping I'd do even if you didn't ask me to — isn't it? And you like it... you like it don't you?'

'Yes,' says Angie who's still having trouble with her breathing. She moves her body closer to his, suddenly pushes towards him and then slowly, after a final series of long and anguished gasps, her breathing subsides, her body relaxes, becomes still — becomes almost but not quite motionless. 'Yes, of course I like it.' She brushes her hair back with her right hand — her free hand. 'It said in this magazine there are rules about American naval personnel — off base as well as on it — rules about what they're not to do and where they're not allowed to do it. The Navy has inspectors. They have inspectors who break into officers' rooms and check — check that they're not doing any of the things they're not supposed to be doing.'

'You're fortunate,' he tells her, 'you're fortunate because I'm not in the American Navy, I've never been in the American Navy and nobody's told me what I'm not supposed to do. Right now isn't one of those particular moments you're talking about, and no one's going to burst in to find out what it is we're doing or, as you put it a moment ago — what we're not doing.'

Angie wriggles into a more comfortable position. 'I didn't know you were the kind of man you are, Harry! I suspected it — well, suspected something like it — but couldn't be certain, didn't know you were exactly like that!'

'Exactly like what?' The question is hypothetical rather than intended to elucidate a reply. There's no way of knowing, even if Angie tells him, what she really thinks, how she really feels — at least, he doesn't believe there's any way of knowing. At the best, he can take what she says at face value, at the worst leave it in that realm of other mysteries where underlying meaning remains vague, undefinable and forever unreachable.

'I didn't know you were exactly like that — like you are!'

'I'm not — it's your imagination — you're imagining it!' And she might be imagining it because he isn't that kind of man (whatever kind of man it is she's referring to), at least he hasn't been that kind of man previously and it's only just now he's discovered there are things about himself he's been unaware of — things he seems able to do with a woman and wants to do with a woman that he's never thought about or if he's thought about them, he's never found anyone except Angie he wanted to do them with.

'But I've never done it — never — it's never happened before!'

'What's never happened before?' Harry doesn't understand what she's saying. He studies her — he studies her because he's thinking about what she's said earlier and he's still not sure she's going to do what she's said she's going to do — move in with him — and he suspects that in a few hours she'll have a shower or go into another room and when he looks for her, tries to find where she is, she'll have disappeared. And he doesn't want her to disappear, doesn't want to lose sight of her, to lose the feel of her body next to his, the whiteness of her skin — her hair on the pillow beside him.

'It's never happened. I haven't had one before... never... and there were seven of them...' She says it in a clinical, an almost detached manner but her delight expresses itself in the way she smiles, the curl and stretch of her body, and then gives way to something else — something he doesn't understand. 'Seven of them, one after the other — it's really something!'

He hears what she says and he doesn't hear it. He's never met a women who talks as openly as Angie does about what's happening to her, what goes on between members of the opposite sex or for that matter, between members of the same sex. And questions are forming in his head, the kind of questions men ask themselves about women: why they do this or do that, what they talk to each other about when there are no men around, why they say one thing instead of another and when they've said it (whatever it is they've said) — the problem of what's meant — of what people mean when they say what they're saying.

'No — no, I've never really had one… an orgasm… not with a man, not even with Gary!'

He doesn't know who Gary is. She hasn't said anything about Gary before and he finds it difficult — difficult to believe what she's saying. 'Everyone does,' he tells her, 'sooner or later everyone has them… orgasms…' It's not a word he finds easy to say — particularly to a woman — and he knows that according to what he's read it's not strictly true everyone has them. He doesn't like talking about such things. It embarrasses him. But he's said what he's said to prevent himself asking about Gary (whoever Gary is) and Angie has a right to privacy — everyone has a right to privacy — to reveal only what they want to reveal.

'The wine,' she says, as if she's able to read his mind, knows what he's thinking and wants to make things easier for him, 'perhaps we should finish the wine.'

He gets the wine and two glasses. And while he's doing it, while he's walking barefoot over the carpet, he remembers a long time ago — when he was a student — walking in a park somewhere, walking over grass in the morning sunlight after long hours of study. Somebody had cut the grass so that it was short and springy and felt like a carpet. In the slanting light of the sun it had looked fresh and clean. And now it seems as he takes the two glasses back to the bedroom that being with her has made everything fresh and clean like the grass was — and right, has made everything right as well.

'If you haven't… if you haven't had an orgasm with a man before, who… if you don't mind… if you don't mind my asking… who…' His voice falls into confusion. It's a question he has no more right to ask of her than he has to enquire about the unknown and mysterious Gary; and it's a situation he hasn't any experience of and he's afraid he mightn't be handling well, a situation in which anything he says could be interpreted as some kind of feeble masculine joke and taken down and used in evidence against him. At least, that's the sort of thing that used to happen during his marriage. The most minor enquiry, the most trivial of comments would suddenly develop into a major catastrophe, escalate into a confrontation — charge and counter-charge — and then into a series of spasmodic exchanges and lingering silences that continued for days and sometimes for so long it seemed they'd last forever. He shouldn't have said anything… or maybe it was Angie who shouldn't have said anything…

'I take it back — I take it all back,' he tells her. 'It's none of my business. It doesn't concern me… I shouldn't have mentioned it.'

'Harry!' She leans back onto the pillows she's piled behind her head and shoulders and sips the wine he's given her. She laughs between sips in an easy, graceful way as if he's said something funny — unbelievably funny. 'Harry, you don't have to be delicate about such things! You don't have to take them so seriously — so terribly seriously! We're not talking about meteorites striking the earth, prime ministers tripping over themselves in Parliament. We're talking about ordinary, common, everyday events — orgasms, Harry — things that happen to thousands of people every night of the week, things that go on everywhere and all over the world.'

She's right, of course — she's right. He takes things too seriously, he's always taken things too seriously. But while it's easy enough to recognise this is what he does, it's not so easy to do anything about it. And he's tried — he's tried every which way! Even what the philosophers, what Plato suggested, although he can't remember exactly where or when he suggested it. Perhaps in *The Republic* or somewhere like that. He might have read it, but it's more likely somebody told him about it, at least, somebody could have told him about it — and that's another fragment of information lost and forgotten. It was something about behaving as if you were courageous or had a sense of humour before you had a sense of humour or were courageous — and he's tried it, but it hasn't worked.

And it didn't work when he had to deal with Tony and the problem of John Stuart Mills — it didn't work at all. He'd kept at it, he'd tried to protect Mills from the foul-ups that seemed to come out of everything he did and he'd tried to make sure the people Mills was responsible for received a fair deal — didn't waste time or the Navy's money and resources. And in the end it had been a waste, the whole god-damn thing had been a waste! And it still worries him, confuses him, so that even now, here with Angie, he keeps thinking of it, his mind drifts back to it — when he should be thinking of what she's talking about, concentrating on what she's saying.

'Orgasms,' she tells him, 'everyone — well almost everyone — ' she corrects herself, 'almost everyone has them and you don't need anyone to help you out. You can have them at home, anywhere at all — do it yourself, the way most people do at some time in their lives, the way I always did it except for — well, it doesn't matter who she was — just wanted to find out what it was like with a... well, it wasn't much different from doing it yourself and then... there was Gary... '

Harry thinks about what she's saying — about Wang Lan and John Stuart Mills — although there's no reason for his thinking about Mills or Wang

Lan at the same time as he's thinking about Angie and the mysterious Gary. In any case most people, and he hates to admit it, most people are scraping around in the dark looking for someone, for something, a bridge to somewhere, the ultimate orgasm — trying to find out if there really is a possibility of becoming millionaires by next Wednesday. But the millionaire bit, that's Angie's idea, her way of describing it, not his — the millionaire bit makes sense. A thousand years ago, people were looking for a short cut to the hereafter — and they were going to the Middle East to find it — fighting against the Muslims (or conversely, if they were themselves Muslims, fighting against the Christians); and even then, they wanted to be millionaires as well — to hedge their bets, make themselves comfortable in the here and now as well as secure and safe in the hereafter.

'Gary,' she says. 'His name was Gary. We weren't very old and my father didn't like him so I left school and we went to live in this commune — well, a sort of a commune — in the country. It was close to the beach, supposed to be provide an alternative — a healthy life style with out-door living — a co-operative society. They were all supposed to do things together, look after the children — their own and other people's — grow their own food, bake their own bread, provide home-made entertainment — no booze of course — and no radio or television.'

'I didn't think people could really do it like that, cut themselves off from everyone else. It's been written about in books — people say they've done it, have written about it…'

'They didn't drink anything but they grew their own marijuana — and there was sex. Everybody was doing it with everybody else except some who didn't want to do it at all — or who didn't do it with anyone except the people they arrived with…'

'It was different in the armed services. There really was a code — not like the one in *Time* magazine. But there were rules that weren't written down, that everyone knew about — usually kept to…'

'And Gary, he was eighteen, a year older than I was, but he knew all about it — at least, he said he knew all about it — and we did everything together, well almost everything… and kept on doing it all the time. But it happened… it happened so quickly…' Angie stares into the distance for a moment and then reaches for the wine bottle and tops up her glass. Harry follows suit, not that he wants anything to drink, but because he needs to do something to conceal his feelings, prevent him saying anything he shouldn't say — that might seem judgemental.

'The Navy was like that,' he tells her. 'It had rules for almost everything — *Queen's Regulations and Admiralty Instructions*. And then there were things that weren't in the book — unwritten rules as important as the written ones — so important that people learnt them before they'd even heard of *Queen's Regulations and Admiralty Instructions*. They weren't about the things *Time* magazine says you're not supposed to do — they were about letting people know what you're doing. I suppose it's like that everywhere — it isn't what you do. Talking about it, letting other people know about it — that's the problem.'

'It was supposed to be an open community, nobody was supposed to conceal anything — everybody knew what everyone else was doing and everybody had to talk about it if they had a problem or thought they had a problem — even if they didn't want to talk about it. And they really were open, completely up front about whatever the difficulty was — talked it through with the whole group — all sorts of stuff. Everybody sat around smoking pot — you had to smoke pot — and talked about it, cleansed themselves.' She gives 'cleansed' a special emphasis as if it's a word of great importance, carries a special significance. 'You had to get it out of your system — tell everyone about it...'

'And did you?' He realises she's talking about a problem she might have had herself, something that still makes her feel uncomfortable. 'Did you have problems?'

'Yes,' she says, 'I didn't know enough, and Gary didn't care very much. He left everything to me. It didn't take long... after a while I became pregnant.'

Sixteen

Wang Lan is also waiting in the dark but unlike Stuart, she's afraid — very much afraid of what might happen. She's tried twice to get through to Harry, but so far she's been unsuccessful — not through any fault of her own, but because employees aren't permitted to use telephones or fax machines for private business during working hours and must book ahead to when normal work breaks occur, or when work has ceased for the day. She's booked in for the end of the working day and because no one has wanted to wait around for her, she's been left in the office to make the call herself. She's switched off the lights because Chen Li knows what floor she works on and she's afraid of what might happen if he finds out where she is.

She's afraid not only because there's a possibility that Chen might be waiting outside to accost her when she leaves to go home, but also because strictly speaking, what she's doing is illegal — not what she's doing with the telephone (she's paid for its use in advance) but what she's been doing privately to recruit students for study overseas and which could get her into trouble with the authorities. It's one of the more recently developed peculiarities of the system: government organisations and agencies are not only free to, but are encouraged to enter into commercial transactions with overseas business companies. Private citizens aren't supposed to. Government agencies are free to profit from contracts with the West, but not individuals. And it's unfair — she knows it's unfair because she's discovered that many of the officials who negotiate such contracts expect under-the-counter payments equivalent to whatever profits they negotiate for the state — thirty percent for the state, and another thirty percent for the negotiator. In fact, she's attended banquets the director she works for has given for important foreign businessmen — really important businessmen — wonderful banquets in the restaurant of the Guibinlou, the distinguished guest building in the west wing of the Beijing Hotel, and she knows what happens. But that's not where she met Mr Houghton.

She was introduced to Harry in the middle wing — only a few doors along from the room in which she met Mr Pierce — not as wonderful as the

Guibinlou, but almost as luxurious and in both places they gave her Coca Cola (genuine American Coca Cola, not the Chinese version). She likes Coca Cola — in fact she likes most things American — almost anything foreign and different. She liked Harry, but not as much as she liked his partner, Frank Pierce. They had sat on opposite sides of the room while Mr Wu Li Xuan had negotiated with Harry and a businessman from Australia. There had been other people there too — Mr Chow had been there — but she could see that Harry (Mr Houghton, as she thought of him at the time) was looking at her — and looking in the way Caucasians look at women when they find them attractive and are hoping their interest is reciprocated and something might come of it. She'd looked back at him because she was interested, and because in contrast to Chinese men, he had pale, slightly yellow hair together with square shoulders and an upright Western military appearance. She had looked back because she wanted to talk to him about the agreement she'd made with his partner, Mr Pierce, when he'd visited Beijing, and about Frank — Mr Pierce himself — as well.

From her desk at the sixth floor window of the Beijing Export Company building, she can see the bright halo of light which usually hangs over the city once the sun has disappeared and which persists through most of the night and continues until it fades into the soft grey colourings of an Asian dawn. She wonders whether Los Angeles, New York and Washington are like that, have the same appearance, and whether the cities and towns of Australia and New Zealand carry the same perpetual night-time glow of coloured lights, signs, restaurants and street markets, of multi-storey office buildings. She would very much like to travel overseas and find out for herself — which is why she's spent so much time studying at the Beijing English Language Club.

English is a difficult language and there are too many students at the Club — all wanting to learn English well enough to get better jobs, to be able to work with foreigners or most desirable of all, to obtain a visa and visit the West, perhaps even remain there. She would learn English much faster if there were fewer students in her class — she knows she would! More than a hundred students in the same room working at the same exercise is far too many, and Mr Pierce has told her in Auckland there are no more than fifteen in a class — that the education authorities won't allow more than fifteen.

She's already faxed Mr Houghton, and she's received an answer from him — not immediately, but it arrived after she'd looked into the facsimile room every twenty minutes or so from mid-morning until noon in the hope there might be an answer — a few words, anything she could show to Chen Li, that would convince him his money was safe and he would get it back.

It's something difficult for Westerners to understand, that such a large amount of money is more than most Chinese can save in a lifetime. The directors of government departments, the people who can travel overseas on business or representing the Government — it's different for them. They can organise things, arrange things — and when they come back they're met at the airport and drive off in Red Flag limousines. Mr Houghton drove about in a Red Flag limousine with a chauffeur, a limousine lent to him by a senior government official who wanted to impress him. 'Chauf-feur,' she repeats to herself in English. It's a difficult word to say — not really English — but she's seen it in a book and heard it in a British film she was shown at the English Club.

Harry has replied to her fax — she knew he would because he's almost always replied within a few days to the letters she's sent him and always given immediate acknowledgement of any of the other documents she's posted him — application forms, student documents, copies of official Embassy correspondence, that kind of thing. But sometimes faxes go missing or don't arrive at all. Secretly, she thinks that while she's been open about it with the people she works with (and they know she pays for any private faxes she sends for the Student Centre), some of them are envious of what she's doing and out of envy sometimes intercept and destroy faxes addressed to her. She's glad it hasn't happened this time, but it could have happened, and if it had and there'd been nothing to show Chen, there would certainly have been trouble — and even now he might not believe what Harry has said — he might still do something serious to her.

And this is why she has to phone Harry and speak to him personally — he has to know re-assurances are no longer enough, that there have been reports that some of the Chinese who have sent money overseas to foreign language schools and lost it, have committed suicide rather than face the anger and vengeance of the people they've borrowed from. That's how they manage to put so much money together: they borrow it — they borrow it from their friends and their family, sometimes at unbelievably high interest rates, rates so high that failing to return the money by due date could put families into debt for several generations while not paying it back could lead to broken bones or even death for the principal borrower.

The office Wang Lan works in is located in a modern Western-style building: its interior partitions consist of off-white and pastel-grey panelling, the floor has been carpeted in beige-coloured Axminster (imported from New Zealand), the desks have been made in the Republic of China, while the electronic and other office equipment — typewriters, computers, word processors, facsimile machines and answerphones — all of this equipment comes from Japan.

The cleanliness of the building is what Wang Lan likes most about it. Originally though, it was the foreign equipment and furnishings which attracted her towards employment with Beijing Export — a company ostensibly capitalist in its methods of operation and similar to its exporting counterparts in England or America but in fact, a subsidiary of the Foreign Affairs Division of the Beijing Higher Education Authority which the Company is responsible to and which receives any profits it makes. She's heard profitability isn't absolutely necessary — it's enough for the Company to acquire foreign currency, to swap renminbi (foreign exchange certificates) for dollars, or even to persuade foreigners to open 'special' accounts and make deposits in the Bank of China.

She can see through her office window that the more distant blobs and points of light have lost the globular appearance they've exhibited over the last few months and have taken on a sharper quality — the sharpness she's always associated with cold air and winter chill, with the frosts of autumn and the hard, brittle crust that sets in over snow in winter. It was cold last winter and she suspects it will be colder this time. She prefers autumn or spring, the time of the year when it's warm — but not too warm.

Wang Lan switches on her desk lamp. Her supervisor has provided her with a desk lamp because she sometimes works late so she can complete the paperwork needed to satisfy the urgency often associated with overseas clients. She takes her telephone number and address book from the briefcase she always carries with her and looks up Houghton Harry. Although she usually records the names of foreigners in English script (there doesn't seem any other way of doing it) she's juxtaposed the family and personal names in accordance with Chinese practice. She knows Harry's number, but she's checking it again from fear that there's been a mistake — in case she's mixed up the digits she's supposed to dial for an international call and this is why she's been unable to get through. When she's confirmed that what she keeps in her head — Harry's phone number and the area code — corresponds to what she's written down, she closes the book, reaches for the telephone and punches the numbers in.

Midnight — it's somewhere near midnight or a little after. Harry reaches for his watch and in the near darkness, glares at the luminescent glow presented by the dial. He can't read the figures but he can tell from the position of the hands what the time is. (He prefers an analogue watch to the digital version because it's easier to read and some dark and dismal night, if he ever gets the engine in his boat fixed, he'll need a watch he can read in the near to impossible conditions of a forty knot gale on the open sea.)

He squints so that he can see better. It's closer to one o'clock than it is to midnight. The telephone — who could be calling at such a hellish hour?

Carefully, in order to avoid disturbing Angie, he eases himself from under the duvet and out onto the floor. When he reaches the phone and picks up the handpiece, the ringing stops. 'Houghton,' he says, 'Harry Houghton,' but there's no answer — nothing except something that sounds like a sudden intake of breath, a muffled voice, some kind of thump, another sound as of a sack of potatoes — something heavy — falling to the floor, and then a click and the steady hum of a disengaged line. Whoever it was who was calling must have dropped the handpiece back onto its cradle, or changed his or her mind and hung up almost at the same time as he was answering the call. A wrong number — it must have been a wrong number because it's too early in the morning to be anything else.

Stuart doesn't like it, he's never really liked it, sitting around waiting for something to happen, and especially sitting around in the dark, but now the waiting's over and he's driving Georgina's car along the motorway towards the Hobsonville turn-off and the Greenhithe bridge, he feels much better — even pleased with himself. There were so many things that could have gone wrong. Georgina might have forgotten to go out and collect the milk. She could have checked the car doors and found them unlocked or looked in and noticed the keys still in the ignition switch. She might have taken a walk and discovered Stuart's car with Stuart still in it — which in itself wouldn't have been much of a problem. Stuart could have found a ready excuse for his being there, but any of these possibilities would have resulted in his having to abandon the project and his losing what was perhaps his one opportunity of ingratiating himself with Sandra's nearest and dearest.

Stealing your future mother-in-law's car (not that Georgina yet recognises or is ready to accept such an agreeable consummation to his relationship with her daughter) — stealing your future mother-in-law's car isn't the sort of crime that's readily detectable. No one expects honest, professional (well, almost professional) people with a good chance of becoming members of Parliament to steal, nor do they expect it of reputable former naval officers (as Stuart still likes to think of himself) and that's the truly ingenious part of the project! The other ingenuity is ditching the car and ensuring its ultimate rediscovery. Well, if it isn't found by the police within a suitable time, he'll have to leak its location anonymously. There's no sense in taking chances — in leaving Georgina's car lying around for such a long time that it might be found by genuine car thieves who'd take it away, dismantle it and sell the parts.

Hiding the car is the most important of the problems he has to deal with, but he's worked it out. The best hiding place is always the one that's least likely. He has to leave the car in a place where it's in plain view and yet won't be recognised. And then, there has to be a back-up, a contingency plan. The worst thing that can happen is that the car will be discovered and returned to Georgina before sufficient time has elapsed for her to be suitably grateful. There's no danger of the car being traced back to him — he's wearing gloves and he's emptied his pockets of anything that's not essential, so that he won't make mistakes and leave clues that might be followed up later. Again, if Georgina doesn't appreciate having a car — a good one — on loan to her, then it will be most unfortunate and she'll never know what happened to her vehicle nor see it again. A car that's been hidden successfully can always be retrieved and permanently disposed of — broken up, scrapped or sold — dropped into the harbour if necessary. He favours the harbour because immersion in salt water is fatal to automobiles and it's the most suitable form of pay-back he can think of.

It was fortunate Georgina didn't come out to her front gate until well after eleven because there aren't many people about between eleven and midnight and there's less chance of them noticing anything. Movie house patrons have gone home, night clubbers may have finished their meals but they're still in the throes of dancing, emptying their wine glasses or settling the question of what happens next — who goes home with whom and to which apartment. It means nobody's likely to see what he's doing or be particularly concerned if they do see him — just another guy who's had no luck, who's driving home alone. And he's been clever. When Georgina went back into the house, he moved his car off to a safer distance and then walked back. By doing that, it was less likely anyone would remember as distinctive a vehicle as a Triumph Stag (mint condition — fully restored and worth a packet) near the scene of the operation. He likes to think of it as an 'operation' rather than a 'crime'. He isn't a criminal nor a thief — he's not actually stealing the car. He's a business man securing his future, working on his family and social relationships.

Georgina, he tells himself and as Georgina so often claims, is 'a self-made woman', and self-made women can easily be unmade, can trip over their own back feet — even their shadows. What she needs is a son-in-law who can protect her from her mistakes, who can do something with her assets, take a small-scale engineering business and turn it into a major enterprise, perhaps a national chain of maintenance and retail shops. And then there's the political side. Politics cost money, yet a political career backed by a reliable business can't go wrong. It's like what's his name says. Political parties do better if they're supported by big business, and if the party's doing well nobody's going to rock the boat, initiate enquiries into how things have happened or who's done what. The difficulty is getting started, winning a seat and getting into Parliament, and the truth, the real truth, is that politicians go further and faster if they have money — successful businesses behind them.

What's unfair is that he has to humiliate himself by playing silly games with Georgina. It's embarrassing even if she's the only person who will ever know of it — it's embarrassing and it's humiliating when people of exceptional ability (and in his case, an ex-serviceman as well — someone who has served his country) are forced through circumstances beyond their control to manipulate and manoeuvre themselves into positions where their abilities can benefit the world. Worse, and although he likes Sandra, he would have preferred Angie — someone better looking, with a sense of humour and a way of dealing with people that always makes anyone with her appear important, at the centre of things. In Angie's case, the problem was her parents — nicer to talk to and more interesting than Sandra's mother but no money, no 'pull'. She'd told him the first time they'd talked with each other that her parents didn't own the house they lived in — they rented it. People who rent the houses they live in always place their daughters at a disadvantage and the disadvantage was made worse in Angie's case by her inability — her refusal — to believe that the wives of business men, of politicians, must occupy a secondary, a supportive role, that they need to know their place.

But right now it's the car that's the problem — the car, and getting it out of sight as soon as possible. Leaving the motorway, he drives through a set of lights that conveniently change from red to green as he reaches them, turns into Hobsonville Road and begins the run towards the Upper Harbour bridge. He increases speed, and the car starts to show what it can do — and it can do quite a lot! It's a conventional vehicle but Georgina, even if she's a woman, is a real engineer and maintains the vehicle herself: the result is an incredibly smooth engine and a remarkably rapid acceleration — the kind of response that only comes from ironing out production-line deficiencies, ensuring exhaust exits and manifold interiors are as smooth as glass and the gas flow uninterrupted by even the most minor of irregularities in the metal it passes over. Georgina has put a lot of time into the car and she's not going to be pleased at losing it — which means, of course, she'll be all that much more appreciative of any assistance he can give in finding it for her.

Half a kilometre from the bridge, where the road is wide and clear, and descends in a gentle slope towards the on-ramp, he pushes his foot down to determine exactly how good the acceleration is, and the car picks up so fast that if it had wings, he can see it would already be airborne. Georgina is obviously something more than an engineer — she's an artist when it comes to engines and their accessories, and can do things with cars most people have never heard of. And she'll want her car back — she really will want it back!

'Who was it on the telephone? An anonymous caller — or someone we happen to know?'

Harry likes it — her use of the first person plural. It makes him feel closer to her, that there's something more than the merely physical (not that he under-rates the pleasure or the importance of the physical aspects of life) going on between them. And he's doubly appreciative that it's Angie and not he who's used it. Yes, it's been a long time since he's heard anyone use the first person plural in connection with himself, and he likes the sound of it, he likes the way it suggests things are changing in his life, that he could go on hearing Angie use the same construction for a considerable time to come.

'No, it must have been a wrong number — someone who's been drinking too much judging from the breathing, who's punched in the wrong number and then suddenly guessed what's happened.'

'That's good. I don't like calls from heavy breathers — people I don't know — who won't give their names. They scare me.'

'You don't have to be scared,' he tells her, 'not when they're on the other end of the line. All you have to do is swear at them, give them something of the same thing they're giving you and they'll hang up — or you can hang up yourself if you'd prefer to.'

'I said I don't like them and they scare me. I didn't say they scare me so much I can't deal with them, can't breathe back at them — and anyway, I know more about heavy breathers than you do — I'm a woman and it's women they call, not men.'

'Yes, but...'

'There was this guy who called once and told me he'd found my telephone number in the book and was making a dirty phone call... said he liked the look of my name, that it read well, was a nice name, an attractive name — that he was tired of having to do the heavy breathing bit and all the talking himself — wanted to know if I'd do it for him, if I'd talk dirty because he'd love to have a woman with a nice name and a nice voice, someone really nice, say dirty things to him.'

'And did you?' He can imagine it, but he can't be sure she'd actually do it.

'No, of course not — of course I didn't — if you let people like that get away with things, they might keep calling you back and you wouldn't be able to stop them.'

'What did you do, then?'

'I told him it was his phone call, not mine — that it was the custom — it was good manners for the person making the phone call to talk dirty and do the heavy breathing, and he'd better get on with it because I was a busy woman, and talking dirty was boring and I didn't have all day to sit there listening to him.'

'What did he do?'

'Exactly what you'd expect — he hung up.' She reaches over and touches him gently, and to his surprise after what's already occurred between them, almost tentatively — in such a way that he doesn't know whether she's seeking reassurance or offering it.

'Getting pregnant,' she asks him, 'you don't mind that I became pregnant, do you?'

'It was clever of you, if it was what you wanted,' he told her, 'but I wasn't there, and even if I'd been there, it shouldn't have concerned me — well... not unless... not unless there had been something happening between us... if I'd been responsible for what happened to you.' Personally, he wishes there had been something between them. He would have liked it and would have preferred it to what was going on in his life at the time — but it wouldn't have been possible. She'd have been too young or conversely, he'd have been too old, and in any case it's more appropriate that people should have their first sexual experiences with others of their own age — that things should be equal...

'Well, it wasn't.' The room is too dark for him to be able to see her face and her voice is so flat and unemotional that he's unable to determine whether she's expressing regret at what happened or is making light of it.

'It wasn't what?'

'It wasn't clever — it was stupid! It's always stupid to do things at the wrong time and with the wrong people — with someone like Gary...' Another pause. 'Coffee,' she suggests. 'If we have to talk about such things — and because we will have to talk about them some time, and it might as well be now — if we're going to talk, we'll need some coffee.'

'Yes,' she says, when he returns with the coffee, 'Gary didn't handle it well. Or perhaps from his point of view, it was the other way round — I didn't handle it well. By the time I knew about it — that I was pregnant — in only a few weeks, everything changed. Gary had discovered there were no strict rules about who could sleep with whom in the group — it was a matter of choice rather than anything else — and he'd already started going off with some of the other women. Just one of them at first, and then a second one — sometimes two of them at the same time. They were older, most of them were older — but not much older — than either of us. And then when he discovered it... found out I was pregnant... he said it was my fault. I was the one who was supposed to look after that part of things and therefore it was my problem, not his, and I'd have to deal with it.'

Her voice is slow and soft, but its undertones are sharp, suggesting suppressed bitterness and pain. Harry reaches over to reassure her, to indicate the sympathy he feels for the predicament she found herself in, and incongruously, her free hand — her left hand — the one not holding her coffee cup, impulsively closes over his and lifts it on to her breast. 'You can feel it — you can feel how much it still upsets me — how my heart beats faster merely from thinking about it.' And indeed, her heart is beating faster. He can feel it under the palm of his hand, and beneath his fingers, her nipple — hard and growing increasingly erect. She rubs his fingers over it and over the lift and swell of her breast. 'Small enough to fit into a champagne glass — and the other one as well — both of them!' She smiles as if sharing a confidence and with a measure of pride. 'French tits, my mother calls them. She says she knows women who would be envious — that big may be beautiful but small is just as good, and maybe more beautiful.' His hand and fingers being where they are and doing what they're doing, Harry doesn't doubt it — he has no doubts about it at all.

'Gary,' she says, 'Gary didn't want to know about it — about my being pregnant — and for a few weeks I'd leave the others each morning and go off to the beach. It was the time of year when the sea is quiet, when there isn't anything more than the ripple of small waves coming up and falling onto the sand and everything is clear and clean and blue. The sky is blue, the sea is blue and there's the beginning of winter in the air...'

'A sort of sadness,' he asks her, 'summer gone and winter about to begin — that sort of thing?'

'Yes,' she says, 'I would sit there just above high water mark where the marram grass and the sand dunes begin, thinking about what was happening inside me, the inevitability of it once it had begun, and wondering what would be the result of it all, what would happen — what would become of the world.'

'You were trying to decide what to do about it?'

'No — nothing like that. I just sat there staring out into space — almost numb — and most of the time not thinking about anything... It would probably have gone on like that indefinitely with no one taking any notice, except that one of the older women — she must have been at least twenty seven! — one of the older women talked to me... I wanted to keep it when it arrived — the child — I really wanted to keep it, but she helped me see it would be better for both of us if I didn't and she knew a family who would adopt it... who would let me visit...'

'And your parents — how did your parents feel about it?'

Angie stops talking and sips her coffee. She's thinking hard, thinking deeply about something — perhaps whether she can trust him, whether she should be telling him as much as she is. And he understands, or more accurately, thinks he understands her reticence: the more people know about others the greater their power over them — and the greater the power they have, the more likely they are to use it.

'Why,' he asks, assuming it's what she wants and changing the subject, 'when we were in the supermarket... I still can't work it out — the telephone number... why did you give me my own telephone number instead of yours?'

'My father,' she tells him, 'it was because of my father. He'd become interested in fundamentalist religion — and rigid — and I was afraid of what he might do — of how he would behave if he discovered what had happened — if he learned I was pregnant.' She sips her coffee. 'And the telephone number,' she says brightly. 'I didn't give you my number — I gave you your own number because I wanted to tell you something... something very simple... like... not to bother finishing your shopping and to be sure to come home in good time... because I was already doing the shopping — that kind of thing — because I wanted to surprise you... and it was a clue. I was giving you, a clue to help you discover something... something that might be important to... to both of us...'

Stuart has already parked his car. The street he's parked it in is quiet and dark, the parking place unmarked, parallel to the kerb and in front of one of several vacant lots in the area. It's a mere two hundred metres from Greenhithe's shopping centre which consists of a mini-market, a milk bar apparently suffering from the current grubbiness which has come with lean and difficult times, and a shop selling fish and chips — euphemistically referred to as 'French fries'. The fish and chip shop has recently been taken over by refugees from South East Asia and now, in addition to its traditional fare, offers a bi-lingual menu and a bewildering variety of Chinese take-aways. Stuart is pleased with himself — everything is going according to plan. The parking place he's chosen is far enough away from the city not to be noticed by searchers for stolen vehicles, and yet close enough to shops and houses to be under local observation and thus prevent Georgina's car from being tampered with by persons foreign to the neighbourhood. Nevertheless, Stuart has to act quickly as he is himself foreign to the area and thus has little time in which to hide the vehicle and depart unobserved.

He checks that the rear doors and the passenger door are locked, takes up the bulky plastic bag he's brought with him and which has been resting on the floor beside him, and then gets out and fastens the driver's door. Quickly and expertly, almost as if he's rehearsed the movement (which in fact, he has), he pulls out the light-weight car cover the bag contains, spreads it over the vehicle and ties it into place, thus concealing the car from public view. He checks his handiwork for a moment and then moving briskly along the footpath, peels off the light leather gloves he's been wearing — 'officers, for the use of', he reminds himself. Well, not exactly, but he likes to imagine that's what they are! Next, the gloves together with the car keys he retrieves from his pocket, are dropped into the bag which he folds neatly and places under his arm for security and ease of carrying.

Seventeen minutes, he tells himself, it will take seventeen minutes to reach the phone box and call for a taxi, and then another five minutes before he arrives at the front of the house he's identified as his pick-up point — twenty-five minutes, including three minutes for the phone call. He knows precisely how much time it requires because he's already walked the route and measured it. Neat — it's a neat and tidy arrangement which will lead the driver into thinking he's just come out of the house behind him, that he's impatient and in a hurry, and wants to get back to the other side of the harbour as quickly as possible. And the last part of it, wanting to get there as quickly as possible, is of course true, but not for any of the conventional reasons like — like just having left someone he's having an affair with and needing to get home to his wife before she begins imagining things, or like having to get some sleep because he works weekends — because he's on shift work, and has to be out and about early next morning.

The driver might imagine any of these as being the reason for his hurry or his wanting to get across the harbour so late at night — but it doesn't matter what the driver thinks providing he doesn't notice anything unusual or distinctive about his passenger. Stuart has tried to make allowances for this. That is, while he's thought that because of the possibility of leaving fingerprints, it's unwise to remove his gloves, he's also turned up his collar to conceal his features as much as possible and practised disguising his voice. He's not sure how much these precautions will help, but he's chosen an unlighted area a few minutes' walk from his own car as the taxi's destination in order to further reduce the likelihood of detection, and taken the precaution of checking out the fare earlier so that he has the required amount of change ready in his pocket. If the fare eventually turns out to be less, he can leave the excess as a tip and thus reduce time the driver might have to observe him — and if it's more, then he has a few extra cents in his pocket.

The one thing that could go wrong is the amount of time he might have to spend waiting for the taxi. If it takes too long to arrive, he'll be standing outside a house whose occupants he doesn't know and who don't know him for long enough to attract their attention. If they notice him and become concerned, they might telephone the police — report him as a suspicious character lurking with intent. He's chosen the pick-up point not only because of its distance away from the Greenhithe shops, but also because it offers a wide verge with well-placed shrubs between the footpath and the house behind it and can thus provide a measure of concealment. If he keeps to the shadows, he shouldn't be noticed but there's always the unexpected — like Harry Houghton's suspicion when he was in the Navy.

If Harry hadn't been so suspicious, if he hadn't been so impatient, it would only have been a matter of time before he got the hang of things and had been able to do the job properly. Harry had been the real source of his misfortunes — and cunning about it, too — pretending to sympathise, to help get him another appointment outside the training group 'where the work might suit you better, Stuart, where things might be less difficult — easier for everyone'. Harry wasn't really helping him, Harry was trying to get him sacked and it was because he hadn't managed it that he'd arranged the transfer. And it was very likely Harry who had checked up on his qualifications — finally lost him his job. If it hadn't happened — yes, if it hadn't happened Stuart might have become somebody. By now, even though he's still younger than Harry was at the time — by now he'd have what must have been Harry's last service appointment — and because he's more intelligent than Harry he'd have made a better job of it — would have been taken more seriously than Harry was — would have got things done better and faster...

When he reaches the call box, Stuart pulls up his sleeve and checks his watch. He's uncomfortably hot and sweaty because he's covered the distance in thirteen and a half minutes — a shorter period than he'd intended and at something more than the brisk walk he'd originally timed himself on. Obviously, he has to watch himself, to be more careful — meticulous in what he's doing. It's when you start thinking of other things that everything goes wrong — which is what happened when he was in the service. He hadn't been careful enough, he'd let his guard down because he hadn't believed anything could go wrong, because he'd thought his initial luck in getting into the Navy would continue. It hadn't — and here he is, standing in a telephone booth in the middle of the night forced into borrowing Georgina's car in order to gain the financial support necessary to advance his political and business careers.

And as for politics, he's gone into politics for the same reasons — because they seem to offer better opportunities, but this area too, is taking longer to develop than he expected. Joining the party is one thing — getting anywhere in it is another, especially when all the official positions of any significance are held by long-term party members who might stress the need for a large membership and broad-based support, but whose real interests are in preserving control and maintaining the tight inner-party structure which will enhance their political future. He's getting support from some of them, but it isn't enough. He needs to become a parliamentary candidate in order to make genuine progress and it looks as if there's a chance — and a chance that could be even better if Richard and Bridget, if Angie and some of the others supported him. Angie particularly, could make it a lot easier for him. She isn't ambitious but people listen to her and take notice of what she says — which is surprising considering how young she is...

He lifts the handset and pushes his phone card into the slot. Silence — nothing happens — no digital display, not even of how many dollars and cents his card might be worth. There has to be something wrong with the equipment. He checks the cord and then bends down and peers under the metal box which contains the telephone's operating equipment. Sometimes vandals pull the wires out, sometimes...

Seventeen

'You shouldn't worry about it,' Bridget tells Richard reassuringly. 'It's a formality. It's the Executive's way of demonstrating the difference between 'us' and 'them', between our party and other political organisations. They're all trying to demonstrate we really care about gender issues and social equity — that people are more important than process. It has to be resolved, there has to be a preliminary discussion before the selection. The gender issue has to be discussed publicly so that justice is seen to be done, so that if a suitable woman is available — if there really is someone like Claudia who's willing to throw her hat into the ring — she has as much chance of being selected as anyone else.'

Richard listens and doesn't listen to what she's saying, not because he doesn't take Bridget's opinion seriously but because he's busy. It's Sunday morning and he's working on policy — a draft that has to be ready for Thursday's policy committee meeting. He's redrafting the youth and young people's section so that it covers the wider field of children and young people as well and complies with the provisions of the United Nations' *Convention on the Rights of the Child*. He's trying to make sure this particular section of the party's policy is firmly centred on UNICEF's principle of first call for children. He should have made sure of it when the policy was originally drafted but he didn't, and he's grateful to Bridget for reminding him of the 1990 World Summit's *Declaration on Children* — which he hadn't been as familiar with as he should have. And he feels pressured because of the preliminary discussion on selection that's been called for by the candidate co-ordinator. He isn't looking forward to an electoral debate with the executive or the private disagreements it will bring into the open.

'They talked her into it,' he says, although he's not sure that 'they' (whoever they are) actually did so, 'they talked Claudia into it when she'd refused — when she'd already taken two days to think about it and told everyone she wanted to stay where she was, to take her chances in her own electorate.' He stares at the screen and thinks about what he's put into the word processor — whether he's put it exactly the way it ought to go: *The*

Party recognises the dignity, equality and inalienable rights of all members of society as the foundation of freedom and justice in the world...

He likes the phrasing, the sound of the words — they have a ring to them, and even though they carry a suggestion (perhaps more than a suggestion) of the American Constitution, they make a statement that applies as much to children as it does to anyone else. He thinks about it for a moment and then adds another sentence to the text he's already typed into the word processor: *The party recognises these rights apply as much, and more so, to children and young people as to anyone else, and that because of their developmental needs and their inability to meet these and their personal needs themselves, children and young people should be given primacy of place in the community, first consideration in all central and local government policies and decisions, and receive priority in the allocation of the nation's resources.*

He reads it aloud not merely because he likes the sound of what he's written, but also because he wants Bridget to hear it and confirm that what he's saying needs to be said and is good enough be taken up by some of the other parties — and by non-political organisations as well — once it's been released and published. As Bridget has said, there are principles that over-ride political considerations and should have a wider distribution, a wider currency than politics can give them, yet might still seem extreme, too revolutionary even for the policy committee to accept.

'Don't make assumptions about people — try to be generous,' Bridget says with a hint of reproof. 'Claudia could have refused the electorate's initial offer for personal reasons — perhaps because of her work situation, because of things going wrong at work — or something that's happening in her private life.'

Richard pushes *Command S*, the 'save' combination on the keyboard. The last thing he wants is to lose what he's written and have to start it again. 'If her circumstances have changed and she's decided to try for the nomination, she should have contacted the convenor — let the electorate know about it first. She has an obligation to contact us directly... she should have contacted us before the executive did. It's courtesy, the correct way of doing things, and she hasn't done it.' He may sound a little pompous, but he knows he has right on his side.

'She could have thought it was too late — that if she'd refused the first offer there was nothing more she could do unless we, unless the electorate invited her a second time.'

'She shouldn't have listened to the Executive. Candidate selection is the electorate's responsibility — not the Executive's.' He stares at the computer screen wondering whether he's misinterpreting things, whether he's missed something or he's being unreasonable — whether he really is in the right.

'You don't mind my saying it Richard, I do hope you don't mind my saying it, but maybe no one on the Executive — maybe no one's spoken to Claudia. Perhaps she's told Sharkey — told somebody on the Executive things have changed. Perhaps that's why they want the meeting — to sound everybody out, discover whether we're willing to reconsider, to accept a woman — another nomination...'

'Stuart doesn't want it — not because it's a woman who's being considered, but because he doesn't want any more competition — and no one else wants it either. They think it's executive interference — an attempt to impose an outsider on the electorate because the Executive doesn't want Colin getting the nomination and losing the party's most winnable seat. They say — and there's a lot of truth in what they say — it's not really a question of equity, of gender balance, it's a question of autonomy — the right of an electorate to make its own decisions, to select its candidate in any way it wishes.'

'Richard,' she says, leaning against his chair, 'they're crooks, Richard — both of them. Colin and Stuart are crooks. They've spent the last three months stacking the electorate's membership with family and friends — family in Colin's case, and Stuart's been grabbing anyone he can get hold of... He's talked about it, told you he has the numbers. The numbers, Richard! He means he's counted heads and he'll win the nomination — which is why he wants you to be his campaign manager. Not 'if', but 'when' he wins! Stuart expects to win... they both expect to win... You have to decide what you're going to do...'

Bridget is still leaning against his chair. She trembles slightly. Her hand creeps onto his shoulder. He knows she's trying to help and yet he doesn't want her to help him. He can't believe that people in the party, people he knows — and knows well — who are working for the benefit of women and children, for ethnic minorities, the poor and the needy, the good of the community, would really do that kind of thing — stack the selection committee — place personal interest ahead of the party's interests, ahead of the democratic process...

'They're crooks,' she tells him, 'they're crooks, Richard... you really have to believe it... They're crooks and someone has to do something. You have to do something...'

For the first time since becoming active in politics Richard feels uneasy — as if the situation has changed for the worst, circumstances are conspiring against him. He began feeling uneasy earlier in the day when Bridget came back to help him with his policy writing or perhaps earlier — when Stuart came to talk to him about Gilbert Sharkey.

It's a feeling that doesn't properly belong in his emotional repertoire. Confidence — yes. A measure of empathy for others — certainly. And it's empathy he's always considered to be the driving force behind his interest in politics, a desire to be of service to others and at the same time (he'd rather not acknowledge it) at the same time, to better himself — to employ his talents not only for the benefit of the community, but for his own benefit as well.

'The labourer is worthy of his hire,' he reminds himself. It's something he'd forgotten — that he was sure he'd forgotten. It's what his father used to tell him and which like many other things his father used to tell him, he's neither wanted to remember nor believe. Yes, there could be a measure of truth in it, and maybe people did get to be like their fathers — and perhaps it was already happening to him even though he was still too young for it. Maybe he was already getting to be like his father...

'Things are more complicated,' he tells Bridget, 'things are more complicated than they used to be.'

'Yes,' she says, 'you'll have to support reopening nominations — speak up on women's issues — speak up for Claudia. If you don't — if someone doesn't — Colin or Stuart will capture the electorate and use it for their own advantage.'

'It's technology,' he says, 'technology complicates things. You can't just write a letter or give a speech. You have to put everything into a word processor — send drafts out by fax, mail printed notices of minutes, motions, agenda — keep a diary, a day runner with different sections for finances, addresses, telephone numbers, appointments, notes, general information, project plans — that kind of thing.'

'You have to make a choice — you have to choose between principle and process, between Claudia and making things easier for Colin or Stuart — whichever of them has the best chance of winning the nomination. And there's Angie. She won't like it if Claudia isn't given an opportunity for the nomination and Stuart wins — and he could — he really could get the nomination if we... I mean, if you don't do something about it...'

When he looks at his bathroom, Harry knows with certainty that changes have occurred in his life. Unfamiliar things (or more correctly, things he's lost familiarity with since the collapse of his marriage) have found their way into the cupboard above his wash basin — face lotions, perfumes, lipsticks, eye liner, eyebrow pencil, insect repellant — someone else's tooth brush and tooth paste. They're not what he expects to see in his bathroom but with the strange and unusual events of the last two days, they tell him he's dealing with someone who knows what she's doing and gets on and does it. He's not sure whether he approves of these attributes — which Angie seems to have in abundance. He's always liked people to be decisive, to make decisions and put them into action — it's one of the things that was expected of him and which he liked being able to do when he was in the Navy; but sometimes (he's discovered it since he returned to the civilian world), sometimes there are advantages in letting things unfold by themselves, develop in their own way and at their own pace — in 'putting them off', but it's a phrase he prefers not to acknowledge.

There's a lot to be said for things developing at their own pace. It leaves a person free to reconsider them, to try them out first — not that he's been aware of anything being tried out. Things have happened — things over which he's had no control and he's gone along with them because he's liked the way they were happening — liked them for themselves. And he likes Angie making decisions, he likes her preparing dinner — well sometimes, but only sometimes because a man needs to look after himself. He's liked her moving into his apartment and assuming he'll go along with it. Broken marriages and businesses that don't go right make it difficult for people to trust themselves and there's a lot to be said for having someone else take charge of things occasionally...

It's been a long time since he's been able to trust his own judgement, a very long time — ever since he left the service and maybe before that — perhaps a long time before... like... like when he began to have trouble with Mills... Stuart Mills... or it could have been earlier, when things started to go wrong with his marriage... maybe the night he played snooker with Tony Poindexter. It's difficult to identify crucial moments in history — especially your own history — and the past is bewildering enough without adding the confusions of the present and the future to it. He used to be good at making decisions but recently he hasn't trusted himself. Frank's noticed it — which is why Frank keeps checking up on him. At least, he suspects it's why Frank does it, checks up on him so often — that it's not just because the business is failing and they're having such a rough time but because he doesn't keep on top of things the way he used to.

He inspects his face in the mirror, lathers up and begins shaving. It's an old-fashioned method of getting rid of bristles but he prefers it to the electric razor he threw away when it broke down and he found himself unable to afford a replacement. It happened during the time he was paying his ex-wife the allowance they'd agreed on (but which he couldn't afford) after they'd been unable to reconcile their differences and she'd asked him to leave. Things had improved since then but the business wasn't earning enough to provide either Frank or himself with a reasonable income and there were no signs of it becoming more profitable in the immediate future.

It was the problem of getting enough students to make sure of a reasonable return — which hadn't happened since the Tiananmen Square incident in Beijing. The hell of it was that while some of the businesses offering programmes to overseas students had failed, those belonging to Languages South Pacific were doing well. He and Frank seemed to be somewhere in the middle, well not really in the middle. They were neither making nor losing money — scarcely holding their own — yet receiving an endless stream of letters from would-be students who claimed they were being held up by the embassy in Beijing, or were refused visas and never received an official explanation. It didn't make sense — not after the Government had encouraged the sale of education to foreign students, had described it as a developing industry and potentially a major source of overseas funds. So far the only thing major about it had been the problems it produced and the work they'd put into it. And they'd had two million — two million dollars in overseas funds in the bank before they'd had to return it! But perhaps things would change, perhaps the agents they'd found in Japan and Taiwan might make a difference.

And then there's Angie, definitely an improvement! She said Bridget invited her to the American Bar, that Bridget had been telling her about him; but it had been the way he decorated his bathroom that had been the critical factor, that had decided things for her — the mural. He hadn't thought of it as a mural, just something to change the appearance of the room, to make it look a less functional: hand basin, cupboard above the hand basin, bath, shower box, mirror... The walls had been pink when he moved in — a pale, insignificant and depressing pink.

It had taken him a while to work out what to do with it, not because he didn't have ideas, but because there hadn't been enough money for any major redecoration. He worked out the answer while he was looking at brochures in a travel agents' office. He'd gone in on impulse — because he'd like to escape, go somewhere, some place where there were no complications and it cost nothing to live, where the weather was always warm, the skies blue and it never rained. And it was at that moment he saw it: a wall-sized blow-up of a tropical beach — sand, sea, and palms in fresh and brilliant colours that in no way corresponded to anyone's personal experience, but which suggested what he might be able to do with his bathroom.

Eventually he unearthed the manufacturer's catalogue and was able to order something. When it arrived he spread the photograph over two walls of the bathroom and sealed it against steam and moisture with a single coat of transparent polyurethane: the temple of Apollo at Delphi — white fluted columns, broken capitals surrounded by flagstones and in the distance, the sea. The scene looks more realistic because of the potted ferns he's placed about the room and at each end of the bath. They tend to give the flat surfaces of the photograph a three-dimensional appearance — a depth they otherwise wouldn't have. The finishing touch is the tiles, the black and white tiles he's spread over the floor and which suggest a three-dimensional extension of the temple itself.

Frank didn't approve of it — didn't approve of it at all. 'Crass,' Frank told him when he saw it, 'cheap and nasty! Looks like those things they have in the foyers of tourist hotels — sailing ships and barrels on waterfronts — nineteenth century blow-ups of draft horses hauling logs — that kind of thing.' He can understand Frank's point of view and that looking at it in the way Frank does, what he's done to the bathroom could be considered a mess. But then, even if he has an interest in such things, Frank isn't the sort of person who would admit to feelings that go with a taste for Greek temples and statues. Harry has different opinions or he wouldn't have gone to so much trouble. There's something about soaring Delphic columns that appeals to him — but he doesn't make a big thing out of it, talk about it very much.

'It's symbolic,' Angie's told him, 'Delphi is symbolic — says something about aspiration — the hopes and fears of the people who lived there... about being pure... about purity even.' Harry isn't so sure. He doesn't think purity has much to do with how anyone feels or with anything else either. There are things people have to do, things they don't have to do — and what they'd like to do. The first and last rarely coincide — which is unfortunate as if they did coincide, life would be much more enjoyable than it actually is. The good thing about the bathroom is that Angie likes it and that it's a factor in her still being in his apartment — so she tells him. As for the other reasons for her being there — whatever they are, they don't matter, they don't matter at all...

He finishes shaving, rinses his shaving gear and using a small, stiff brush, scrubs the inside of the hand basin so that it becomes as starkly white as it was before he began shaving. It's an habitual procedure that comes from living alone — cleaning up immediately after doing anything so there's no accumulation of work that will need to be attended to later.

Eighteen

Richard isn't looking forward to it — he isn't looking forward to the preliminary argument over calling for further nominations and he keeps thinking of the discussion he had with Bridget earlier before the third nominee — before Colin phoned. And now unexpectedly, the meeting isn't going to be chaired by the electorate convenor, but an outsider — someone from the Central City electorate. The majority of the forty-one people who have so far arrived (he's counted them) are party members who have recently joined, who won't notice anything unusual in Gilbert having arranged for an outside chairman to run the meeting. 'It's a precaution,' Gilbert told Richard and is now telling everyone else, 'it's a precaution to make sure every aspect of the question is given full and proper consideration — that each one of us — that we all understand the situation.'

Gilbert exudes his usual confidence — the confidence of someone accustomed to getting his own way — and a slight but perceptible impatience at the amount of time it takes to ensure people understand the subtleties and sophistication of politics and the democratic processes involved. His wish is for complete objectivity — to 'make sure all aspects of the question receive a complete airing and are given all the consideration due to them'. In these terms Richard tells himself, Gilbert's views differ very little from those Colin presented to him on the telephone before the meeting and remind him of how much the two of them have in common.

'It's not just a question of gender,' Colin pointed out to him, 'It's more complicated than that. We have to think of party members at the local level, we have to think of their autonomy — of the electorate's right to decide what procedures will be used, its right to select a candidate without interference from the regional executive or the Council.'

'Yes,' Richard came back at him, because he agrees (although he doesn't like doing it and suspects there's something going on he doesn't know about), 'yes, it's not only the electorate. There's the community. We represent the community and the Party has an obligation to express the views of the community — to push the community's views forward at the political level. Not our personal views, but the views of the community.'

'Of course — of course,' Colin hurries to reassure him, 'no one's going to argue about the party's obligations to the community but there's this other question, the question of process — of the electorate's right to decide things for itself, of grass-roots' decision-making. It's in the Charter — we have a right to select our own candidate in our own way. It's what we should tell Gilbert and the regional executive we're doing — it's what we have to tell them if our rank and file members are to retain their right to decision making at the local level, before it's taken over by the Executive or even by the national council.'

'Equity,' Richard reminds him, 'fair representation of all ethnic groups and everyone in the community... equity's more important than process. We have to keep talking about it, reminding people about it.'

It makes him feel a bit of a wimp talking like that, talking about equity and community responsibility — spelling it out, but he says it because it has to be said and because he doesn't want Colin to think he's been getting at him personally.

'Both points of view are valid,' he tells Colin, 'but it's the Executive and Gilbert who are doing the stirring. Gilbert should have done something about it before nominations closed — made sure there was enough time to consider extending the closing date. If they'd done that — if the Executive had suggested it at the right time — Claudia's nomination would already have been accepted and the whole thing would have been resolved.

'Someone has to speak up for the electorate.' Colin keeps the conversation going even when Richard has had enough of it. 'Someone has to put the electorate's point of view — make sure ordinary party members have a chance to put their views to the Executive. And there has to be a spokesperson — someone who can make it clear for them, resolve the issue.'

'What we ought to do,' Richard says — the idea has just come to him, 'what we ought to do, is to persuade people to turn down any proposal the Executive makes, vote against executive interference and then have the electorate re-open nominations of its own volition so Claudia can come in as a possible candidate. Four nominees would make the meeting more interesting and give everyone a wider choice.'

'Yes, but who's going to persuade them — who's going to persuade Gilbert and the Executive they're exceeding their rights, who's going to convince them? They'll have to be convinced first — before the electorate decides what to do about Claudia.'

Richard can see the difficulty — someone has to convince the hierarchy that the electorate's autonomy takes priority...

'Would you do it?' Colin asks him. He seems to have reached the point he's been working up to. 'No one could do it as well as you could, and it has to be someone who has credibility with the Executive. You have it, Richard — and you could do it.'

Although he isn't interested in politics and has never been a member of the party, Harry as well as Richard is attending the meeting. Angie has insisted he attend, 'As an observer, Harry, because you might — you just might want to join the Party later. And if you did — if you joined, you'd be useful, *really* useful... you'd learn how everything works — and you'd get things done...' He could see from the way she's said it and from the suggestion that he'd get things done, that she was trying to flatter him into going with her — but he had no objections, no objections at all. 'Besides,' she told him, once he'd agreed to it, 'now I've managed to catch you — and I have caught you! — I'm not taking any risks — I'm not going to let you escape.'

It's a flattery Harry enjoys because it comes from Angie — and because he needs flattery or something like it to counteract what's been happening in the other parts of his life. Frank has been to the airport and after picking up the two who have just arrived from China and having delivered them to their homestays — the homestays Bridget has arranged for them — he's dropped in at the post office to collect the mail. 'Nothing much in the box,' he tells Harry when he phones him. 'They're settling into their digs — can't speak English — not a word of it — but still, they're pleased to be here — obviously pleased — and we'll see them on Monday...'

'If they can't speak English, how do you know they're pleased?' It's Harry's usual joke — clumsy, but still a joke. He's picked up enough newcomers from the airport to be on familiar terms with the nervous excitement they always bring with them.

And these letters... three of them from China... two with our logo on them and the return address...'

'Perhaps they're from Wang Lan,' Harry suggests, 'or they could be new enrolments — and we need them, we really need them.'

'A moment.' He visualises Frank hunching a shoulder in order to hold the handpiece to his ear so he can free his hands and tear the ends off the envelopes. It's a clumsy way of opening mail, but Chinese envelopes don't have paste on their flaps — they're sealed with the aid of a pot of paste and a brush. They have to be torn at one end or cut open with a pair of scissors. In the absence of scissors, Frank has to tear them open as best he can — and it's not always easy. Trying to keep the telephone up to his ear would make it more difficult than it usually is and explain why the operation is taking longer than it normally would.

'The first is from — from Guangcai Hu — you remember Guangcai Hu? He's with the Meteorological Bureau in Beijing.' Indeed, Harry remembers him. Guangcai Hu is persistent — incredibly persistent — didn't give up even when the embassy in Beijing turned down him down for a visa — wrote and asked what else he could do, whether there was anyone he could appeal to. The Minister of External Relations, Harry suggested — perhaps he could write to the Minister and get an explanation. Guangcai Hu had done exactly that but so far hadn't received a reply.

'I'll read it to you, the whole letter,' Frank says. 'It goes like this... damn! — just a minute.' There's a metallic clang suggesting he hasn't been able to keep the ear piece in place and has dropped it, and then another — a less definable sound suggesting he's having trouble in retrieving it. 'Just a moment... hold on ,' he says, 'This is how it goes — there's not much — just a few paragraphs. 'Dear Mr Houghton,' Frank reads out to him...

Dear Mr Houghton, Thank you for writing to me on 30 November. I feel encouraged by your letter. After writing to you on 12 November, I received the Minister's letter of 30 October. But he tell me , "... the language school you wish to study at has since collapsed, and there is therefore no question of your being able to take up the course..."

I don't believe the speech, don't believe the collapsed. I think there is a lot of way to maintain courses such as developing side occupation, looking for the investment company... If the Government would make suitable policy for Chinese, courses for Chinese would be flourishing.

Mr Houghton, I now write to the Prime Minister and the Leader of Opposition, and send the relevant copy to the Embassy. Good luck to you. Sincerely, Guangcai Hu.

'What do you think of it, what do you think's going on?'

'We're out of business — or close to it — that's what's going on,' Harry tells him. Guangcai's discovered why we haven't been doing very well — it's because the Embassy thinks we've closed down — has been told by the Ministry and is telling people we've closed down. That's why they're not getting visas, no-one's coming to us from China.' He wishes there were another explanation, but he can't think of one, not at the moment. 'The other two letters,' he says into the phone, 'if they have our logo on them — we must have sent them to somebody. Check the names and addresses. Who did we send them to?'

'They're from Beijing... they've been returned... God knows why! There's nothing on the envelopes... wait a minute... rubber stamps... they're smudged, hard to read... *Gone... no address...* that's what they say and... just a moment, Harry, just a moment... they're the cheques we sent Chen Li and Zhang Jie — the two guys Wang Lan's been going on about.'

Harry feels unwell. The letters and what might be happening to Wang Lan — they make him feel sick in the stomach. 'When you get to the office,' he tells Frank, 'you're going there aren't you? Send another fax — tell Wang Lan what's happened, tell her that if she sends us new addresses we'll post the cheques back to them — and tell her to show the fax to Chen... he'll need to see it...' He knows there's no need to tell Frank what he should be doing, but Harry's telling him anyway to tide himself over the conflicting emotions the three letters have aroused — anger, guilt — the emotions that arise when things go seriously wrong and solutions are hard to find.

'It's Harry — Harry Houghton,' Angie introduces him to people he's never seen before, and is unlikely to and has no desire to see again. Three or four faces slide past and are replaced by another three or four faces. A murmur of conversation fills the room and hangs over everything and everyone in it — not a comfortable or relaxed sound suggestive of the common interests and shared values a political party might be expected to have, but a sound reflecting underlying tensions and divisions. Trying not to think of what Frank has told him, Harry attempts to single out individual exchanges from the medley of conversations going on around him. He studies people and faces. Some of the men wear ties, some have beards, most are informally dressed in loose-fitting jackets and open-necked shirts; the women are similarly attired — a few are elegant, but most are otherwise. Angie introduces them in pairs. 'Beverly and Jim... Barbara and Geoffery,' she smiles at them. He shakes hands, nods acknowledgement, offers polite and inconsequential replies to Geoffery's comments on the weather, Jim's observations on the state of the nation.

He tries to compare what's happening with naval cocktail parties and the more official diplomatic receptions he's attended in the past and overseas — in Bangkok, Seoul, Honolulu — but it's difficult to make comparisons, and it's even more confusing when he reminds himself that politicians have to fight their way through an endless series of such meetings before they become Members of Parliament or gain any influence over political events. It explains why the most urbane and sophisticated of parliamentarians can exude complete confidence and exemplary panache at one moment and then at the next, lapse into the crudities and crassness of a language employed by black market money launderers and back alley drug pushers. They fight their way through a jungle of damaged egos, frustrated ambitions and distorted sensibilities before they get anywhere. It explains why politicians are impossible to talk to, why they constantly fall back on cliche, catch-phrases and hollow self-righteousnous rather than risk an honest and open exchange of opinion.

He tells himself, he'll have to talk to Angie and some of her friends about it — explain how it appears to a newcomer; but they'll probably disagree, tell him it's not the selection process but the way Parliament operates that's the problem, that people can't speak freely when the system insists they do otherwise — that they support whatever views and opinions Cabinet and the Prime Minister require them to support...

'Harry,' Angie introduces him, 'Harry, this is Helen — Helen and Peter Wilkins...' He acknowledges an elderly couple, each of them very like the other in appearance — both thin, alert, with intelligent eyes that miss nothing and immediately take in his jacket, tie, and perhaps his reluctance to be there as well. They shake hands. Helen sums him up immediately and neatly. 'Not a politician are you, Mr Houghton — a business man.' She turns to her husband, 'Exactly what the party needs — a man of action, someone who can take over the fund raising... do it properly...'

'Yes,' Wilkins responds, coming in on cue and launching into what appears to be a well-rehearsed and perhaps often repeated political speech, 'new and developing parties have difficulties with money — they need it to develop public support, yet they can't get into a sound financial situation until they have the support they need the money to develop... it's the cart and the horse... the cart and the horse all over again... that kind of situation...'

'And Harry,' Angie interrupts, 'here's someone I'd like you to meet — one of the three nominees for the candidature — someone who might become the candidate.'

He shrugs to Wilkins and his wife suggesting polite reluctance at discontinuing the conversation, and turns towards Angie... There's a man standing close to her, a man with his right arm around Angie's waist in a gesture of affection and familiarity — a man he recognises — who looks at him with his jaw slightly open, who wears a fixed and frozen smile not dissimilar to the one he's sure he's suddenly acquired himself.

'Harry,' Angie says to him, 'I'd like you to meet Stuart. This is Stuart Mills — John Stuart Mills — one of the our more enthusiastic party members...'

His initial surprise gives way to disbelief — disbelief that after the difficulties Stuart's caused him and the time that's passed since he left the Navy, Stuart is here in the same room with him — standing right here with his arm around Angie's waist. Almost as quickly surprise gives way to a feeling of disconnection — of disassociation — the feeling he's had almost continually since leaving the Navy and since his divorce — perhaps longer.

He'd thought it was wearing off, that over the last day or so it had fully and finally disappeared. But now what's going on around him, the people coming towards him, moving away from him, seem more than ever — distant, unreal, two-dimensional, as if they're paper cut-outs and liable to disappear if a window is opened, a fan switched on. Automatically, his hand moves towards Stuart who takes his arm from Angie's waist, extends his hand for a moment and then changes his mind and withdraws it.

'We've already met,' Stuart tells her, 'we met... when we were in the Navy.' He makes small talk, speaks in that strangely incongruous and deep baritone Harry remembers so well, and speaks as if the Navy's something he's still associated with, as if it's something they both have a fondness for — have a shared interest in — and he'd like to talk about it — he'd really like to discuss it with Harry — but can't just now because there isn't time. 'The meeting,' he tells Angie, 'it's about to begin...'

Angie sits next to Harry and whispers explanations of what's going on. He finds it difficult to understand what's happening — what the speakers' motives are and what they're getting at — and in spite of Angie's whispered comments, can't make sense out of it. It's his own fault — he knows it's his own fault. He's let his emotions get in the way, take over — allowed himself be disturbed at seeing someone else in such close proximity to Angie, and he's been shocked at that someone being Stuart. He can't understand it — it doesn't make sense — there's no sense in it. He can't understand how Stuart has suddenly re-appeared — and with sufficient status to be accepted as a potential parliamentary candidate! And the business — what Frank's told him about the Minister's letter to Guangcai Hu — what might happen to Wang Lan...

'There has to be a decision, it has to be decided before the selection takes place — we have to know the rules we're working to and recognise what we're losing if the gender issue isn't addressed...'

'Gilbert,' Angie whispers to him, 'it's Gilbert, the party convenor. He wants nominations to be re-opened — to include Claudia in the selection.'

Harry isn't sure who Claudia and Gilbert are and doesn't much care. Stuart and Angie know each other — that's what matters — and that arm, the arm Stuart had round her waist, suggests Mills hasn't only gained in confidence and reputation over the last few years but that his relationship with Angie is something more than might be expected from a mutual interest in politics. Harry doesn't like it — he doesn't like what he's seen — he doesn't like it at all.

'And that's Richard,' Angie nudges him with her elbow. 'Richard is arguing against the proposal, he's saying Claudia's had her chance and the electorate is solidly behind him, solidly against outsiders coming in and making decisions for them — whether it's the regional executive or anyone else — he says it's the electorate which has to make the decisions — that the Alliance isn't the Labour Party...'

Harry hears and doesn't hear what she's saying. He's thinking of Stuart, thinking that if it hadn't been for Stuart, he wouldn't be in a business that was falling apart — that had worked up to being worth more than two million dollars and was now worth nothing at all; if it hadn't been for Stuart he'd have been able to afford a new engine for his boat — would have had the job he'd almost obtained when he was leaving the Navy but which he'd lost because Tony hadn't backed him up... because it was Tony he'd named as his referee, and who hadn't supported his application, had said he wasn't up to it... And he wouldn't have known what Tony had said, if Tony hadn't told him 'as a friend', that he was doing him a favour, telling the truth about Harry and preventing him from getting into something that was 'too deep' for him, over his head, a job he wouldn't be able to keep up with. 'It's not your thing, Harry,' he'd said, 'management isn't your thing — not after the way you handled Mills. You're not cut out for it, wouldn't be able to hack it...'

He's tried to stop thinking about it — the way he handled Mills — but more especially he's tried and sometimes he's succeeded in forgetting Tony's part in losing him the job he really wanted. Now there's something else to stop thinking about — Stuart's arm around Angie's waist — and he's not sure he's going to succeed in forgetting it.

'They're winding it up,' Angie whispers, 'at least, Richard's winding it up — the first part of the meeting... He's asking them to take a vote on it.'

Harry isn't sure what it is they're putting to the vote and he doesn't much care. He knows he has no personal claim on Angie, that she's her own person, free to go where she likes, do what she likes — associate with whoever she wants to associate with. But he can't believe anything could happen or has happened between Angie and Stuart. Thinking about it brings an unbearable coldness into the room, makes him feel that although he's sitting next to Angie, he's not actually there — that the physical distance between them has ceased to be a matter of centimetres and has suddenly become light years. He doesn't belong here, has no business here — should be at the office trying to do something about Wang Lan — doing something useful for the business, for Frank, for himself, for the Chinese kids who have paid more than they can afford and haven't been able to, and won't be able to get visas...

Stuart also is unhappy but not merely at seeing Harry again. He hadn't expected Richard to play such a major part in events, to stand up and argue so convincingly a case which would pull everyone in behind it and indirectly and as a consequence lead to Richard having a better chance of being selected. Stuart has worked hard at gaining new members for the party and he has their assurances — their promises — they'll vote for him. The danger is that Richard's rhetoric will have persuaded some of them to move in his direction — something Richard doesn't deserve because he isn't politically astute enough, hasn't lobbied enough, hasn't brought new people into the party — people who have sworn to vote for him. Richard doesn't understand politics and tends to talk nonsense, tells people he believes in the integrity of party members, that they'll select whoever they think will make the best candidate — not the person who recruited them. The party they belong to, Richard keeps telling people, is different from other parties — it stands for honesty, integrity, grass-roots decision making... What Richard says shows the kind of politician he'll make — that he doesn't deserve to become the candidate... !

And the car — the trouble he went to with the car! He spent half the night looking for a phone box, trying to get a taxi, and even then it hadn't worked out because this morning when he called on Sandra, Georgina refused to accept the offer he made her — his offer of a vehicle — and told him she always paid her own way and didn't intend to stop doing it just because someone had stolen her car. It was insured she told him, and what kind of a woman did Stuart think she was that she wasn't able to look after herself — that she'd take a hand-out from a scruffy little runt of a second-hand car salesman who hadn't done anything with his life and wasn't likely to do much more with it in the future? If people thought she needed that kind of help, they'd better start thinking again! And what was more, Sandra wasn't interested in him, had never been interested in him, and he could keep away from her... keep well away... and permanently!

'There — do you see!' Angie is still trying to help Harry understand what's happening. 'Richard's persuaded everyone to vote against re-opening nominations and now they're going to start the selection process. Each nominee has to make a formal speech, and everyone has to ask questions — attempt to prove the person they support will make the best candidate there's been since the discovery of toasted cheese sandwiches. Then the people who support the other candidates have to demonstrate the opposite — that he tells lies, has ripped off his grandmother, beats his children, cheats on his wife, comes home drunk every night...'

Stuart's immediate problem — and suddenly it looms larger and more important than before, is that he'd thought that the past — even if it couldn't be forgiven — had at least been forgotten, would somehow have disappeared. And up until half an hour ago, he'd assumed it had disappeared. Harry's reappearance has changed the situation — brought back to mind the small print at the bottom of the nomination form he'd had to sign as as a possible parliamentary candidate: *Criminal convictions or other matters possibly damaging to the party: if any such circumstances exist, the nominee shall give a full and complete statement, seal the statement in a plain envelope, mark the envelope 'Confidential' and forward it with his or her application form to the candidate co-ordinator.*

Unless it's a major criminal matter, Stuart's been told, the whole thing is just a formality — a means of the party being forewarned, able to protect itself against the unexpected. Whether it's a formality or otherwise, Stuart hasn't taken the risk of preparing such an envelope and what's more, has no intention of preparing one. But now there's the possibility that Harry might — just might — stand up and say something, disclose what's best left undisclosed and in limbo where it belongs. Thinking about it makes his hands shake, brings him out in a cold sweat.

But Harry isn't listening to what the nominees are saying. In comparison with what's happened between Angie and himself and his fear of the discontinuance of their developing relationship, in comparison with his suspicion of what might or might not have occurred between Stuart and Angie, everything else seems trivial. But then he might be imagining it, and perhaps nothing happened at all — perhaps the alarms and excursions, the disasters of the last few years have so distorted his judgement, so much soured him, destroyed the confidence he used to have in himself, that he's unable to see things clearly, has lost the ability to believe in people, to trust anyone. Even Frank, he reminds himself — Frank who's happily married and has three young children — even Frank — Frank mightn't really be trustworthy and who's to know what went on or didn't go on between Wang Lan and Frank in Beijing?

'Honesty and integrity,' Richard is saying, 'honesty and integrity — ours is a party that stands for the management of public affairs not in accordance with the wishes and self-interest of politicians, not for the comfort of public servants nor for the profit of big business and private investors... We're not the kind of men and women who give in to the blandishments of lobbyists or the persuasions of pressure groups...' He steps forward and leans across the lectern in order to emphasise what he's saying and heighten the intimacy, the effect of his final phrases. 'This party — the party we belong to...' (applause), '... this party stands for the accurate and truthful representation of the wishes of the people, for the aspirations of ordinary men and women — for the translation of those aspirations into living reality, into a society all of us can live with, all of us can enjoy…' He stops speaking and stands in front of them for a moment, silent, without moving, with an air of humility and then steps away from the lectern to an explosive clapping of hands — a standing ovation.

'He's going to win — Richard's going to win!' Angie whispers. 'Colin's a terrible speaker and Stuart's even worse.'

And Colin and Stuart are indeed terrible speakers. Stuart doesn't make much of a fist of it at all. Despite his surprise at seeing Harry, his voice, although it lacks humour and warmth, still retains the depth and timbre Harry remembers and his hands if they're shaking, don't visibly seem to be doing so. He begins with a few halting banalities and an apology for not being as good a speaker as Richard — not being as sophisticated nor as concerned with elegant language and fancy words as Richard is. But he offers, he tells them, something they might prefer: straight talk in plain language — the language ordinary people are familiar with — and an assurance of something he's certain, he tells them, they're already aware of — his ability to get on with things, to get things done and get them done properly.

'But he hasn't done anything,' Bridget hisses, 'he hasn't done anything!'

According to Stuart however, he's done a great deal. He's a foundation member and the current chairman of *Mountains and Streams (Inc)*, which he claims is a new and developing ecological association with a national and growing network of sub-associations and working groups — 'already making representations to local bodies and beautification groups — to *The Rose Society* and its sister organisations — organisations increasingly concerned at the growing pollution of the harbours and waterways, shocked by the unpardonable, the inexcusably sordid untidiness of waterfront buildings, the ecological insult industry continues to impose on the environment…'

'Nobody's heard of it!' Bridget whispers to Angie. 'He's making it up — he's inventing it!'

Harry doesn't believe in such an organisation as *Mountains and Streams (Inc)* either. He doesn't believe Stuart could organise his way out of a paper bag and he doesn't believe — struggles against believing — that at some time something might have gone on (could still be going on) between Angie and the possible candidate. The thought of Stuart being involved with Angie is intolerable to him. The rational part of his mind informs him of the impossibility of such a circumstance but another part — the part which remembers Stuart's arm around Angie's waist (and which has fastened the image into his mind as if it were a snap-shot taken by a camera with fast film — a very fast film, indeed — inside it) — insists otherwise.

'Angie,' he whispers to her, 'have you known Stuart very long — how long have you known him?

'Not now, Harry — the voting comes next. It's the most important part of the meeting. They're taking the vote!'

Angie's interest in politics isn't something he'd normally have difficulty with, but because of Stuart's involvement, it disturbs him. 'Is Stuart a close friend of yours,' Harry asks her. 'I mean — have you... have you ever been... with him... in... the physical sense?' She makes a tick on the voting paper when it's given to her and hands it back to one of the scrutineers. 'A very successful meeting,' the woman on her right informs them, 'and such a wonderful occasion — such remarkably able speakers.'

Eventually the murmur of conversation fades and is replaced by a ripple of excitement which spreads rapidly throughout the room. Angie seizes his elbow. 'I don't believe it — it's not possible, not after the speech Richard gave — not after the way people responded!' And indeed, impossible though it might be, it appears from the comments being made in front, on his left, and behind Harry, Richard's attempt at the party nomination has been knocked flat in the first round. The survivors are Stuart and Colin, and already the scrutineers and their two assistants are issuing voting slips for the final selection.

'It's rigged,' Angie insists in case he hasn't worked it out, 'Stuart and Colin have stacked the meeting and now we're going to see which of them has made the best job of it!' She turns round and shows her voting slip to Bridget. 'Look,' she says, 'There are only two names on it — and they haven't had time to write them out — the voting slips must have been ready before the meeting.'

'No — no,' Bridget turns towards her, 'no one would have cheated — they'd have printed voting papers to cover every possibility. The scrutineers have issued the slips that were printed for Stuart and Colin. If Richard was still in the running, they'd have put out papers with his name on them.'

'The secretary,' Angie comes back at her, 'the party secretary arranged it — arranged for the voting slips to be printed, and you know she's against Richard — she favours Colin. You can't vote for them, Bridget — you can't vote for Stuart or Colin!'

Bridget looks at the voting paper she's holding, and then at Angie and across to Harry.

Harry tries not to think of Angie with Stuart's arm round her, tries not to think of anything else that might have happened between the two of them and for the moment manages to blot such thoughts out of his mind. Everybody is either talking to a neighbour or marking off a name on one of the voting slips. Richard has moved into the corner near the door, and is conversing with a small, dark woman and a man standing next to her. The woman is speaking earnestly to him and the man nods occasionally in agreement. Gilbert and the other members of the regional executive who earlier tried to persuade the electorate to re-open nominations appear as equally disconcerted as Richard is. They too, have found themselves a corner and are whispering quietly together. The scrutineers collect the voting slips and retire.

'There has to be a better way of doing things,' Colin's voice carries across the room. 'New procedures — that's what we need — new parliamentary procedures and real accountability...'

'Political acumen,' the party secretary insists, 'of course Richard speaks well, but it's political acumen that really counts, that gets results.'

'Political acumen...' Colin's voice repeats over the general hubbub.

'Shhh... .' Conversation falters, the ripple of voices falls away.

The chief scrutineer has come back, goes up the three steps onto the dais and stares out at the assembly. There is a serious and slightly disapproving expression on his face and in his voice. 'Two votes,' the chief scrutineer announces, 'two votes are missing. Is there anyone who hasn't returned a voting slip?' He's not only disapproving, Harry notices, but is also anxious, nervous, and peers round the room almost short-sightedly. 'Is there anyone who hasn't voted — anyone here at all?'

Bridget and Angie stare at each other. Angie and then Bridget, slowly at first, and then more quickly, put their hands into the air. 'Two abstentions!' Bridget calls out. And then to make sure she has the scrutineer's attention, 'Over here!' she says, 'Two abstentions!'

'In that case,' he says loudly and clearly after a short silence, and looking and sounding Harry thinks, like the chief undertaker at a bankrupt's funeral in mid-winter, 'in that case I'm pleased to tell you that this electorate has selected Colin as its candidate for the coming general election and... as we all know... with everybody's help... a Member of Parliament... our next parliamentary representative. Well done, Colin — well done!' Silence from the electorate and its assembled selectors, hierarchy, party members, friends and associates. 'Now, everyone — a big hand . . .' his voice carries to every corner of the room, '. . . and now a big hand for the candidate... let's all give Colin a very big hand!'

Nineteen

Harry doesn't get it — indeed, he doesn't get it at all! In the first place, he doesn't understand how Angie and Bridget could have known in advance that if they didn't vote for either of the candidates things would come out the way they did. 'It's a secret,' Angie insists afterwards, 'a secret between the two of us — between Bridget and me — female intuition, that's what it is, not the kind of stuff men understand. We just know things like that, and we knew it would work out that way.'

'But you couldn't have known,' he says now they're back in his apartment and the major new and recognisable disaster that might have eclipsed almost all other disasters, has been allayed — perhaps not permanently but at least and in spite of a residual feeling of unease, for the immediate and foreseeable future. 'How did you work it out — how did you know that was what would happen?'

'Because we did,' she tells him, 'because we worked it out and there are things women understand that men don't. It's part of their mystique — their ability to see things men can't see.' He doesn't believe her, but then their relationship has moved on to another, a second — a more relaxed, an easier stage — and she doesn't expect him to believe her.

He's told her about the language school business he's operating with Frank — that it will almost certainly fold — especially now Languages South Pacific has a monopoly on the Japanese market and there's no chance of their receiving any further students from China. He's told her about Wang Lan and his fears for what might happen to her — what might already have happened to her, about the bank drafts, about Mills and the things that took place before he left the Navy — how he felt when he saw Mills with his arm round her waist — when he thought there was something going on between them. But he hasn't told her about his sense of guilt, his irrational fear that these threats and misfortunes are the inevitable outcomes of his inability to anticipate the future — the result of some inexplicable flaw in his character — his lingering suspicion that he deserves what's happened and deserves as well anything similar that's likely to occur in the future.

'It didn't make sense,' he explained to her. 'I mean — it just didn't seem possible Mills was the sort of person you'd...' he remembers hesitating in his search for the right way of saying it, '. . . the sort of person you'd be interested in...' And maybe he shouldn't have told her as much as he's told her... maybe he's said too much already...

'It was partly because Stuart was so confident he was going to win,' she says, not precisely answering the questions he'd like to ask her, that are still uppermost in his mind, 'and partly because he'd already asked Richard to vote for him if Richard didn't get into the second round...'

'I still don't get it, how you could know for sure how everything would work out, what Stuart was really like...'

'Stuart manipulates things, he lobbies people, he's probably taken a course in it, on how to be a successful politician — he's always taking courses, he boasts about them — and he's done the rounds of all the party members, talked to them, shaken their hands, and given them an opportunity to get to know him, as he puts it... Bridget says, he even went as far as asking Richard if he'd mind his doing it... and trying to get Richard to vote for him... wanted to know if Richard would be dropping in to see everyone as well. And some of the people in the party — the older ones — they have great respect for candidates like Stuart, candidates who have been in the armed services, who are young and might have a long career ahead of them — they take candidates like that very seriously...'

'They don't know about those other things,' Harry reminds her, recognising that some questions are unanswerable, some things are best left to the future and some of them are unknown and perhaps unknowable. 'The things you said you read about in *Time* magazine?' he suggests. He still hasn't recovered from the shock of seeing Stuart, but he's trying not to think of it, to make light of recent events.

'I'm being serious — I'm talking to you about politics. I'm telling you how politics really work, about something that affects the nation.' Her face is serious and her eyes, wider than usual, stare directly into his. 'And besides, it was the best way to get back at everybody,' she tells him, 'Stuart didn't get the nomination despite stacking the meeting, the hierarchy didn't establish a precedent that would consolidate its power over the local electorate, and the party got a candidate it doesn't really want — which is why the chief scrutineer hoped the two missing votes would turn up and put Colin out of the running — because the scrutineer was on the side of the hierarchy which didn't want Colin but might have put up with Stuart because it doesn't know enough about him — doesn't realise what a little shit he is.' She's still staring at him in the direct, disconcerting way Harry's beginning to become familiar with. 'It's simple!' she tells him. 'It's all so simple!'

'Angie, I'm not into politics... I'd rather talk about...'

'Colin, remember — Colin didn't play fair either. He brought his relatives in to vote for him and stacked the meeting, and even if he's now the official candidate, he doesn't have the panache — he's not going to win the election. And Richard gets his own back — he gets it back on the electorate for not supporting him, on Stuart and Colin for cheating, and on the party for trying to change the rules and manipulate the selection process... which of course, they were doing because they thought they would get a better candidate and it would be fairer for the voters.'

'And Stuart, why did he put his arm around you? Why did you let him put his arm around you...' It's an image that haunts him, that remains in his mind — that will stay there forever.

'He wanted me to vote for him, Harry. He knew he couldn't rely on Richard, so he wanted — he expected Bridget to vote against Colin — and he knew he needed one more vote if he was to get the nomination... and he wanted me to give him mine...'

'It's too confusing, I'm lost, I don't understand what you're talking about.' It isn't entirely true he doesn't understand what she's saying — he gets the general drift even if the details tend to be a little confusing, to elude him. He just doesn't want to go on talking politics, especially when there are other problems in the world like — like what will happen to Wang Lan, whether any serious harm will come to her. In comparison with that, the selection of a political candidate who's not going to get elected (and even if he were elected, in the current political climate and under the present parliamentary system would have little or no influence on social or economic events) — the selection of a candidate who isn't going to get elected isn't earth shattering and has no connection with anything he's interested in.

'Was there anything more to it — I mean, anything more between Stuart and...' He can't finish the sentence. He doesn't have the right. There's been no exchange of assurances, neither of them has offered any assurance to the other... and they aren't at a stage with whatever's going on between them, that requires promises or gives him a right to ask that kind of question.

'Does it make any difference? Would it matter?' The humour fades from her face. She seems uncertain, a little disappointed, and her eyes are steady, unblinking — ice-blue and cold. At least it seems to Harry they're cold but he suspects it's not because she has any feelings of that kind towards him — but because the colour sometimes makes her eyes look that way. At least, he hopes it's the case — that there's no other reason for it.

'You said — you said you already had a boyfriend, and I thought... it seemed...'

'The telephone number I gave you in the supermarket was your telephone number — your own telephone number, Harry — it was you I was talking about. What I kept on trying to tell you was the same thing, exactly the same... and haven't you noticed? You should have noticed... I didn't just bring an overnight bag with me... I brought two suitcases... most of my stuff...'

'Yes,' he says, 'I should have been more observant, taken a good look at what you brought with you and worked out what you were doing, but then,' he notices her mouth is beginning to crinkle at the corners, 'but then, maybe you should give it more thought, maybe you should think about it again. It looks — it looks as if I'm not going to... to be a millionaire... not in the foreseeable future.'

'No,' she says, 'at least — well, not by next Wednesday! In the meantime, there are other things — there are things we can both think about apart from business and politics. And you've got some reading to do — a lot of it — and homework... You have to catch up on your homework, your *Time* magazines — learn a little more about the things the American Navy says its personnel aren't supposed to do — the things I told you about.' She reaches over and slowly and methodically begins loosening his tie. 'And you don't have to do the reading part of it immediately — well, not straight away — not tonight. We could start... we could start with the practical work... yes, practical work... yes, that's it... like that... exactly the way you're doing it... the way you're doing it right... now... !'